Carnage in D minor

There is no applause.
There is no audience.
There are no musicians and no conductor.
In the warm, soft light of the empty stage,
there is only the magnificent piano, the beautiful woman,
and the tears streaming down her face.

Carnage in D minor

A novel by
Stacey Alan Spivey

Stacey Alan Spivey

ISBN: Carnage in D minor (paperback) 979-8-9934942-0-3

ISBN: Carnage in D minor (hardcover) 979-8-9934942-1-0

ISBN: Carnage in D minor / The Screenplay (paperback) 979-8-9934942-2-7

ISBN: Dissension / The Screenplay (paperback) 979-8-9934942-3-4

ISBN: Carnage in D minor (paperback B&N press) 979-8-9934942-5-8

ISBN: Carnage in D minor (hardcover B&N press) 979-8-9934942-6-5

The Writers Guild of America, West Reg 2270475, 2238001

A brief history...

The novel *Carnage in D minor* was adapted from the award-winning screenplay, *Dissension*. I knew early on that I wanted to bring this story to a wider audience, and the acclaim *Dissension* received fueled my determination. The primary difference between the two is the reimagining of the characters—from Ryan, a white male in *Dissension*, to Leeza, a Black female, taking the lead role in *Carnage*.

In the novel, I wanted to explore the same powerful themes of trauma, addiction, and redemption through the eyes of a new and underrepresented cast of characters. Both Leeza and her predecessor, Ryan, are haunted by military service in the form of PTSD—souvenirs of a deployment to a war zone. How will they cope with their pasts? And how much will they risk to save themselves and their families from evil forces that want to see them destroyed? Their childhoods may have been worlds apart, but the choices they face as adults are tragically the same.

To my inspirations and my cheerleaders:
Christina Nichole
Conrad
Miss Tana
Rasha & Mike

Shout out to my grandsons:
Devin, Michael, & Alex

To everyone who ever offered the words "It gets better"—
You were right. Just sayin'.

Carnage in D minor
A novel by
Stacey Alan Spivey

Stacey Alan Spivey

Prelude

Carnegie Hall

Anticipation is palpable. The young, world-renowned pianist approaches the Steinway in the Neo-Italian Renaissance auditorium, set against stately stone columns and ornamental plaster ceilings. Warm lighting and her ivory silk gown, the color of worn piano keys, accentuate her dark brown skin. As the house lights dim, an ethereal silence envelops the concert hall.

Piano Concerto No. 1 in B-flat minor, Op. 23 fills the prestigious venue, each note commanding authority over the room. Her hands move with an athlete's focus and agility, while the masterpiece evokes nineteenth-century nostalgia.

Soon, her fingers blur, dancing over the keys with the quiet confidence of a child prodigy. She sways and lunges with the rhythm, her energy pushing the grand instrument to its limits. She channels Tchaikovsky's soul as a sustained dramatic bass chord underlines the crescendo. Triumphantly, she raises her hands from the keyboard as the final notes dissolve into the cavernous hall.

There is no applause. There is no audience. There are no musicians and no conductor. In the warm, soft light of the empty stage, there is only the magnificent piano, the beautiful woman, and the tears streaming down her face.

Part 1

1

That Young'un Can Play the Piana!
Beaufort, South Carolina - early spring, 1999

Teachers loved to hype the biannual talent shows at Beaufort Middle School, billing them as the most popular and exciting events of the year. But to the barely teens, it was another unfair assault on their precious time. In their collective indifference, they secretly ninja-texted on their flip phones while enduring readings from drama team nerds, a jazz-dancing gymnast, a violinist, and some dork with an act called "Blake-the-Great's Magic Tricks." And, of course, there was the ever-popular stream of "Britney Army" wannabes; a swarm of peripubescents with wide-open mouths dancing to anything from the Britney Spears Mall Tour with meticulously rehearsed routines. If their parents only knew the lyrics, fewer tweens would be in Britney's Army at BMS.

Then came the prodigious twelve-year-old from Port Royal. She had started sixth grade the previous fall and won first place with a classical piano performance of *Mozart's Piano Sonata No. 10 in C Major, 3rd Movement*. Beaufort Middle School found itself in the local headlines, and the young Black girl named Leeza Allen found herself giving recitals at the old auditorium. Even Britney's Army came to see her rock some Chopin and Rachmaninoff. And she always ended with an encore by a guy she called Scott Joplin.

March 26th was the last Friday before spring break. Leeza, the third of three soloists at the increasingly popular recital, followed two eighth-grade sibling violinists whose family, the Nguyens, represented Beaufort's entire Asian population.

Known for its military base and National Cemetery, Beaufort was not a natural melting pot of ethnicity and culture. It was, however, a reasonably safe place to raise your young'uns, and Beaufort Middle School was known to encourage those with the wherewithal and internal fortitude to help themselves. According to Principal McStanley, the recitals were a significant event for the school, and he made sure the local paper got a copy of the program, followed by reminder emails and a snail-mail copy, just in case the new computer was on the fritz again. He also made the Friday afternoon performances mandatory for all teachers, "plus-one encouraged."

Ginnie Nguyen finished her halting, slower-than-intended execution of Mendelssohn's *Opening Violin Concerto* and gave several deep bows for each section of the audience. She flashed a well-rehearsed toothy grin and waved like a gymnast who had just dismounted the uneven parallel bars at the Olympics. The polite applause was short. The audience was there to see the little Black girl—the one who played piano like Liberace but without the jewelry or showmanship of a white man with a freeze-dried face and fabulous outfits.

The crowd had come to see the piano prodigy in their midst. Little Miss Allen was the kind of kid they featured on TV shows like *60 Minutes*. There are kids who are born with God-given talents, but not a Black kid, and definitely not a Black kid from Beaufort, Port Royal, or even Charleston. But they imagined reading stories someday, about her jetting around the world from concert to concert, playing in all the fancy theaters, in all the fancy countries, eating fancy food with fancy white people, and they would be able to say they saw her playing the piano when she was twelve years old in Beaufort, South Carolina. "Bless her little heart," someone in the crowd murmured.

Their prophecies were right on track. Inspired by her daughter's talent and motivation, Leeza's mama, Catherine, brought her to The Juilliard School for Music in New York City to audition for the pre-college conservatory-style music program for students under eighteen. Driven by hope for a brighter future, Catherine believed Leeza would get accepted into the young artists' program, followed by a full-ride scholarship after high school. A single mother and an LPN, she had worked three jobs to pay for private lessons since Leeza began showing surprising talent at the age of five. Once Leeza became a headlining classical pianist, they would travel the world together. And Beaufort, South Carolina, would become a distant memory for both of them.

Whispers of anticipation floated in the air before Leeza's performance.

"How can that little Black girl do that?" a large elderly woman asked the man next to her.

"I never seen such a thang," he responded.

"The Lord sure is smilin' on that little young'un," she added.

The old man smiled faintly. "For *some* reason."

Ginnie Nguyen stomped triumphantly toward stage right as Principal McStanley appeared from the wings of stage left, tapping and blowing into the microphone.

"Testing," he said, like he did every time, fumbling for the on/off switch. He cleared his throat, searching for the perfect distance between his mouth and the bulbous head of the microphone. "That was outstanding, wuden't it?" He shuffled his index cards; his discomfort was palpable as he struggled to read the siblings' names. "Help me in congratulating Ginnie... bee... uh... by... byee... bang... inguin, and shine... shy... ang... sheen... yang... inguin." He mopped his forehead with a handkerchief. "Lord in heaven," he whispered, with the mic a little too close to his mouth.

The 1950s-era auditorium, with its scuffed and worn brown tile flooring, was crammed with tan folding metal chairs. Creaky wood bleachers lined the walls. Leeza had an aisle seat next to her mama at the back of the room.

"Now, for any of you here this afternoon who haven't yet seen our next performer, you all are in for a special treat, yes indeed," Principal McStanley continued.

Catherine kissed her daughter's hand as they listened to him describe her as a young "whiz kid," who was born right up the road in Port Royal. His voice boomed through the speakers and echoed off the back wall. With a mischievous grin, he added, "I wonder if her daddy was stationed at Parris Island." The wisecrack was met with chuckles and back-of-the-hand whispers. Catherine fixed a cold, icy glare on the sweaty white man at center stage.

"Our next performer dreams of being a famous piano player and playin' with orchestras all over the place."

"I didn't say famous," Leeza whispered.

"Please welcome Miss Lisa Allen." The room erupted. "Where you at, Lisa?"

"Knock 'em dead, baby," said Catherine, kissing her forehead.

Leeza made her way through the applause and cheering to the old blond-wood baby grand piano at center stage. Principal McStanley beamed as she walked past. She turned to the audience with a humble smile, then positioned the bench as if she, the piano, and the bench were a dynamic trio, each with a crucial part to play. The auditorium took a collective deep breath. Leeza's hands rose ceremoniously above the keyboard. Seconds later, the agonizing radio silence was replaced by a brilliant performance of Beethoven's *Piano Sonata No. 17, Tempest, 3rd Movement*.

Leeza had been best friends with a white girl named Davina since they were toddlers, and Davina's mom and "aunt" moved in next door. Neither girl ever saw a man walk through the front door of either house, and it didn't dawn on them at the time that perhaps that wasn't completely normal. But over the years, they realized their moms and Davina's aunt were completely at peace with their arrangements. The girls were never told anything about their own fathers, and the one time Leeza asked about hers, her mama cried, then yelled, then cried again. Davina explained that her aunt, a Beaufort County police detective, referred to men as "non-essential personnel."

Early spring in Beaufort meant mild weather—soft sunlight across the neighborhood—before the stifling heat and humidity waterboarded the Deep South for months on end. On Wednesday, March 31, four days before the end of spring break, Leeza and Davina spent the afternoon in the park just up the street from their houses. Leeza studied a music journal while Davina read *The Hitchhiker's Guide to the Galaxy* by Douglas Adams.

Leeza hummed and tapped her fingers with fastidious accuracy across the pages of handwritten musical compositions as she played an imaginary keyboard. "Oh fudge!" cried Leeza, jumping up from the blanket. "I totally forgot!" She frantically shoved the journal into her backpack and tugged on the blanket Davina was still lying on. "We need to go!"

"What the hell?" cried Davina, rolling off. "What happened?"

"Nothing happened," Leeza said, speed walking toward her house. "I have to check the mail!"

"You scared the shit out of me because you have to check the mail? Are you even serious right now?" Davina bookmarked her page and trailed her worked-up friend.

Finally at the mailbox, Leeza snatched out the contents and rifled through grocery store coupons and business flyers. When she found the only envelope that wasn't a bill, she stared at the return address:

The Juilliard School of Music
60 Lincoln Center Plaza
New York, NY 10023

She clutched it to her chest.

"Open it! Open it!" cried Davina.

"Oh my god, oh my god, oh my god!" Leeza rocked back and forth. "I can't do it!"

"I'll open it!" exclaimed Davina, trying to snatch the envelope.

"I should wait for Mama!"

"That ain't likely, now is it?" said Davina, crossing her arms.

"Okay, okay, okay!" Leeza stopped breathing. She tore the envelope with trembling hands, revealing the letter inside—the letter whose words would shape her destiny. She started pulling the letter from the envelope, stopping often.

Davina swallowed hard in anticipation. "Could ya do that any slower?"

Leeza managed to free the letter and held it in front of her face, then very slowly, opened her eyes and tried to focus. She read to herself before looking up at the blue sky with the pillowy white clouds and mouthing the words, "Thank you!"

The girls gripped each other's shoulders as they screamed and jumped up and down. Leeza pulled back and looked at the letter again, then hugged her friend. "I gotta go! Love ya, mean it!"

"Love ya, mean it!" said Davina, cupping her own face. She knew how much Leeza wanted this and how dedicated she and her mama were. Leeza ran up the steps into the old wooden house with the peeling paint and broken porch swing, stormed through the door, and flung her backpack onto the piano bench. Inside, she immediately noticed the unusual quiet.

"Mama!" she yelled, scanning the front rooms for any sign of her mother. "Mama!" There was always music: if not piano, then the radio, especially since Mama was always home by four on Wednesdays. *Why is the door unlocked if she ain't here?* Leeza looked at the fading mahogany skin of the second-hand baby grand piano that commanded the center of the small living room. Her mama had bought it at an estate sale when Leeza was seven and was still making payments. When a coworker once asked why she was picking up an overnighter, Catherine had replied, *"Time to tune the piana."*

Leeza walked slowly toward the hallway. It was early afternoon, and the inside of the house always seemed darker than it should have at that time of day, especially after coming in from the bright sunlight. The beams of light from the kitchen window were filled with omnipresent dust, lingering in the air like the fine silt in the lake when you opened your eyes underwater. *Lake dust*, she called it. She moved from room to room, her voice softening each time she called for her mother. "Mama? Are you home?" She made it to the end of the hall to the doorway of her mother's bedroom. As she peered around the doorframe, she saw two women sitting on the bed with their arms wrapped around one another, rocking each other gently. Her mother was crying. The strange woman saw Leeza in the doorway. She kissed Catherine's forehead and helped her lie down, covering her with a crocheted throw made years ago from leftover yarn. The large woman wore a colorful apron, as if she had come straight from cooking supper somewhere. She swept Leeza from the room and closed the door behind them.

As they walked down the hall, Leeza tried to read the strange woman's face. Her eyes were half-shut, and her clothes smelled of stale cigarettes and biscuit dough. She walked very slowly, her whole body rocking from side to side with each step, as the wood floor creaked beneath her weight. She motioned for Leeza to sit on the front steps. They didn't notice the kids screaming in the park where Leeza and Davina had spent the afternoon. Leeza fidgeted with the letter from Juilliard.

The woman introduced herself as Mrs. Beasley, a member of First African Baptist Church on Craven Street. She had finished with the fellowship brunch in the church hall's cafeteria, where she volunteered as a cook, and was headed toward the bus stop when she saw a woman sitting in a car across the street. She could tell the woman was crying. She went up and knocked on the window. "Is you okay?" she asked. The woman in the car looked familiar, but not recently familiar—more like somebody you knew years ago and then you ran into them at the Harris Teeter. The woman in the car wiped her nose and rolled down the window. Mrs. Beasley leaned in for a closer look. "Is that you, Miss Catherine?" Catherine used to take Leeza to the Baptist church when she was a baby, shortly after moving to Beaufort from Port Royal. Mrs. Beasley took pity on the young mother and would give them diapers and saltine crackers, but by the time Leeza was a toddler, they had stopped going to church. Catherine had shown up a handful of times but always left before the congregation could get to her. "Your mama was sittin' in the car over by the church," said Mrs. Beasley. "She was in no condition, so I says let me ride with you. Told me she'd been drivin' round for hours."

"What is it?" Leeza asked, bracing herself for what the woman was about to tell her. "Did somebody die?" A nervous grimace crossed her face. "Did my daddy call?"

Mrs. Beasley looked at Leeza. "You was a baby last time I seen you," she said, cupping Leeza's chin. She looked toward heaven and muttered a prayer that Leeza couldn't hear. "Your mama got the breast cansa, real bad like." Mrs. Beasley wiped her nose again, followed by a robust sniff. "They say she can have some chemicals and some eksrays or somethin' but it don't look too good, baby girl."

Leeza tried to remember if she'd ever heard anything about cancer. *Do we know anybody with cancer? Isn't there an operation they can do for cancer?* Her eyes darted wildly as she searched for an answer. *That's it! An operation! It's no big deal! It's no big deal!* A feeling of relief consumed her as she breathed deeply, in through the nose, out through the mouth, like she and her piano teacher, Mr. Brathwaite, did during warm-ups.

Leeza touched the old woman's shoulder. "It'll be okay. They'll do an operation, then I'll take care of her. They'll cut it out, and I'll take care of her." She imagined herself standing next to her mama during the operation. The doctor would pull out the cancer, the size of a lima bean, and drop it in the trash next to the operating room table. She could see a slight smile forming on her mama's lips as the cancerous blob hit the pail. Her mama would come to New York City to see her recitals, and they would travel together to Europe. Leeza looked at the envelope from Juilliard.

Mrs. Beasley rocked forward and back several times, each time a little farther, then reached out and grabbed the railing, heaving herself up from the steps. She offered both hands to Leeza and pulled her up. The woman and the young girl stood face-to-face on the porch of the old wooden house, with dust suspended in the sunbeams and the tired mahogany piano waiting patiently in the living room. There was a deep emptiness in the strange woman's expression. As they stared into each other's eyes, Leeza sensed the woman's head moving very slightly from side to side, as if she were saying, *"No"* to a voice inside her own head. *"No, it's not okay."*

The letter from The Juilliard School of Music in New York fluttered to the ground.

2

Terrorists on My Mind
Twenty years later...

The primal screams of a demented toddler pierced the cabin of the crowded flight to Charleston. Dark-gray clouds harassed the city as the aircraft shook in the turbulence of an April storm. Military personnel, looking like foreigners in their own country, were stuffed into a section of economy class. The overhead announcement from a late-career flight attendant muffled the groan of the engines.

"Ladies and gentlemen, we're about fifty miles from Charleston. It's gonna be a bit bumpy for the duration, so please keep those seatbelts snug, and we'll see y'all on the ground."

Eyes closed but still awake, Army Captain Leeza Allen-Byron was immersed in a classical orchestral piece through her earbuds. But the eighteenth-century masterpiece was violently interrupted by the toddler's rage-fueled tantrum, caused on this particular occasion by the fact that her mother had put away her snacks "for now." Poor little Vivian. The entire flight knew little Vivian, having heard her mama try to talk her down for the past six hours.

"You're gonna sleep like an angel tonight," the amateur mother cooed between her daughter's screams.

"We all will," muttered a passing flight attendant.

"That young'un reminds me of the hollerin' contest over at Spivey's Corner back in the day," said the soldier next to Leeza. "Prob'ly scare the bejesus out of them poor hogs."

Leeza's hair was in a tight ponytail. Military fatigues did little to camouflage her beauty. She took out her earbuds, wiped her eyes, and stared expressionless out the window. She could see the lights in the terminal through the pounding rain. The plane decelerated as it rocked from side to side.

Another announcement interrupted her attempt at dissociation.

"I'd like to welcome you all to Charleston, where the local time is four fifty p.m. It's currently sixty-eight degrees and rainy as all get out."

The seatbelt sign disappeared with a loud ding. The metallic clicking of unbuckling seat belts filled the fuselage. Another announcement blared through the speakers.

"If I could please ask that everyone remain seated and allow our military personnel to deplane first. Please remain in your seats unless you are military."

A large chunk of camouflaged economy class was quickly on their feet as cheers and applause erupted.

"And if you're not sure if you're military or not, just look down at your outfit and you'll figure it out."

Tempestuous Vivian screeched on; but this time she would have to compete with the sounds of laughter.

Even after a year away, Leeza knew it would be easy to spot her family in the terminal—just look for the handsome white guy with a pair of ten-year-old Black twins. She saw them before they saw her. Grant made eye contact from fifty yards away and started running.

"Leesie! Leesie! Leesie!" yelled Grant, a skinny Black boy sporting a fuchsia fedora, running full-throttle through the crowded airport toward a camouflaged woman at the far end of the Alaska terminal.

He sobbed as he wrapped his arms around his mama. "I missed you, Leesie."

"I missed you too, baby," said Leeza, her voice thick with emotion.

"Mama!" cried Charlotte. Leeza stretched out an arm and pulled her into the group hug. The three of them rocked in the embrace as Artie watched.

Leeza looked up at Artie, his chin trembling. With his perfect, fair skin and gym-toned body, he wore a Tom Ford double-breasted peacoat paired with Ralph Lauren straight-fit selvedge jeans. He looked more like a magazine cover than ever. He embraced the three of them and caressed Leeza's head. As soon as she stood, he lifted her into the air, spinning around, half laughing, half crying.

She cradled his face. "Hey, it's okay, I'm here now."

"Are you really?" said Artie, his voice halting with emotion. "Let me look at that face."

"We're okay," she said, brushing his hair aside.

Leeza held the kids' hands as they walked through the terminal. Grant and Charlotte talked incessantly, each desperate for her attention.

Artie squeezed her waist. "Did you miss me?"

"Always," she replied, just like every time he asked that question.

At the baggage carousel, Leeza handed her carry-on to Grant.

"How long this time?" Grant asked.

Leeza shot a puzzled glance at Artie. "You didn't tell them?"

"Tell us what?" Charlotte asked.

"Yeah, what?" Grant added.

Leeza kneeled down in front of the kids and playfully hesitated.

"Yeah?" said Charlotte.

"I'm back at my old job at the clinic. You're stuck with me." The kids squealed. "Nicely played," she whispered to Artie.

Leeza's Army duffel bag sauntered along the carousel until Artie was able to grab it. He threw it onto his back and motioned for the kids to head outside.

The family huddled together on the wet sidewalk as cars pulled up while others left. Travelers exchanged hugs as loved ones were picked up or dropped off. Some embraces were farewells, the kind that begged seconds to turn into years. Others were joyous reunions. Leeza looked down the street at the shuttles and taxis. A sea of windshield wipers waved hypnotically in the persistent drizzle. The sky was still menacingly gray.

A large black SUV slowly approached. As it crept closer, and the deeply tinted windows slowly lowered, Leeza saw the four men inside. They had olive complexions and were dressed in camouflage shirts and black berets. They were staring directly at her. In slow motion, she watched as they lifted their military rifles and took aim. She dropped her carry-on as they opened fire, hitting her chest. The family screamed as they watched her fall. A pool of blood formed around her body almost as soon as she hit the ground.

Artie let out a tortured cry as Leeza's blood sprayed across his anguished face. He dropped to his knees and wrapped her body in his arms as panic-stricken onlookers fled the horrific scene, screaming and running for their lives. Shocked and helpless, Artie and the twins stared at Leeza's lifeless body as the pool of blood seeped and spread further from beneath her.

The nightmare shattered as Leeza's entire body arched in a shuddering, silent scream. Her eyes stuck wide as she fought for each breath, the horror still beating against her ribs. Artie grabbed her by the shoulders and used his weight to hold her as she fought to break free.

"Leeza!" cried Artie. "You're home! You're home!"

She struggled to free herself from his grasp, still fighting for her life. She looked right through him, her eyes darting around the room, desperately searching for the enemy.

"You're okay, Leeza. You're home!" He steadied her shoulders, their faces inches apart. "It's okay, baby. It's okay."

Leeza pulled away and darted for the bathroom. She splashed her face with cold water, then threw open the medicine cabinet lined with prescription drug bottles and miniatures of alcohol. Her hands trembled violently as she opened a bottle of pills and poured several into her hand, chasing them with a tiny bottle of Jack Daniel's. She stared at her reflection in the mirror, chest heaving. Water dripped down her face, or was it sweat? Her hair was tangled in a wild mess. She slid to the floor as her legs gave way without her orders. Her vacant eyes stared, not at anything recognizable—and definitely not *from* anything recognizable.

A rtie gazed from the kitchen window across the frosted lawn while the smell of blueberry pancakes filled the house. The kids waited at the table, engrossed in their devices. Leeza's steps were slow and deliberate as she waded into the kitchen through faded consciousness. Jack and diazepam for breakfast, mingled with the lingering effects of yesterday's Ativan, had her teetering between numb and somnolent. She made it to the table and kissed each twin on the forehead. A Welsh Corgi rubbed against her leg. One hand firmly on the counter, she leaned down and vigorously rubbed the dog's neck and back.

"Well, good morning, Colonel," Leeza murmured. "The perimeter's secure, I see. Strong work."

Grant's face was a mix of sadness and concern. "Leesie?" he asked softly.

"Yes, baby?"

"Are you okay?"

"Of course. Just checkin' on the Colonel," she said, half convincingly.

"Why do you still call him Colonel?"

"Well, he acts like he's in charge, wouldn't you agree?"

"We've talked about this. You do know his name is Inspector Frisky, right?"

Leeza kissed the dog and ruffled his head, then pulled herself upright.

"You're such a dork," Charlotte said to Grant.

"Guilty as charged, ma'am," Leeza replied.

She reached for the plates, but Artie blocked her path.

"I'll take care of it." He put the breakfast on the table as Leeza slid into a chair.

"Best five things about school in twenty seconds—who's first?" Leeza said, forcing her eyelids all the way open.

"Girls first," said Grant.

"Whatever," said Charlotte with an eye roll. "Spelling bee club, science field trips, art history, study period."

"That's four things," Leeza said.

"Mr. Khosravi," said Charlotte.

"What about Mr. Khosravi?"

"He's hot."

Grant cracked up. "Mr. Khosravi is definitely hot! He's husband material."

"He has a wedding ring, sooo..." said Charlotte.

"Still hot."

"Acknowledged."

"Okay, this is awkward," said Artie. "Bus in fifteen."

"Your turn, Dr. G.," Leeza said.

"Study period, Mr. Khosravi, field trips, and... that's all I got."

"Homework didn't make the top four?" said Artie. He leaned behind Leeza and whispered, "You okay?" She forced a half-smile.

"Study period *is* for homework," said Grant.

"Love you," she whispered back. She pushed herself up and poured a glass of cranberry juice. "What kind of day are we having?"

"Best day ever!" said Grant, with two thumbs up.

"Best day ever," said Charlotte, adding under her breath, "Do we have to do this every friggin' morning?"

Leeza kissed Artie on the lips, then opened the coat closet. She froze when she saw the yellow binder on the floor. She shoved it back into her backpack.

"Correct answer. I expect to hear all about it when I get home." She grabbed her helmet and jacket, then flung the backpack across her shoulder.

Artie pressed against her back. "Don't even think about it," he whispered. She spun around and squeezed his behind. "I have patients," she said, with her own forceful whisper. Leeza knew her tolerance for drugs and alcohol, and she knew she would be fine before the first appointment. This wasn't the first time.

"Bye, Leesie," said Grant.

"Stay home," said Artie. "Reschedule the morning, and I'll drive you later. That was the plan, remember?"

Leeza's lips tightened as a familiar frustration grabbed her. She hated justifying herself. And she hated the idea that anyone might see her as weak—especially at work. What would they think if she didn't show up when there were patients on the schedule? She'd covered for other people who did that, but she never could. Besides, last night wasn't her fault, and the morning cocktail wasn't her fault. She refused to use them as excuses. She was leaving, like it or not.

"No bike," Artie said.

He followed her into the cavernous garage where the motorcycle was sandwiched between a spotless red Jaguar SUV and a silver F-150 with all-terrain tires and a lift kit. As one of the three garage doors rose, Leeza started the bike, savoring the roar of the Yamaha Star Venture Touring edition. She twisted the throttle twice and relished the moment as the monstrous vroom and thumping vibration filled her senses. *Never gets old.*

Artie hit the start/stop button. The bike died as silence reclaimed the space. He leaned his body into hers. "I'm fine!" cried Leeza. Artie was still. "I'm fine," she repeated, calmly.

"Just needed to look at that face again." He put his head on her chest; he loved the feel of her breasts through that leather jacket, loved the way it accentuated her perfect body, the smell of the leather, and her skin. "I wish I could do something."

"You are. You're here," said Leeza, rubbing her fingers through his morning hair. "I got you on my squad. There's nothing we can't do. I swear." The lethargy had eased, and she was able to focus.

Artie kissed her, then stepped back. "What kind of husband lets his wife drive in this condition?"

Leeza laughed. "Lets?"

He knew better than to argue. "Love you, sweet pea. Be careful."

Leeza winked as she restarted the motorcycle and pulled on her helmet. "Love ya, mean it," she told him. She headed down the driveway and onto the street. Artie gave himself a moment alone in the garage before lowering the door.

Back inside, Grant methodically rearranged his food. He could stack mini pancakes two feet high if only he could hide enough of his first three servings before getting busted. Artie took his plate. "I can tell when you're done."

"I wasn't done creating," Grant protested.

"Wash up. Y'all need to get moving."

"Jimmy Norlander says school is for losers," said Grant.

"Jimmy Norlander's a creep," added Charlotte.

"No, he's not. He's husband material. But he does smell awful funny."

"Be nice," said Artie, suppressing a laugh. "And no more 'accidentally' forgetting your homework. Got it?"

Grant headed toward the stairs with his signature dance moves. "Shantay, you stay, and sashay away!" he exclaimed, flipping long locks of imaginary hair and thrusting his hips from side to side.

"You need to be more like your brother," said Artie.

"Gay?" said Charlotte.

"He doesn't care what people think."

"Uh, I have two thoughts," said Charlotte.

Artie was amazed by how much Charlotte sounded like her mama when she had a point to make—or an argument to win. She wouldn't let it go until her opponent conceded that her point was at least valid, if not the absolute truth. Their stamina for arguing had to sit somewhere near the 98th percentile.

"First of all, he's a lot more fragile than you think. But he'd rather get hit by a bus than let anyone know that, especially you and Mama. And second, just because I try to maintain somewhere between being a stuck-up brainiac and a brain-dead slacker doesn't mean I'm obsessed with what people think of me."

Artie put the last of the dishes in the sink. "Whatever you say," he whispered to himself before turning back to her. "You obviously care what the popular girls think. Nobody's going to accuse you of being a brain-dead anything. But you can't be a hundred percent perfect at everything all the time. You're the spitting image of your mama." As usual, the conversation spiraled. It should have gone like this: strike up a conversation—work in some compliments to gain points—walk away. But as usual, it turned into a battle of wits. His best strategy was still his first strategy: walk away, grasshopper.

Charlotte was remarkably mature for her age, and Artie felt increasingly self-conscious when she asked him questions. The thought of raising a teenage girl—especially when dealing with Leeza's issues—left him feeling unprepared and exposed. And Charlotte was not just any teenage girl; she was a prodigy. A Black girl prodigy. A Black girl prodigy with boobs, glasses, and straight

A's. The older the kids got, the more his imposter syndrome worsened. He had a recurring dream that he was a teacher, floundering in front of a room full of students, and one of them was way smarter than he was. How was he supposed to keep from looking like an idiot in front of the class?

"Mama? Or you?"

"Beg your pardon?"

"You're projecting."

"You lost me."

"That's what they call it when people say other people do things, but *they* actually do it."

"I know what projecting is; my point was—"

"You get tied in knots every time you have to go to Gramma's house. You're not a little kid. You're a grown-up."

"Remember who you're talking to, baby girl," said the idiot teacher to the star pupil. He searched for an exit from the conversation *he'd* initiated. His face softened as he looked into her eyes. "They should be jealous of you, not the other way around." *That was pretty good.* "Now go get ready, I have tennis. And by the way, no more talking about hot teachers. You're twelve."

"Almost thirteen."

God help me.

3

Cornbread and Craniotomies

Mid-spring rolled out the red carpet to stunning blue skies and gentle breezes, charming the senses with luscious scents of flowering dogwood and magnolia. It was a beautiful slice of the calendar, reminiscent of sweet potato pie cooling on an open windowsill—a fitting prelude to the apocalyptic days of summer, when the charming exotica of spring would be traded for the smell of expired Piggly Wiggly mincemeat that had been left out too long. But that was still a few months away.

People wandered the historic streets, some hand in hand. There were picnics on the expansive green lawns, framed by gently swaying Spanish moss that hung from neighboring trees, proud historic buildings, and the famous Pineapple Fountain at Waterfront Park. Canada geese roamed freely, leaving poop landmines in their wake as they meandered along the waterfront—they had given up migrating centuries ago. Heaven on earth.

Leeza passed the University Medical Center and arrived at the Rutledge Tower on the corner of Rutledge Avenue. She parked, killed the engine, and pulled off her helmet, rolling her eyes at the sight of the business sign:

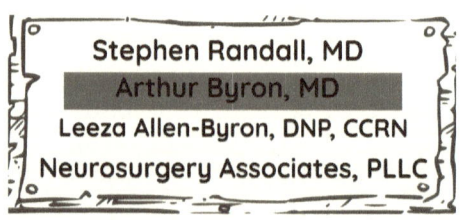

Her father-in-law, Dr. Arthur Byron, had moved out eight months ago, leaving Leeza, Dr. Randall, and an RN named Tana to manage the busy practice. Dr. Byron decided to join the famous group of academics from New York that had bought out University Neurosurgery after they offered him a million-dollar sign-on bonus and partnership within three years. Truth be told, they were pariahs, buying out smaller practices left and right to get their talons into more "communities." Artie's mother, Miranda, got to keep the million bucks when pancreatic cancer took his daddy a few months after the move. *Serves 'em right,* Leeza thought when she found out. *Rich lady got something for nothing, but at least the jackals screwed themselves.*

The large, gray void where her father-in-law's name used to be looked like a filthy band-aid, covering his name like an infected wound. Leeza had tried to convince Stephen to update the sign with just their names, but he refused to talk about it. She grabbed her backpack and headed up the steps through the double glass doors.

She closed her office door and pulled the yellow binder from the backpack, dropping it onto the leather swivel chair behind her desk. She cherished the daily ritual of arriving at her office and closing the door behind her; it was the day's first true moment of solitude. There was an azure accent wall, setting the mood for the rest of the room, which was done in flawless cottage white. The space was immersed in soothing classical music from the Mark Levinson stereo on the crowded, floor-to-ceiling bookshelves behind her desk, and the surround-sound Bose speakers across the room. Framed diplomas, certificates, and artwork, including abstract tribal dancers, pencil-and-ink drawings of ancient musical instruments, and nineteenth-century pianos and harpsichords, hung on the other walls. A multi-colored area rug with a distinctly

African vibe lent its blessing to the floor of the striking lair. *I Know Why the Caged Bird Sings* by Maya Angelou was prominently displayed on a retro burl-wood credenza, flanked by two barrel chairs.

Leeza slid into her white lab coat with her name embroidered in navy blue above the left chest pocket. A sterling silver caduceus lapel pin, received upon graduation from the nurse practitioner program at Georgetown University, graced the left lapel. She draped a stethoscope over her shoulders and took a chart from the inbox on her desk. Closing her eyes, she self-assessed her mental clarity. *It's all good.* She perused the patient information, then stopped in front of the three-quarter-length mirror on the back of her office door. She stared at her own face, waiting for the reflection to say something.

"*You got this,*" she heard it whisper. She opened the door and looked right and then left, as if Cujo himself could jump out at any second.

Leeza knocked lightly on the exam room door and entered with a smile and greetings all around. She was confident and genuine, with a bedside manner that made you feel important.

Inside the cramped exam room, a nurse was removing staples from a large, C-shaped craniotomy incision on the scalp of a middle-aged man as he reclined in a bulky electric wheelchair. His wife sat on a rolling stool in the corner, fast at work on a knitting project.

"Richard and Celeste," Leeza said on her way into the room. "Good morning, good to see you."

"Hey, Leeza," Celeste said.

"How are you two holding up?" She slid a stool next to the exam table.

"He's a handful."

"It'll get easier, I promise."

Leeza watched as the nurse skillfully plied each staple from its place in the incision. "Good morning, Tana," she said.

Tana was an RN in her early forties with the assurance and attitude of someone who'd been around the block. If not for the five-year age difference, the women could be twins.

"Mornin'," said Tana as she methodically extracted the final staple. She examined every centimeter of the long, curving wound. "Gonna look just fine when that head of hair grows back." She dropped the staples and staple remover into a red sharps container.

Leeza pulled on a glove, leaned in, and ran a finger slowly along the large incision. "Beautiful." She peeled off the glove and examined his pupils with a penlight.

"His taste buds have done changed," said Celeste. "Smell of cornbread and collards makes him hurl. Used to be all he wanted."

"Unfortunately, that's not unusual, tragic as it is," said Leeza. "Surgery went well." She pressed the stethoscope against his chest. "Dr. Randall was able to resect most of it." She lifted his shirt and pressed on his belly.

Celeste wiped tears from both cheeks.

"Therapy starts on the fifteenth," Leeza said as she thumbed through his chart. "We'll get another PET/CT scan in three months to monitor for metastasis. So far, so good. We'll do everything in our power, Celeste."

"I know you will."

"He still has some swelling. You'll start seeing changes soon." Leeza nodded at Celeste's project. "Another scarf?"

"Helps with the tremors, I think."

Leeza smiled as she studied Richard's face. "See you soon, amigo. Call if you need anything at all. Thank you, Tana."

Leeza was charting on her computer, surrounded by a collection of framed photos: Artie and the twins, a wedding photo of her in a white gown and Artie in a black and white tux, an old, faded black and white photo of her mother, and a photo of her in camouflage fatigues standing in front of an Army hospital tent—a large red cross claiming its roof. The expressionless platoon of medics and infantry soldiers were resolute, their faces unreadable.

Dr. Stephen Randall, a stodgy white man in his early sixties, appeared in the doorway. He wore dark-rimmed glasses and a white lab coat with his name embroidered above the left pocket, like Leeza's. He was direct, abrupt, and always eating crackers and cheese from the break room, but he never seemed to notice the crumbs clinging to the front of his tie.

"You're scrubbing in on the spine case next Friday. That sucker's gonna be a bitch," he barked. "Name's Smith or Smoot, or something like that."

"It's on my calendar, but—" He was gone before she could finish.

His tone got under her skin.

"A practitioner is a nurse with a prescription pad," she'd overheard Arthur tell him before he jumped ship. *"They don't know which end of the scalpel is the sharp end."*

She didn't know which was worse—that her father-in-law said that about practitioners, or that his partner didn't defend her. Without her and Tana, they wouldn't have a practice. That is, unless they learned to talk to patients while they were still conscious, and God forbid, take out their own staples, and actually saw patients before the anesthesiologist knocked them out, and did consults at the hospital, and set up therapy and home health care appointments. She was always defending them to the floor nurses who complained endlessly about how they talked to them.

One thing that recentered her was her photos. She had seen them a thousand times, but looking at them brought her right back to the moment in time when each one was taken. She could remember the exact feelings captured in each frame as if they were happening all over again. Except for the one in front of the medic tent. She never stared at that one, even though people asked her about it the most. She'd move it off the desk one of these days.

A sudden knock startled Leeza, sending her into an instant panic: gasping, eyes clenching shut, heart racing. Unexpected noises caused a violent flight-or-fight response, jolting her into a horrified state, as if defending herself against very real and present danger. She had experienced this full-body panic response countless times since returning from deployment less than two years ago. The gut-pounding reactions were triggered when she least expected it by the most insignificant things, and were gone as soon as they happened, but were infuriating, nonetheless. There could be no timers or analog clocks in the house or office; the sound of seconds ticking or an alarm going off could drop her to the floor.

She slowly wrestled her mind back.

Tana's restless energy didn't have an off switch. It served her well in a fast-paced work environment, but she had no patience for people who were prone to lollygagging. She stopped in her tracks. "Christ, I am so sorry," she said. "I never learn." Scaring Leeza was easy for Tana to do, even when she consciously tried not to.

Leeza took calming breaths, in through the nose, out through the mouth. Tana gently delivered the stack of charts to Leeza's desk.

"Only one consult tonight. New admit in ICU. Sixty-five-year-old female, history of ground-level fall. CT showed a frontal lobe mass, MRI scheduled for tomorrow morning. Liver labs slightly elevated, fatty liver on ultrasound."

Tana handed the chart to Leeza. "Fastest friggin' thing that ever happens in a hospital is a liver ultrasound for elevated LFTs. This is the South, people; that shit is incidental!"

"This is America, people; that shit is incidental," Leeza agreed.

"Uh-huh," exclaimed Tana. "Try to get an MRI on Saturday night, your ass outta luck. Granny eats a cheeseburger at Chuck E. Cheese and an hour later she's gettin' a gallbladder ultrasound!"

"Pizza," said Leeza. "Chuck E. Cheese is pizza."

"Granny ain't got no business at Chuck E. Cheese anyways," cried Tana.

The consultation was highlighted in yellow. At the top of the document, Tana had written a daily affirmation for Leeza, as always. And Leeza always read it aloud.

> "I consider that the sufferings of this present time are not worthy to be compared with the glory that is to be revealed to me."

"Thank you, Miss Tana."

"You get some rest. You can't be workin' all the time like you do," said Tana.

"Yes, ma'am."

As Tana turned to leave, Leeza made a call.

Artie picked up. *"Did you miss me?"*

Leeza stared at the avatar, the one she took of him in Monaco with the tweed newsboy cap and racing gloves. She adored that picture. "Always," was her answer every time he asked that question. "I'll see you after my appointment. I'll be home in time for supper."

She opened the top drawer of her desk and pulled out the bright yellow binder, thick with worn pages. The cover was filled with notes, formulas, and drawings. She pulled back the cover and ran her fingertips over the first page, every centimeter was filled with mathematical equations, chemical compounds, scratched-out words, underlined words, highlighted words. She lingered on the pages before sliding it back into her backpack.

She took off the stethoscope and lab coat and hung them next to the door. Staring into the mirror, she took a slow, deliberate cleansing breath. Her reflection spoke back: *"It's all you."*

4

You Ever Slept with a Cop?

Listening to Claude Debussy's *Arabesque No. 1* while riding a motorcycle through the backroads of Charleston, Savannah, or Hilton Head Island—that was one of life's greatest pleasures, and it should be on everyone's bucket list. The symphony of vibrations, the saltwater breeze, and the masterpiece in E major consumed Leeza's senses, banishing the ever-present toxicity, trauma, and fear—if only for a few moments. It was crucial for her to experience such transcendence as often as possible.

She guided the bike through the streets of Charleston, consumed by the masterpiece. She made a detour to the tent city under the Arthur Ravenel Jr. Bridge, where a hundred and sixty people existed with only a sliver of polyethylene between them and the world. A recent article titled "Homeless in the Holy City" had affected her deeply, although nothing in the story really surprised her. Not far from the five-star restaurants, tourist shops, and historic buildings on King and Calhoun streets, humanity lived on the fringe. There were a thousand reasons why they ended up here, but so many of those reasons—like addiction, mental illness, and poverty—were preventable, or at least treatable. *How is this still happening in this country?* She slowed the bike to a crawl as she stared into the faces of the residents. "This shall change," she promised herself. "This bullshit's gonna change."

Society was quick to blame bureaucracy—Big Pharma, the Veterans Administration, Congress. But those were merely pawns in the game. Administrators and politicians would never refuse a paycheck they had done nothing to earn, showing zero interest in actually learning and understanding the root causes that put those people in tents in the first place. They were obstructionists, and Leeza had no expectations of them.

Most of the homeless were there because of their own actions and their own decisions. The question for Leeza was—what happened inside their brains that led them to those choices? Nobody grows up dreaming of the day they can go and live in a tent under a bridge. What went wrong? Was it an organic process that altered their mental reality? Or unsuccessfully treated psychological trauma that led to addiction and anti-social behavior? This limb of society is broken, but it can be fixed. The answer is out there. A cure is, too. *I'll figure it out if it kills me.*

Leeza parked in front of The Nomad Club on King Street. The doors had just opened, and it wouldn't be hopping for several more hours. She paused just inside, allowing her eyes to adjust to the darkness, then followed the plaid wallpaper down to the bar.

The Nomad was known for its open-mic nights, which attracted only the best out-of-work musicians. Every act had to audition for a slot in the "open" lineup to ensure the best (free) talent, which attracted swarms of regulars and tourists. There was a drag show every third Tuesday night, and the house was packed with women celebrating bachelorette parties and divorces by getting drunk and shoving dollar bills into the corsets of men dressed as women, belting out Cher, Taylor, Tina, and the occasional Aretha.

Some of the employees performed at the open mic during their breaks—that was a house favorite. Watching a hot young guy make you a cosmopolitan and then stare into your eyes while singing "Perfect" by Ed Sheeran was an orgasmic experience for a lonely sophomore from Waynesville, Ohio. The owner figured that out two decades ago and was still laughing all the way to the bank.

The stage hadn't changed since the last time Leeza was there, before her deployment. The owner spared no expense on the sound system, including the Yamaha Clavinova CVP-909 digital piano, which could be heard four blocks away. Black velvet curtains covered the back wall of the stage, and the overhead recessed lighting peeked out from the shiny purple ceiling. *Who uses gloss enamel on a ceiling? And purple?* she remembered thinking the first time she saw it.

A young musician wearing tight jeans and a cowboy hat played guitar and sang "You Shouldn't Kiss Me Like This" by Toby Keith. Josh was a bartender in his early thirties, but he looked twenty-four. He worked full-time while taking poli-sci classes at Charleston Southern University. His boyish face, beautiful voice, mesmerizing stage presence, and impossibly tight jeans made him a favorite during open mics. He finished his rendition to thin applause, mostly from coworkers—and Leeza, who was standing at the bar.

"Leeza!" Josh yelled from the stage when he realized the source of the sustained ovation.

"Bravo!" cried Leeza, with a huge grin and animated applause. "I miss that!"

Josh tipped his hat before giving her a huge hug, then headed behind the bar.

"Still doing double duty, I see," said Leeza.

"Want your regular?"

"Why not?"

"What are you doin' here this time of morning?" he asked as he poured a Jack and Coke.

"It's almost four o'clock... P.M.," said Leeza.

"Early as hell for some of us."

"Is Sammie here? She said she would meet me here."

"Oh, she's here all right. You're all she's been talkin' about." Josh motioned toward the bathroom at the far end of the club as a young woman emerged.

Sammie was Latina, in her mid-thirties, with a youthful face and short, spiked black hair. She wore jeans and an AC/DC t-shirt with cut-off sleeves. They had known each other since high school, but they had chosen severely different paths.

Sammie sprinted across the room. "Leeza!" she squealed. She cupped Leeza's face, looked into her eyes, then kissed her passionately. "Welcome home, soldier. What took you so long?"

"Been a little hectic."

"Excuses!"

Josh parked three shot glasses between them. "You made it home in one piece. We got us a real-life war veteran." He poured the ouzo and lifted one in a toast.

"A *hot* real-life war veteran!" said Sammie.

"To the long-awaited return of Charleston's finest!" said Josh. The three toasted, threw back the shots, and slammed the glasses.

Leeza grabbed her cocktail and motioned for Sammie to follow her to the outdoor patio. "Don't you leave without sayin' bye," said Josh. Leeza blew him a kiss as she and Sammie joined arms.

"Staying out of trouble?" Leeza asked as they settled at a bar-height table in the covered space. A half-wall separated them from the sidewalk, where pedestrians went about their day from the waist up.

"It's a full-time job."

"I worry about you."

"I could stop by. Y'all could use an old-fashioned wellness check," Sammie said with a wink.

"I'm serious."

Sammie took a long drag from her vape pen. "You ever slept with a cop?"

Leeza scoffed. "What the actual hell? You really haven't changed."

"Dudes are... meh. The chicks?"

Leeza felt her face cringe. "Don't make me ask."

"Selfish bitches," said Sammie. "Emphasis on selfish."

"Note to self."

"Just sayin'." Sammie's eyes performed a quick, but obvious, scan of Leeza's body. "Might be useful someday. You never know." She took another satisfying drag from the vape.

One-track mind, Leeza thought. "You're looking healthy, Sammie."

"Yeah, well, the judge gave me an offer I couldn't refuse."

"Look, I wanna get together."

"Finally!" Sammie exclaimed. "You don't know how much I missed you guys, both of you. I know I ruined it with Artie, but maybe you can talk to him. We had a good thing, you know we did."

"A good thing that ended badly," said Leeza. "You're a different person when you're using. It's not pretty. And there's the trust issue."

Sammie leaned her elbows on the table and watched the tops of cars creep along King Street; her enthusiasm having been knocked down a peg. "So why did you call?"

"I'm working on something, and I need your expertise..." Leeza said, before catching herself. "And I wanted to see how you're doing."

"You need something." Sammie scoffed. "Figures." She took another hit from her vape. "Fine. Time and place."

Josh arrived with three more ouzos. "I can't believe I'm looking at the two of you together again right now," he said.

Sammie raised her glass. "To the old times and the new!"

"Old times and the new," chimed Josh and Leeza as they downed the shots.

"New chances, new beginnings!" added Sammie, waving her glass in the air. "Woohoo!"

"I've gotta go," said Leeza. "I'll text you soon. Give me a hug." Leeza leaned in, wrapped her arms around Sammie, and whispered into her ear. "This is between us." She held Sammie's shoulders and looked into her eyes, waiting for a nod.

"Yes, ma'am," said Sammie.

Leeza grabbed her helmet and headed for the exit as Josh and Sammie watched. "Whatever you say, ma'am," Sammie called out. "Just don't ignore me."

5

Pesky Side Effects

D r. Kashvi Singh and Leeza sat facing each other in the cavernous brown-and-beige office. No external sounds could be heard; even their own voices were strangely muted. Massive wooden bookshelves loaded with medical journals, encyclopedic collections, and classic novels dominated the walls. The patient's chair was a large, tufted leather chaise, which allowed one to lie down when the situation called for it. The doctor's chair was unnecessarily large and upholstered in matching tufted leather. Between them, a huge wooden coffee table, which looked as if it had been commissioned by King George III. A thick candle, encased in hardened wax that had dripped down its sides, stood proudly in the center, a relic used for exorcisms—or, more commonly, regression therapy. When the patient was sufficiently hypnotized and working through long-buried memories but suddenly needed to stop, they could blow out the candle and sit in silence until they were ready to move on—or until their time was up.

"How are you doing, Leeza?" asked Dr. Singh.

Dr. Singh, a second-generation immigrant, was dressed in colorful, albeit Indo-Western, clothing. Deceptively young-looking, her demeanor was direct but assuasive. She spoke with the residual Indian accent of a native Indian speaker who learned English as a second language from a young age. Leeza found the red bindi on her forehead oddly distracting.

"Bordering on acceptable," Leeza said.

"Let's aim a little higher, shall we?"

"Staying busy with projects and chemical castration as prescribed."

"Ah, pesky side effects," Dr. Singh noted, scribbling in her notepad.

"Yoga and meditation only work so well without a Jack and Coke," said Leeza.

"Well, those are adjunct therapies," said Dr. Singh. "We're steering a barge here." She took an academic pause. "You used the word acceptable. I'd say that's measurable progress. And yoga beats the hell out of crocheting."

"I have no problem with crocheting," Leeza said, remembering the old woman covering her mama with the crocheted throw made of leftover yarn.

Dr. Singh's voice was unwavering. "But not with a Jack and Coke."

Leeza shrugged. "It's the more pragmatic choice."

"Got it." Dr. Singh searched Leeza's face for a sign that she was joking.

The large windows in the psychiatrist's office were hidden behind thick drapes that might have been created by an Indian cousin of Jackson Pollock. When the dust-filled sunbeams crossed the room during the late afternoon, it reminded Leeza of her and her mama's house in Beaufort.

"I think it's prudent to consider changing course at this juncture," Dr. Singh continued. "Given that you have endured repeated episodes of traumatic emotional injury, which began after an otherwise exemplary early childhood, the treatment plan must be carefully calculated. We'll have to remain diligent in monitoring measurable progress, even small victories. You may discover benefits in exploring more unconventional therapy methods to ensure the greatest opportunity for success. Ultimately, we need you to be less dependent on chemical therapy. I have some thoughts along that avenue."

"Lock and load."

"Great." She set the pad on the giant coffee table and again tried to read Leeza. "I need you to elaborate on something," she said. "I gathered from remarks you made previously that you had feelings of guilt when you first learned of your mother's diagnosis."

Leeza leaned back into the leather chaise. *Here we go.*

"Let's revisit that."

"I thought we were moving forward."

"I want to be certain," Dr. Singh pressed gently. "We can stop at any time." She struck a match and lit the candle.

Sandalwood and sage, Leeza thought. *At least it's not charcoal and driftwood.* She instinctively drew a deep breath, knowing that what was about to happen would be both unpleasant and potentially dangerous. "It wasn't the cancer I felt guilty about."

"We may need to open some wounds, and we'll need to do this without the dark passenger, and by that, I mean—"

"The lie?" Leeza asked.

"I have to remind myself I'm working with a neuroscientist."

"Just a nurse."

"The lie in the sense that you harbor the misbelief that the repeated episodes of trauma are somehow of your own doing. We tend to blame ourselves for things that happened *to* us." She pushed the candle across the table closer to Leeza. "I want you to recount what happened objectively. None of your scars are there because of anything you did. Once that is established in your mind, we can work on your inner motivation to change the way you process and deal with the horrible things that are beyond your control, past and future." She leaned back into the enormous doctor's chair, crossing her legs. "Take several moments."

Leeza settled back and closed her eyes. She could replay the scene in her mind as if she were still living it, like an eight-track tape player that started over after the last song, relooping forever: Friday afternoon. The recital. *Beethoven's Sonata No. 17, Tempest, 3rd Movement.* The blond-wood baby grand. *My God, that piano was ugly.* Principal McStanley called her Lisa instead of Leeza. She remembered spending that Wednesday in the park with Davina. She could feel the sunlight and see the pillowy clouds against a brilliant blue backdrop. She remembered getting the letter from the mailbox and running into the house to find her mama. It was always the same.

Leeza's eyes fluttered behind closed lids as she watched the scene unfold in Beaufort.

Mrs. Beasley's eyes were fixed on Leeza's as the woman and the young girl stood face to face on the porch of the old wooden house, dust dancing in the sunbeams, and the tired mahogany piano waiting patiently in the living room. There was a deep emptiness in the strange woman's expression. As they stared into each other's eyes, Leeza sensed the woman's head moving very slightly from side to side, as if she were saying "No" to a voice inside her own head. "No, it's not okay." The letter from the Juilliard School of Music in New York slipped from Leeza's hand, fluttering to the ground.

Leeza broke the silence. "She knew the piano would get me out of that town. She worked three jobs to pay for my lessons. She never did anything for herself. Never asked a single fool for help. Left alone with a baby by some military coward, but she did it anyway." A tear slipped from Leeza's eye. "She gave me everything. And all of a sudden, she's helpless." Leeza's chest heaved.

"Take several moments, Leeza," said Dr. Singh. "Take several moments."

"And all I did was take."

"Leeza—" said Dr. Singh calmly.

"All I did was take!" Leeza repeated more forcefully.

"Your mother's dream for you was in your music."

"ALL. I. DID. WAS. TAKE!" Leeza screamed.

"She chose that sacrifice," said Dr. Singh. "Giving you that gift was important to her." She noticed Leeza's trembling hands. "Take a moment, Leeza." She tried to redirect her. "Sounds like you hit the ground running at your old job. That must feel good." She moved toward the candle, but then—

"I did everything you said!" exclaimed Leeza, eyes open and staring directly at the psychiatrist. The red bindi was brighter than before—and bigger. "Everything you told me to do!"

"You've been home for a relatively short time. All things considered, I—"

Leeza grabbed the sides of her head and squeezed her eyes shut. *The unrelenting, deafening sound of artillery and bombs exploded all around. The air was thick with smoke, and the sounds of men yelling, chaos, and cries of agony. Two soldiers rushed into the medic tent with a stretcher carrying a wounded soldier in his early twenties, placing him on a cot in front of Leeza. The soldier's head was covered with blood-soaked gauze. Through the sound of the explosions, Leeza slowly lifted the dressings to reveal an eye staring at her in horror. As she peeled back the rest of the dressing, she saw that the other side of his head had been blown off. The soldier desperately grabbed Leeza's hand!*

A gut-wrenching wail tore itself from Leeza's body as she snatched her hand away from the dying soldier. Her body was trembling as Dr. Singh blew out the candle and rushed to her side.

"Leeza, you're safe," Dr. Singh told her. "You're safe."

Leeza's eyes darted from side to side, searching for enemy soldiers in the far corners of the room. "Shhh! Shhh! Shhh! We have to be quiet!" she whispered frantically. "We have to be quiet!" Her body shivered as she squeezed her face in her hands, fingers digging into her temples. "Stay down! Be quiet!" She pulled her knees tightly against her chest.

Dr. Singh rubbed her back and rocked her. "How often now?"

Leeza whimpered softly as reality slowly crept back. She glared at the ceiling, sucked in a long breath and released it as slowly. "Been a while," she lied.

"Leeza, you need to—"

"I know!" she snapped. "Focus on your goals!"

"Focus on your future," Dr. Singh added. "And see your past objectively."

"People would hate me if they knew what I did."

"What happened to you happened *to* you," Dr. Singh said. "The dark passenger—"

"Why did I come back from there?"

"You *did* come back, and now—"

Leeza raised a hand as if to say, "*Stop!*" "I am a literal zombie. Dying would have been the *only* way to..." her voice trailed off. "All I do is move from one expectation to another, one responsibility to the next, and I can't keep doing it like this."

"I know you're exhausted, but you should be proud of your progress. We're going to help you to see your entire existence through a new paradigm." Dr. Singh glanced at her watch. "Let that be your takeaway for today."

Leeza wiped her face. "I'm in quicksand," she said. "And I'm stuck."

"You're not stuck. You're not stuck." Dr. Singh went to the bookcase and found a thin paperback. "I'm going to send you home with a tool to help you recognize and regulate levels of your emotions, everything from bliss to rage to depression." She sat next to Leeza and thumbed through the book. "You picture each of these emotions in your mind as a ladder. When you're angry, you visualize the ladder as anger, then you assign the level of anger you are feeling to a rung on the ladder. For instance, on rung one, you might feel irritated. On rung five, you might be really upset about something, but you're analyzing it, seeing yourself, and talking yourself down without escalating. You can see these rungs clearly and you know exactly where you are. Rung ten is rage. At that level, you're unable to rationalize what is happening, and you've lost control of your ability to de-escalate. But you can still see the tenth rung, all lit up; pulsating with bright, fiery flames. You know what you have to do. You can never let yourself stay above the first rung for long; you should always de-escalate in your mind to get off the ladder. Always be aware of the ladder."

"Homework," said Leeza.

"Don't memorize it—just peruse it before you see me again, and we'll take a deeper dive together." Dr. Singh smiled. "This is progress. We know that emotions are forever changing."

Leeza grabbed her jacket and helmet and headed for the door. She slid the paperback next to the yellow binder and rolled her eyes. *As if I would memorize this crap.*

Inspector Frisky gnawed on a bone in the corner while Leeza and Artie worked on dinner.

"Leesie, guess what?" said Grant.

"What, boyfriend?"

"I'm helping Charlotte study for the spelling bee, and when she wins, she's giving me half the money."

"I told you, the money is for college tuition, and I might not even win," said Charlotte, staring at the food Artie had set in front of her.

"Oh, you're gonna win, alright. With me helping you, you *have* to win. Right, Leesie?"

"If you work really hard."

"We practice every night. Watch this," he said, turning to Charlotte. "Sequin."

Charlotte rolled her eyes. "Could you use it in a sentence?"

"Trixie wore a silver sequin gown with matching lace-up sandals."

"Sequin," Charlotte began. "S.E.Q.U.I.N. Sequin."

Grant beamed with a toothy grin and gave two thumbs up.

"I'm proud of both of you."

"I'm not hungry," Charlotte said.

"You haven't even tried it," said Artie.

"That's brain food, ya know," Leeza added.

"What's brain food?" Grant asked.

"It's what parents tell kids to make them eat, 'cause food makes you smart," Charlotte explained, rolling her eyes. "Whatever. And I did eat some."

"When I grow up, I want to be the First Lady of the United States," said Grant.

"First Gentleman," Charlotte corrected.

"Or President," Artie suggested.

"Have you *seen* the outfits they wear?" Grant asked, with a dramatic flip of the wrists.

"Maybe by the time you're old enough, presidents can also wear fabulous outfits," said Leeza. Grant's face lit up at the idea.

"God help us," Charlotte mumbled.

"Three more bites, no negotiating," Artie told Charlotte.

An enormous fart suddenly ripped through the room, causing everyone to turn and stare at Inspector Frisky, still happily gnawing on his bone. Grant howled with laughter while Charlotte rolled her eyes and dropped her fork onto her plate.

"Now I really am done!" she exclaimed, dropping her plate in the sink before heading for the stairs.

Artie shook his head as Grant lost his mind. Leeza smiled, desperately trying to suppress her laughter.

Getting tucked into bed was Grant's favorite time of day, and he was hell-bent on dragging it out as long as possible. Leesie did it best. She let him talk about anything he wanted without interjecting like Daddy. He had a wildly vivid imagination and loved making up lyrics to new songs, even if they sounded more like something William S. Burroughs wrote during his heroin phase. His poems landed squarely between childish ramblings and literary brilliance.

"Leesie?" asked Grant.

"Yes, Dr. G?"

"Why does everything have to be a competition?"

Leeza often had to think before answering Grant's questions; they sounded completely random, but she could usually figure out where they came from. "So there can be winners, like you." She kissed him on the forehead.

"I'm fine if everybody wins," said Grant.

"I know you are, sweetheart. Me too."

"Leesie?"

"What, baby?"

"Jimmy Norlander pushed Alicia Swenton down at school, and the next day he said he told his dad it was Alicia's fault and that nothing bad was going to happen to him."

Leeza's bottom lip slid between her teeth. "Is Alicia okay?"

"Her elbow was bleeding."

"Is he still your friend?"

"I like him some of the time," Grant answered thoughtfully.

"I love you *all* of the time." Leeza kissed him on the forehead. "To the moon and back." The moment Grant started to laugh, Leeza realized what she'd done. She put her hand over his mouth as he tried to talk through the building laughter.

"Don't you dare say it." She put her finger on his lips and leaned in close. "Don't you dare, I mean it."

Grant laughed even harder as Leeza moved her hand away and stood to leave.

"I love you to Uranus and back!" exclaimed Grant, followed by hysterical laughter and logrolling across the bed. Leeza shook her head and turned out the light before heading to Charlotte's room.

"He's going to hell, ya know," said Charlotte.

"I can hear you!" yelled Grant through his laughter.

Leeza kissed her on the forehead. "That boy is a mess, indeed."

By bedtime, Charlotte was usually agitated by whatever had happened that day at school, whether it was because the popular girls were going to a party she wasn't invited to or because Daddy asked a question but didn't let her finish her answer. It was always something, and Leeza was usually wrong when she tried to guess what it might be that night.

"Is everything good with you?"

"All good," said Charlotte, arms crossed.

"Except?" Leeza asked, knowing she wanted to talk, but they would have to play the game first.

"It'll wait," Charlotte taunted.

Leeza called her bluff and stood to leave. "Okay, night, sweetie."

"You know what it is," said Charlotte.

"You're gonna have to give me a hint," she said as she sat back down.

Charlotte grabbed her phone from the nightstand, opened her calendar, and held it up.

"A little more of a hint, please."

Charlotte pointed to a date on the calendar.

"That's your birthday, which is three months away."

"That's the day you tell me who our real parents are. You promised."

Leeza knew Charlotte had been told for years by her classmates that she and Grant were adopted because their skin was different from their daddy's. Some kids had a Black parent and a white parent, but those kids' skin was in between, not Black and not white. But she and Grant were Black like Leeza, even though Daddy was like totally white. Leeza and Artie agreed they would have 'the talk' when the twins became teenagers.

Leeza nodded. "I won't forget. I love you so much. Sweet dreams."

"Love you."

Leeza's home office radiated a warm glow, with an azure accent wall, music-themed artwork, and ever-present classical music, just like her office at work. A Yamaha upright piano in flame mahogany was flanked by floor-to-ceiling bookshelves. Framed family photos adorned the desk on the opposite wall. A crystal whiskey decanter and rocks glasses were on perpetual standby on a small cocktail table under the window.

She poured a drink and took a long sip, then quietly locked the door. She peered out the window, then turned the cocktail table around and opened a drawer that faced the back, removing a wooden box. Inside, there was a clear plastic bag with white powder, a straw, a syringe with a tiny needle, a vial, and a spoon with a bent handle. She stared at the contents of the box, as if memories poured from each of them. She put the box back in the drawer and turned the table back toward the window. She unlocked the door, took another sip, went to the piano, and set the drink on the yellow binder next to her. Her gaze was fixed on the black-and-white piano keys. She let her fingertips hover over them, barely skimming their perfectly smooth surfaces. She looked up at the sheet music waiting in front of her: *Sonata No. 17, Tempest, 3rd Movement.*

Leeza made her way through the applause and cheers to the old blond-wood baby grand piano at center stage. Principal McStanley beamed as she walked by. She turned to the audience with a humble smile, then positioned the bench as if she, the piano, and the bench formed a dynamic trio, each with a crucial part to play. The auditorium took a collective deep breath. Leeza's hands rose ceremoniously above the keyboard. Seconds later, the agonizing radio silence was replaced by a brilliant performance of Beethoven's Sonata No. 17, Tempest, 3rd Movement.

That was then. Tonight was different. She slid the yellow binder from under the rocks glass and placed it in front of Beethoven's masterpiece. She stared at the wrinkled, scribbled binder and started playing. But it wasn't Ludwig's Tempest; tonight, she pampered herself with *Hope Springs* by Roy Todd. Calming. Uplifting. Transcendent. Easy.

6

If That's Code for Something, I Don't Wanna Know What It Is

A haunting soprano solo of *O Patria Mia* from Aida serenaded the house in the early morning as Grant and Charlotte had breakfast.

"Leesie's in the shower," said Grant.

"Aida," said Charlotte. "Again."

"How many kids do you know that get opera for breakfast while waiting for the bus?" Artie asked.

"None," they chimed in unison.

"Precisely. You are the chosen ones. Thirteen minutes; eat up. I'll be right back," he said as he disappeared up the stairs.

Charlotte eyed Inspector Frisky gnawing on his bone. "He is so gross," she said.

"He's a dog," said Grant.

"Who does that?"

"Dogs... and people."

"It's supposed to be private," Charlotte muttered.

"Not for dogs."

The outline of Leeza's body was barely visible through the steam as she belted out the aria. She had told Artie about the time her mama took them to see Aida when they were in New York for the Juilliard audition, and within a week, she had memorized every female solo piece. Singing opera in the shower was a good way for her to get out of her own head, if only for a few minutes a day.

She shut off the shower and turned around to find Artie staring at her. "Mornin' sweet pea," he said with a grin. Leeza grabbed his shirt, pulled him toward her wet body, and kissed him. The air was warm and dense. "You're obnoxious," she said.

Artie slid his hand between her legs. "I'll show you obnoxious."

Leeza's chest heaved as she thrust her pelvis into his hand. She closed her eyes and allowed herself to revel in the pleasure between her legs. "You got thirteen minutes?" he asked.

"Only need ten," she replied, before dropping to her knees and pulling down his pants.

Downstairs, Grant and Charlotte were scraping their plates when Artie returned. "The bus should be rolling up the street," he said.

"What were you doing?" Grant asked.

"Building a spaceship."

"If that's code for something, I don't wanna know what it is," said Charlotte.

"Leesie is gonna be late for work," said Grant.

"She's working half a day."

"No fair!" Grant protested.

"Go!" said Artie. "And have a great day. Love ya, mean it!"

"Love ya, mean it!" yelled Grant as he slammed the door.

Leeza lay waiting for Artie on the bed. The earlier playful mood had settled back into its usual contemplative, pensive quiet. She needed to talk.

He plopped down next to her. "You spoil me," he said, adjusting his underwear before turning onto his side to face her. He used his fingertips to trace circles on her belly. "How's Leeza?"

"She's still here. And she's determined to stay here even if she has to..." Her voice trailed off. "I'm still working on the rest of that sentence."

"You'll figure it out." His eyes lingered on her belly for a moment longer before he slid the towel down to expose her breasts.

"I remember the first time I saw you naked. That black skin on those white sheets, nothing but candlelight in a pitch-black room. Your eyes were closed. Jesus Christ. I could have stared at you all night long... our third date. I think about that all the time."

"I wish I could have been a fly on the wall when you told your mama and daddy about me," she said. "That's what *I* think about all the time."

Artie chuckled. "You really didn't want to be there, trust me. My mama invented pearl clutching that night."

"Bless her heart."

"I guess you didn't exactly align with her vision for me."

"Still can't believe you went against her like that."

"I knew she'd come around, eventually."

"And has she?"

The question hung between them. Both wanted to break the tension, but neither could.

Leeza half-smiled as she stared at the ceiling; her words were tentative: "Speaking of how Leeza is doing, I think I've kind of plateaued with Dr. Singh. She has some unconventional drug combinations developed in the mid-eighties that most psychiatrists don't even use anymore." Forcing a half-hearted chuckle, as if levity would help her case, she added: "And she's got me playing Chutes and Ladders for homework."

Artie rubbed his jaw. "I don't even know what that means. You can change psychiatrists or therapists or PCPs or whatever, but you promised me you would do what they recommended and that you wouldn't self-diagnose or self-prescribe. This is serious, Leeza. We've talked about it quite a bit."

"Not enough."

"Yes, enough," he insisted. "You remember what happened the last time you decided to tweak your meds."

"Last time you knew about," she mumbled.

"Didn't hear you."

"I told you—I decided to wean myself off an antidepressant from that drug trial, and you flipped out. You ran home to Mama for two days. I wasn't even acting any differently. You wouldn't have known if—"

"There are two people in there," he said, touching her forehead. "I fell in love with one of them. It's the other one we're trying to fix. You said it yourself; it's a team effort."

But they hadn't discussed it enough, and she wasn't done—she was just getting started. And someday he would have to admit he was wrong.

7

Grampa Was a Real Doctor

Leeza was charting, but she couldn't get the conversation with Artie out of her head. He was the only thing in the world as important to her as her mama was. He was the only other person in her life who made her feel like she was worth a damn thing. He was a sensitive guy, and Leeza loved that about him. She also loved his intelligence, curiosity, and zest for adventure. He was genuine. And he wasn't a redneck—*and* he was straight. He was also an outspoken activist for the less fortunate, even though Miranda thought volunteering at the legal aid office was "misguided."

She loved staring at his profile. She remembered the moment when they were taking their vows and the minister said, "Do you take Leeza..." Artie turned and looked at him for a second—and in that moment, she memorized his profile. The minister finished the line, "...to be your wife?" And as Artie turned back to her, his face softened, and his smile touched her soul. As they both finally exhaled, he answered "I do."

Leeza had been trying to think of a way to tell him about her ideas on managing the flashbacks and night terrors, desperately needing his support, but unsure if he could accept the unorthodox methods she would be using. She'd been diligently researching and logging every detail of her hypotheses and planned experiments in the yellow binder, and she was ready to move on to the next phase. She'd finally gotten up the nerve to tell him Dr. Singh wasn't helping, but Artie made it clear she was to follow the advice of her therapists and physicians religiously: end of discussion.

Tana knocked lightly and peered inside before entering. "Two consults tonight. First one is a head injury in the E.R., male, seventeen. Ortho cut in line again and they want him in pre-op STAT, so he'll be in PACU by the time you get to him."

Leeza rolled her eyes. "Post-anesthesia consult? That'll wait till morning."

"And a new admit with a brainstem tumor, female, fifty, Neuro room 331." She handed over the list with the two consults highlighted in yellow. Leeza saw her daily affirmation with a smiley face and read it aloud.

> "I make a difference in the
> world by simply existing in it."

Leeza smiled. "Priceless."

"Tomorrow morning, you have your pre-op class in the third-floor conference room, then at 10:00, you're scrubbing in with Dr. Randall on the spine case on Clarence Smoot, OR fifteen. Then later, you have an add-on outpatient consult for Parkinson's back here at 4:30. Dr. Randall wants him worked up for a deep brain stimulator and scheduled ASAP."

"What would I do without you?" Leeza asked.

"Oh, you'd be just fine. Text me if you need somethin'," said Tana on her way out.

Leeza checked her phone. There was a text from Sammie.

did u forget about me

call u tomorrow, promise

Sammie sent a hugging emoji and three hearts.

tell artie hey please please please

"What part of 'just between you and me' kicked your ass?" Leeza said to herself as she grabbed her helmet. She peered into the hallway, looked in both directions, and took a cleansing breath, in through the nose, out through the mouth.

C harlotte was warming up for her 5:00 formal lesson with Leeza while Grant and Inspector Frisky lay on the floor under the seven-foot Steinway grand. Grant had some serious abandonment issues and would never think of hanging out in his room when the rest of the family was downstairs. Besides, he loved writing his own song lyrics while Charlotte played.

Artie was finishing up his mise en place. He wore citronella Tommy Hilfiger Brooklyn shorts and a royal blue Polo top and had spent the afternoon at a retreat for stay-at-home dads called "daddy daycare," which, predictably, was followed by happy hour at Jack's Tavern and Oyster Bar on Crescent Drive.

Leeza got home from work and kissed Artie on the neck. "Sweet pea," she whispered. He didn't turn around. "What did I do this time?"

"Why do you keep asking me that?" Artie asked.

"Just checking."

"Mama keeps asking when I'm coming over. It's been nonstop since Daddy passed."

"You know you can go anytime." Artie shrugged. "You know that, right?"

"Of course. It's just really different over there now."

"Take care of you. I'll be fine."

Artie turned around and pulled her pelvis into his. "I love you."

"Love you back."

"By the way, Sammie texted me out of the blue," said Artie. "What part of we're done does she not get? It's not hard."

Leeza hesitated before kissing his cheek. "Don't respond. It'll sink in."

A rtie backed out in the Jag SUV as Leeza and the kids waved. "See you in three days."

"Let me know when you get there," said Leeza.

"Bye, Daddy!" yelled Grant.

"And be sure to text me when you're on your way home," Leeza added. "Don't forget."

He blew a kiss. "Will do."

I ndaco on King Street was one of those fancy restaurants where Grant learned you could ask for whatever you wanted, even if it wasn't on the menu. Tonight, he commanded the skinny noodles with baloney sauce, which Leeza translated into beef Bolognese with tagliatelle. He would wait till it was delivered to ask for his very own side of grated parmesan. Charlotte and Leeza ordered the beet salad with feta.

"I want to hear all about school," said Leeza.

"Boring," said Grant.

"Is not," Charlotte countered.

"Still dealing with sixth graders," Grant added.

His comment earned a melodramatic eye roll from Charlotte. "You really should consider being an actor, ya know."

"How about you?" Leeza asked Charlotte.

"Miss White says I have a good chance in the spelling bee."

"'Cause of me," Grant interjected, snapping his fingers. "Shantay, you stay!"

"Remember, the recital is in two weeks. Promise you'll be there," said Charlotte.

"You know I would never miss that."

"What kind of nurse did you say you were, Leesie?" Grant asked.

Charlotte sighed. "Again?"

"Say it with me. Neuro..."

Charlotte and Grant answered in unison. "Neuro..."

"Surgical..."

"Surgical," the kids repeated.

"Nurse practitioner."

"Nurse practitioner."

"Excellent."

"Still a nurse," said Grant matter-of-factly.

"Well, actually," said Charlotte, holding up a finger to emphasize her point, "there is such a thing as a doctor's degree for nurses."

"Grampa was a real doctor."

Charlotte rolled her eyes. "Christ on a cracker."

"Leesie?" asked Grant.

"Grant?"

"What kind of movies are there in Afghanistan?"

"I didn't go to the movies, but probably the same as here," she said.

"Did you watch Drag Race?"

"Every Sunday," Leeza chuckled.

"Here you go, young man, chef's special," said the waiter as he presented Grant with his skinny noodles and baloney sauce.

"Have you heard of a book called *ALIVE*?" asked Charlotte.

"About the plane that crashed in the Andes mountains?"

"I don't know what it's about. I haven't read it yet."

"Why do you have that book?"

"Miss White picked a different book for each kid in AP English, and she said she wants to talk to me after I read it. She says the class is too easy for me."

"And you don't know anything about it?" Leeza asked.

"No."

Leeza was stunned that a teacher would give Charlotte a book about survival and cannibalism without consulting her parents. *Catcher in the Rye is banned, but we're gonna give this to our sixth graders?* "Where's the book now?"

"At home."

"Miss White's going to have to pick another book for you. I'll call her tomorrow."

"I can handle reading about sex, if that's what you're worried about." Charlotte said.

"If only."

"I told her I might want to be a writer."

"What happened to experimental psychology?" Leeza asked.

"I can do both."

"You're gross," Grant interjected. "Who reads about sex?"

"Eat your Bolognese," said Leeza. She knew that girls matured faster than boys, but the difference between these two was profound.

"Leesie?"

"Grant."

"What do brains look like?"

Leeza looked at his plate, then responded with a posh English accent. "Well, Dr. G, they look like your dinner."

"AHHHHHHHHHHH!!!!" Grant unleashed his *HOME ALONE* scream—eyes and mouth stretched to capacity—hands over his ears, emitting a crystal-shattering, 120-decibel frequency. Leeza slammed her hands over her ears as his scream tore through her head. *She was in the medic tent. Bombs hammered the earth outside as soldiers were carried past her, screaming and crying out in agony.*

Several agonizing moments later—she forced her eyes open. Grant looked like a black Macaulay Culkin as startled customers stared. The waiter rushed to the table as Charlotte snorted with laughter.

L eeza looked at her watch as she tucked Grant in. She was expecting a text from Sammie and wanted to make sure the kids were asleep if she showed up unannounced. It was the first of three nights she would have the house to herself without Artie.

"We scared each other, didn't we, Leesie?" asked Grant.

"We did indeed."

"It wasn't funny at first, but then it was."

"I'm so glad you thought so."

"Leesie?" asked Grant.

"Yes, Dr. G?"

"How come you're a nurse?"

She hated that question. If an adult asked you something you didn't feel like answering, you could tell them to fuck off, but that wasn't generally an appropriate response with kids, especially since they repeated everything to their teachers and anyone else who would listen. Being a nurse had never crossed her mind when her mama was still alive. She was going to be traveling the world as a pianist, after all.

"Best way I know to help people," she said.

"But Grampa was a doctor, and he helped people."

Your grampa was an asshole. "How would you like to hear a secret?"

"Yes!" cried Grant.

"My mama was a nurse. The best nurse in the whole wide world. Everybody who met my mama fell in love with her. And she took care of people every day, and she made it look easy because she loved it so much. So, I decided I wanted to be like her."

"When I was little, I heard Daddy say you were practicing to be a piano player, and that's why we have two pianos."

"Alright, young man, that's enough for one night," said Leeza. "Go to sleep."

"Wait! Wait!" Grant pleaded. Leeza kissed his forehead and pulled the blanket up tight to his chin. "I can hear you playing the piano in your office at night," he went on. "Mostly sad stuff, but I can tell you're almost as good as Charlotte."

Leeza felt the sting shoot from her gut up through her heart. *I'm the one teaching Charlotte*, she reminded herself. She knew it was inevitable she would lose some skills as the years passed without consistent, regimented practice, but it was the first time she heard it out loud, and it was a bitter pill to swallow—even if it was from a kid.

"That's awfully sweet of you to say," she told him. "Love ya, mean it."

"Love ya, mean it," said Grant.

As she pulled the door closed, she could hear Charlotte sniffling.

"What's the matter, baby?"

"Nothing," said Charlotte, wiping her eyes.

"What is it?"

"We can talk later."

"You're not going to change your mind when I close the door?"

"I'm sure," said Charlotte.

"You know I'm here forever, right? I'm not leaving again."

"I know."

"Do you wanna give me a hint?" Leeza asked as Charlotte rolled away. Leeza kissed the back of her head, then closed the door and texted Sammie.

busy?

uh, busy waiting

i've been wanting to pick your brain about something

on my way

come to the back door the kids are passed out

Leeza poured a drink from the decanter. She sat at the piano and thumbed through the yellow binder.

Phase two.

8

Buried Battle Wounds

Italian cypress trees lined the cobblestone drive that wound its way to the top of a knoll. The stunning mansion, with its meticulously manicured lawn, awaited like the queen of the realm herself, inviting only the worthiest of subjects to approach.

Artie let himself in through the massive double front doors, walked into the grand foyer, and set his things on an Edwardian-style side table in the entry hall. The soaring ceilings and priceless artworks screamed old money. A colossal portrait of Jesus greeted mortal sinners at the top of the double staircase. His face, painted with pity and forgiveness, seemed illuminated by some ethereal spotlight Artie could never figure out the source of.

His out-of-state college friends used to say, "Southerners who got money want everybody to know they got money." Even after all the years since he moved out, Artie wouldn't think of visiting wearing anything less than Armani, Berluti loafers, and a close shave. He went to the kitchen and looked around the expansive, eerily quiet space.

"Mama?"

Dishes were strewn over the counter and sink—something that wouldn't have been tolerated when he lived there. He turned on the water and started rinsing. He felt a silent presence across the room behind him.

"Where's Yolanda?" he asked.

"Retired."

"Gonna replace her?"

He heard her scoff. "Hardly worth it. Just me now."

Miranda was in her mid-sixties, but she clung to her youth with all the latest treatments, products, and services money could buy. A facelift or tummy tuck or two had made their way into her fountain-of-youth arsenal at some point, but she would deny it on her deathbed. *"Why have it done if you're just going to blab to everybody that you had it done? Let 'em wonder, for chrissakes!"* she was known to have said.

As for replacing Yolanda, her longest-serving maid, Artie knew his mother wouldn't last long without an attendant chasing behind her like an indentured servant, constantly thanking her for the honor of cleaning up her mess.

"You hungry?" he asked.

"I could eat," she said as he kissed her cheek.

He had never seen his mother without makeup. The death of his father had taken its toll on her after forty-three years of marriage.

"Clean yourself up," he said. "I'll fix something." He rummaged through the fridge as Miranda walked toward Jesus and disappeared up the stairs.

The back veranda featured a large pool that glittered under the evening lights. A bronze statue of a little boy peeing in the water was prominently featured at one end, while a silver and gold 'Lion and Maid' fountain that Miranda found while vacationing in Italy guarded the opposing side. Artie and Miranda were having their dinner under a trio of lazy ceiling fans.

"Are you going to Europe this year?" Artie asked.

"Of course not."

"You've traveled alone before. I used to think you preferred it." They pushed around the leftovers on their plates and picked over whatever small talk they could think up.

But then the small talk came to an abrupt end. "Marlie asked about you," Miranda said.

Artie let out a laugh, tinged with disbelief and agitation, even before he fully processed how ridiculous that sounded. Married for fourteen years with two preteens, and his mother was still convinced there was hope yet that he would end up with her idea of what a wife should be.

"Tell her I said hello, that I'm still happily married, and that I have kids."

"You were obsessed with her in high school," said Miranda. "It was always Marlie this and Marlie that. I just don't understand how—"

"That was years ago. Obviously, she wasn't the one, Mama."

"The one?" Miranda balked. "She's the editor-in-chief of the Charleston National News."

"Ah, yes, the position you *gave* her."

"What difference does it make? She's successful. You could be successful. You have a law degree, and you're a whadda ya call it?... a stay-at-home dad for chrissakes."

"I studied corporate law because it was either that or neuro-surgery, remember? Oh wait, I could've been an orthopedist if I wanted to 'scrape the bottom of the barrel.'"

Miranda shoved back her chair and started pacing, her voice rising with each point to be made. Her face tightened as she spoke. "You married this woman, this African woman, because you were 'in love?'" She emphasized 'in love' with melodramatic air quotes. "Then *she* decided to adopt two Black babies and then she up and left you with them for a year. All those were *her* decisions."

In the South, old wounds waited patiently, only to be ripped open at the most unfortunate of moments—and Miranda sound-ed like she was literally wounded. Over the years, Artie left every conversation with his mother thinking—I've said too much, or this will come back to bite me. This was shaping up to be one of those times.

"Jesus, Mama, she was deployed to Afghanistan for chrissakes!"

"As what? A nurse? Do you know how ridiculous that sounds?"

The little bronze boy peeing in the pool was the only sound for the next five seconds. Artie was shocked by his mother's language.

She never cursed. Ever. The only time his father cursed was when he was going off about 'nursing mistakes.' He was convinced that if he ever got sued, it would be because of all the "goddamn nursing mistakes!"

"I can't believe this," said Artie. "You know she was in a war zone!"

"Do you have any idea what your father and I have endured?"

"What have you endured?" *Are you even serious right now?* "Do share, Mama."

"People whispering at the table right next to us at the club! I know you did that to spite me. You had the world at your fingertips, and you did all that out of spite!"

Artie grabbed the plates and stormed into the kitchen, dropping them into the sink. He could feel the heat rising from his neck, turning his pale skin redder by the second. He'd never talked back to his mother, even when she berated him in front of his friends from school. She followed him into the house.

"This stops now," he said, tempering his anger. "I know you're upset about Daddy, but you're walking a fine line."

"I'm walking a fine line?" Miranda scoffed, then laughed. "Look around you, Arthur. Do I look like I give a shit? You are an ingrate!"

Artie headed for the foyer with Miranda on his heels. He grabbed his keys, then spun around and faced her, furious but calculated.

"My wife was an orphan at fourteen. My wife is a United States Army officer, has a doctorate degree, and is fluent in three languages. She also has PTSD and can't even hear a fucking dog bark without having a fucking flashback because of that hellhole she was in while you and Daddy were drinking Grey Goose martinis with a blood-orange twist and listening to your 'friends' talk about the fact that your daughter-in-law is an African woman! And it's AFRICAN AMERICAN!" The words come out louder than he had intended.

He swallowed hard as he wrestled to control himself. "And I just want you to know, since we're on the subject, Daddy was an asshole to her at work from day one. Nobody in that office misses him." He finally managed to dial it down to a whisper as he realized just how bad that made his father sound. "Some legacy, huh?"

Miranda looked at him as if she might shapeshift into Indominus Rex.

"I know you're hurting," said Artie. "But if you want any kind of relationship with your son, this ends here and now." He took a deep breath as the mansion returned to its default sound of dead silence.

A painfully long pause hung between them.

Miranda buried her face in her hands and began to cry, her shoulders shaking with deep sobs that shattered years of composure. Arthur watched his mother slide down the wall to the floor, overwhelmed by grief. He sat next to her and rocked her in his arms, allowing a raw mix of sympathy and sadness to wash over him. There they sat; son holding mother in the entry hall of the palatial mansion, with the little boy peeing in the pool, and Jesus watching over them, bathed in a heavenly spotlight from atop the double staircase.

He decided to go home early. No way was he staying there for three days.

9

Apothecary

With the kids tucked in and her glass refreshed, Leeza retired to the sofa on the back porch. Determined to confront some of her many fears, she had started challenging herself to experience the back porch at night with the lights off. For most people, the chirping and rustling of night critters beyond the edge of darkness would sound soothing. But for Leeza, every snap of a branch ricocheted through her chest like the sound of a charging handle on a sniper rifle; every acorn hitting the ground was the click of a grenade pin twisting free. Panic simmered beneath her skin.

Mind over matter, she repeated to herself; nothing in her own backyard was going to hurt her. To most people, being in an MRI tube was just uncomfortable, but for a claustrophobe, it was a waking nightmare—the same as being buried alive. Still, she reminded herself, it was utterly harmless. And this, too, was harmless. She just wanted to feel normal again.

But that night, she fell asleep shortly into the challenge, and the soft, yellow glow of the indoor lights illuminated both the vulnerable space and her body. A snoring Colonel (aka Inspector Frisky) stretched out on the basketweave jute rug next to her.

Deep inside her dream, it was Leeza's turn to play the voyeur. She watched the action from a chair in the corner of the room. She dipped a finger into her iced Sauvignon Blanc and let the wine drip onto her lips and tongue as she stared at the couple on their bed. The moaning and heavy breathing from the lovers grew more intense. Her body flushed with arousal as she watched Artie and Sammie kiss passionately. Sammie slid her tongue down Artie's chest, to his belly, to his groin. He winked at Leeza, motioning for her to join. She moved toward the bed, joining Sammie at midship. Artie's breathing deepened as he watched the girls share him and exchange kisses between turns.

A sudden, terrifying sound ripped through the silence, jolting Leeza upright. The Colonel's bark—that of a cornered animal—assailed something lurking next to them, just out of sight. Terror seized Leeza's body; she was unable to scream, and too terrified to look. *The unrelenting, deafening sound of artillery and bombs exploded all around. The air was thick with smoke, filled with the sounds of men yelling through the chaos and cries of agony. Two soldiers rushed into the medic tent with a stretcher carrying a wounded soldier in his early twenties and placed him on a cot in front of Leeza. The desperate soldier grabbed Leeza's hand!*

She forced her eyes open, desperately trying to focus on the direction of the Colonel's attention. Barking was replaced by angry growls; someone stood over them. She felt her body thrust upward and slam backward into the house, knocking over the end table and shattering the rocks glass. In front of her stood a human form. She forced her eyes upward, scanning the body slowly, all the way up to its face—Sammie, and a very upset Welsh Corgi.

"I'm sorry, I'm so sorry!" cried Sammie. "I didn't know you were asleep, I swear!"

Leeza's chest heaved as she processed the growling dog, the crashing furniture, the intruder at the edge of the darkness. "Jesus Christ! What the fuck!"

"You knew I was coming!"

"You can't do that!" Leeza screamed.

"I was literally just standing here!" Sammie pleaded. "It was the dog!"

Leeza struggled to focus as the Colonel sniffed Sammie's leg. Sammie offered her hand, but it was met with another growl.

Leeza rushed to her office and poured herself a double. Whiskey sloshed over the rim as the glass approached her lips. She downed the shot then forced a deep breath. Sammie was close behind.

"Goddammit!" Leeza yelled, pressing the heel of her hand to her forehead and trying desperately to stop the tears before they started.

"That's not normal, Leeza," Sammie said.

Leeza shot back: "Ya THINK?!"

It took her a while to recenter. She turned on some classical music and took five or six deliberate breaths—in through the nose, out through the mouth—as Sammie watched.

"Do you want a drink?" she finally managed.

"Thought you'd never ask."

Leeza poured the whiskey, then refilled her own. Sammie leaned in behind her, pressing herself against Leeza's body. "Who were you dreaming about?"

Leeza pushed her away. "Give me some space."

"I *really* missed you guys. You have no idea," Sammie persisted.

"Look, time is not on my side, and I need your help. It's important."

"No time for a wellness check?" Sammie said, pulling her shoulders back and offering her chest. Leeza allowed herself to gaze at Sammie's breasts. Their three-ways with Artie were hot as hell, even if they were fueled by drugs and alcohol.

"I need you to focus," Leeza said firmly.

"Where is the big guy, by the way?" Sammie asked.

"His mother has tightened the umbilical cord since the house fell on Daddy."

"I can't even pretend to know what the hell that means." Sammie took her drink to the piano bench. "But anyway, what can I help you with?"

"Apothecary."

"English?"

"Drugs."

"That's what I get paid for—well, mostly."

"I'm serious. I have these really bad flashbacks."

"Yeah... I noticed." The Colonel planted himself at Leeza's feet. "Isn't that, like, normal for military dudes?"

"They're like nightmares that can start any time, except..."

"Except?"

"Nightmares of actual memories." The room took a beat as the realization settled over both of them. "No matter what I'm doing—a dog barks, the clicking of a freakin' lamp."

"You want stronger drugs? You know I can hook you up."

"I'm working on something that's going to change the way PTSD is treated," Leeza said as she opened the yellow binder. "And not just PTSD. And not just for soldiers." She dropped the binder onto Sammie's lap. "Imagine no more tent cities. No more panhandlers."

Sammie shook her head as she thumbed through the binder. "You've got some splainin' to do, Ricky."

"There's the perfect compound, the perfect marriage of prescription and street drugs."

"And how exactly—"

"Coupled with adjunct therapies, of course. I know it exists, and I know I can find it."

"Of course." Sammie was lost.

"Psychiatric healthcare is pigeonholed, and addicts are often viewed as sanctimonious losers," Leeza explained. "We need to be better at getting to the underlying cause of the affliction. Is there a proportional, algorithmic relationship between addictive personality disorder and the different classes of mental illnesses?"

"You're asking me?"

"We have to focus on managing thought patterns and behaviors during treatment—a paradigm shift in the individual's reality, finding and nurturing the psychological motivation to return to their pre-trauma psyche. From identifying vulnerabilities and triggers, to intercepting the fall to rock bottom. We can figure all this out. All of this is measurable. All of it is possible."

"That's harsh," Sammie said.

"What's harsh?"

"Addicts are sanctimonious losers?"

"I speak from experience."

"So, if shrinks and drug addicts would get together and share their secrets—"

"Can't happen."

"Ya think?"

Leeza took the binder from Sammie. "Once all that is accomplished, I intend to redirect and supercharge the research on organic mental distortion."

"Such as?" Sammie asked, cringing.

"Autism. They're barking up the wrong tree with that."

"Jesus."

"Do you know why primates don't get schizophrenia?"

"Will that question be on the test?"

"The correct answer is 'no,' you do not know."

"I was gonna guess that." A look of concern replaced Sammie's fading surprise. "You're either crazy as hell or a genius. I'm leaning towards—you need to take a step back."

Leeza knew she was wasting her breath having this conversation with Sammie. "It's just... the treatment shouldn't be worse than the disease and pretending that prescription drugs are some kind of holy grail is bullshit."

"Speaking of drugs, did you know cops have split personalities?" Sammie asked.

Leeza shot her a WTF look.

"It's true. One minute they're like..." She put a finger to her cheek and spoke in a sweet voice, "Good evening, ma'am. Do you know why I stopped you? And the next minute they're like, GET ON THE GROUND! GET ON THE GROUND! HANDS

WHERE I CAN SEE THEM! GET ON THE GROUND!
NOW!"

Leeza stared at her incredulously and tossed the binder at her
again. "Look at this."

Sammie flipped through the pages filled with handwritten math
equations, generic drug names, and chemical compounds. She
tried to pronounce some of the words. "What the—"

"I've listed every prescription psychotropic drug on the market
and the top twenty street drugs in the world, broken down by
active ingredients, how they're metabolized, side effects, and their
intended uses, both legal and illegal."

"Obsessed much?"

"I calculated the actual effective dose versus what it would take
to O.D. based on body habitus, plus or minus a few milligrams for
liver disease. Ignore the bullshit printed on the labels."

"Of course."

"Some of the best-known drugs are used for their side effects."

Sammie raised her hand. "Ooh, I know, I know... Viagra!"

"A hard-on made a lot of old farts forget about their chest pain.
There's already a lot of data out there. The perfect drug cocktail and competent therapy could make virtually all non-organic
mental illnesses more successfully managed. Then, as the brain
becomes reprogrammed, there is a chemical weaning phase during
the paradigm shift."

"When you get rich and famous, don't forget about your
friends."

"It's not about that. We've been dicking patients around for
decades. Big Pharma is a multi-billion-dollar industry. When was
the last time you saw a news article about a revolutionary treatment
for mental illness? It's always the same old commercials: talk to
your doctor about this, talk to your doctor about that, this new
drug might cause diarrhea, that new drug might fucking kill you,
don't eat grapefruit with your statins, don't mix alcohol with your
opiates." Leeza poured a shot of Jack.

"What exactly do you want?"

"There was a study in Amsterdam that combined minute amounts of heroin with a combination of antipsychotic medications called paliperidone and brexpiprazole, along with methylphenidate, also known as Ritalin. The drugs were synergized and suspended in an ethanol solution, then made into a chewable—butterscotch rum, no less—with customized doses based on habitus, overall health, and condition severity. Can you imagine that with holistic psychosocial therapy?"

"I cannot."

"It's just a small piece, but the research is fascinating."

"I keep thinking you're gonna yell April Fools! any second. You've got that look you had in science class when we got a new experiment. Wait, did you say heroin?"

"This isn't your grandma's ketamine," said Leeza, even more focused. "We're talking about treating different mental illnesses, including stress-induced panic disorder, with natural derivatives of opium, benzodiazepines, midazolam, caffeine, vitamin B12."

"And a partridge in a pear tree," Sammie joked.

"Do you know what happens when you take a stimulant and a depressant at the same time?"

"I do—it's called tantric fucking sex."

"Sorry, I know the pharmacology lesson is a bit overkill."

"Not at all." Sammie finished her shot, but her eyes never left Leeza's face.

"The beauty of synergism," Leeza continued. "Think Valium and steroids. Cialis and opium meet the exorcist." She slowed her pace, making each word deliberate: "It's the controlled distraction that facilitates opening your mind to the catharsis. We have to remove all hesitation, remove the fear."

Sammie held up her glass for a refill.

"And then you wake up, realizing you were in a thick fog, thinking, 'What the hell was wrong with me?' Mental conflict remission."

"Mental conflict remission," Sammie repeated. "M.C.R. Now *that's* heavy. But I think vodka and Red Bull do the same thing—unless it's sugar-free."

"I'm glossing over it, I know. The therapy will be a huge part of the process."

"Honey, if that's what you call glossing over, I would hate to hear the details."

"It's about the capacity for reintegration into society with a clarity you haven't experienced in years, maybe never. Imagine the impact on their quality of life."

"Like waking up in the operating room with a new set of tits. I've heard *that* will change your quality of life."

Sammie's comments were background noise. Leeza was staring into her eyes with the intensity of a mad scientist. It was the first time she had been able to say it all out loud, and it was exhilarating. She decided to conclude the lecture with the simplest metaphor possible.

"What if I could convince you that all your phobias, childhood traumas, and worst memories were nothing more than cartoon characters on Saturday morning TV? You are the writer and director, and you have the power to rewrite your own story."

"You're creeping me out just a tiny bit over here," said Sammie.

"It's like this: the perfect chemical cocktail combined with intensive life coaching. Music therapy, psychodynamic therapy, and cognitive behavioral therapy—including aversion and diversion—are administered by competent, specially trained therapists. And voilà! Paradigm reprogramming of motivation and goal-directed behaviors!" She ended with a triumphant grin.

"Music therapy?" Sammie asked.

"That's all you heard?"

"That's all I understood. Can we rewind for just a second?" Sammie scratched her head. "So, you think you can cure PTSD?"

"I'll take effective management for two hundred, Alex."

"And I'll be supplying the 'nonprescription' ingredients for your experimentations."

"Precisely."

"Easy peasy, but I don't understand all the Greek, so—"

"Latin."

Sammie crossed her arms. "Seriously, bitch?"

"Sorry," said Leeza, handing Sammie a piece of paper. "We'll start with these."

Sammie read the list. "I can do that."

"Tomorrow, 8:30 sharp. We'll work in the garage."

Leeza took Sammie's empty glass and kissed her cheek. "Sammie, I need you to not contact Artie again, please. He can't know."

Sammie hesitated. "What did they do to you?"

Leeza held the door for her.

A torrential rainstorm had seized control of the Charleston night. Random bolts of lightning lit up the night sky, followed by deafening claps of thunder. Classical music filled the garage, competing with the clamorous rain. The truck and motorcycle were parked in two of the three spaces. Sammie sat alone at the reclaimed wood workbench against the back wall, waiting.

Leeza joined her, carrying a tray covered with an autumn-themed towel with prints of red and orange leaves, gourds, and bales of hay. Sammie cleared some space on the workbench as she approached.

"Dinner?" Sammie asked.

"It's a visual aid—then it's dinner."

"Of course it is." Sammie chuckled as Leeza pulled off the festive towel to expose two salads, two forks, and three bottles; the kind you get salad dressing in at the store, but these had been washed clean, labels removed. Two of the bottles contained liquid, and one was empty.

Sammie eyed the presentation. "I like Ranch."

"You'll eat what I give you, and you'll love it." Leeza held up the empty jar. "I'm going to make last night easier to understand."

Sammie shrugged. "You used big words for half an hour, so that would be great."

A bolt of lightning lit the room. Leeza held up a finger and waited until the accompanying thunder landed and then dissipated.

"This will make it simple. Ready?" She presented the empty jar in her palm. "Imagine that this is a mental diagnosis: depression, schizophrenia, bipolar, ADHD, alcoholism, drug addiction—or even a combination." She handed the bottle to Sammie and picked up one with liquid. "Now, imagine this is therapy." Leeza swirled the viscous liquid—the consistency of olive oil. "This is oil. You with me?"

"Ask me again when the salad's ready," Sammie replied.

Leeza poured the oil into Sammie's bottle and grabbed the next one; the rose-tinged liquid was the consistency of water. "This is red wine vinegar," she explained. "You could use anything with the molecular weight of water, but we'll be eating it, so..."

Leeza poured the vinegar into the oil, set the bottle on the table, and handed Sammie the lid for her bottle. "What's happening in your bottle?" Leeza asked.

"Nothing," Sammie said. "They're separate, like jocks and geeks at a school dance."

"Precisely. The vinegar is the formula that we're after."

"Therapy and drugs."

"Diagnosis. Therapy. Medication. Now shake it."

Sammie looked at the separate liquids, then started shaking the bottle.

"Harder," Leeza instructed.

Sammie shook the bottle with animated zeal, over both shoulders, like a bartender with a martini shaker.

"Now look at it," Leeza said.

Sammie held the bottle of emulsified salad dressing in front of her. "*That's* how they do that!"

Leeza took the dressing, opened the bottle and poured it onto the salads. "Do you know what the salad represents?"

Sammie stared at the dressing as it drizzled across the fresh, green lettuce and sliced cherry tomatoes.

"Life."

"Precisely."

Leeza poured Jack Daniel's into two glasses. She downed hers in one shot.

The rain hammered the house as the women sat in silence. Sammie's face was stoic, her mind still working through the demonstration, but Leeza wore a look of self-satisfied calm, confident she had chipped away at Sammie's skepticism.

Several open prescription bottles and a dozen scattered pills covered the table's well-worn surface. A mortar and pestle, along with a small wooden box from the home office, rounded out their grocery list. Jack Daniel's and rocks glasses stood ready nearby. Leeza studied the pills, arranging them meticulously before holding out her hand. Sammie handed her a small, clear plastic bag of white powder and some more pills. A bolt of lightning illuminated the room like three flashes of a strobe light in a nightclub, followed a few seconds later by a monstrous wave of thunder.

"Integrated medicine at its finest," said Leeza.

Sammie watched as the scientist arranged her ingredients. "Last night, I asked you a question."

Leeza leaned back, fixing her gaze on Sammie. She was feeling the effects of the double Jack, moving her hands up and down with the music as if conducting an orchestra. A thin, satisfied smile graced her face.

"I am taking control of my destiny. That's why we're here, my lovely."

"Okay, that's hot."

"We are on the threshold of greatness."

"And if 'we' don't achieve this greatness?" Sammie asked.

"The people with the power to fix this are doing nothing. Everyone has their own agenda, and people like me—people like us—we are not high on their list. And to answer your question, failure is not an option. It is unfathomable."

Leeza pushed herself upright, her legs faltering as she grabbed the bench for support. Sammie caught her by the waist to steady her. "It's not an option for the medics of the Destroyer Aid Station at Forward Operating Base Pasab, Afghanistan. It's not an option for the lovely residents of the tent city under the Arthur Ravenel Bridge. It's not an option for people with clinical depression, or addictive personality disorder, or ANY OF IT!" Leeza's agitation suddenly mounted as she considered the needless suffering around her: homelessness, untreated depression, debilitating addiction, hungry families begging for money on street corners. *If I hear about one more goddamn suicide!*

"What if you get caught?" Sammie asked.

"The angels are sleeping, and the castle's all mine for two more days."

Another flash of lightning exploded, followed seconds later by thunder that shook the house.

"I doubt they're sleeping," said Sammie.

Leeza drew fluid from a vial into a syringe, then sprayed the solution into the mortar and added the white powder.

"Answer my question. Why? There's already—"

Leeza slammed her hands onto the workbench, sending the pills hopping into the air. "I won't lose my family because of something I brought back from that place! Why can't you understand that? You saw it for yourself!"

Sammie backed off for a moment before pressing calmly. "I'm just saying, you have a damn good support system—unlike most of us."

"Tell that to a war veteran with a bedsheet around his neck."

Sammie grabbed Leeza's arms and locked eyes with hers. "I hear you, and I get it, I swear." Sammie's concern was becoming emotional. "But this is just drugs, Leeza. There's no bedsheet around your neck."

Leeza's chest rose and her eyes narrowed as she started to speak, but Sammie continued: "Explain to me how you can take your own drug concoction and still go to work and raise your kids?"

"My whole existence is a freaking haunted house, and I can't get out!" Leeza yelled. She paused, then forced her tone back down. "Apparently, I can't make you understand that. I'm either a zombie or I'm in full-on panic mode—there's no in-between. I can't do my job or raise my kids like this. There are no other options. I don't know how to simplify it any more."

Leeza tried to focus on her breathing exercises as she poured the mixture from the mortar into a rocks glass. She added Jack Daniel's to the powdered mixture, followed by two ice cubes. She cut a lemon in half and squeezed it into the glass. "Martha prefers lemon."

"You seemed like you were in control."

"This is what control looks like, baby." Leeza turned up the music, glass in hand, and began to sway. Her movements were wobbly as she motioned for Sammie to join her. Sammie followed reluctantly, spinning in slow circles, her arms dancing above her head, feigning a smile. Leeza sipped the formula and twirled around, head back, trancelike, humming along with the orchestra; she knew every note. Another flash of lightning lit up the room, followed by a rumble of thunder.

Sammie laid her head on Leeza's shoulder and closed her eyes. As the women slow danced to the classical performance, swaying in a gentle circle, their bodies intertwined. The violin concerto, the rain, and the cavernous space felt magical to Leeza through the increasing haze of the drug cocktail. Then, without warning, the dizzying effects hit her like an ocean wave. The conversation in her head fell silent, as if she had just absorbed a bolus of propofol through an IV. She held Sammie tighter as the feelings in her legs began to dissolve.

Through dwindling consciousness and half-open eyes, Leeza thought she saw lights. She squinted at the windows as they passed by with each full rotation of the slow dance. *Why. Are. There. Lights?* She barely managed to form the thought. They made another full turn as Mozart continued his serenade, but the beautiful violins had dissolved into distant car horns. As the garage doors came into view again, she tried to focus on the lights coming from the windows lined up across the top. *Headlights? Somebody's here?* Sammie's eyes were closed. *Somebody's here.*

Leeza's body suddenly became a dead weight on Sammie's arms as she collapsed, the glass exploding onto the concrete around them. Sammie dropped frantically to her knees, her heart racing, and cradled her.

A flash of lightning bleached Leeza's face. "Leeza!" Sammie screamed.

The garage door moaned as it rose, amplifying the sound of the rain across the room. Headlights flooded the garage, shining through the raging wall of water between them and Artie, who sat in the SUV behind the frantic wipers. Leeza could see him through a blurred reality—a high-pitched ringing flooded her ears, and numbness had taken over her hands and feet. Their eyes locked as he slid from the seat and stepped into the rain.

He stood in the downpour, staring back at her, his face a mixture of confusion and disbelief. He was drenched, but he didn't seem to notice. He burst into the garage and shoved Sammie away, pushing her onto the concrete covered with shards of glass. He tried desperately to wake Leeza, shaking her and slapping her face.

"Leeza! Leeza!" She was listless, motionless. The pleading expression on his face was inches from hers. Her world shook violently as he slapped her face over and over. She watched as he looked around the room, taking in the broken glass on the floor and the prescription bottles on the workbench. And Sammie. He glared at Sammie with the full weight of his fury and disgust.

"WHAT DID YOU DO TO HER?!" he screamed. "WHY?! WHY?!"

Leeza watched, detached and frozen, as the surreal horror flick played out above her face, and Artie's anger morphed into rage.

"She asked me for help! She called me!" Sammie pleaded.

Leeza struggled to follow Sammie's lips, but they seemed distorted, as if looking through murky water or an unfocused camera lens. She could still make out the words—barely; their voices competed with the ringing noise.

"You're a liar!" Artie shouted.

"She's trying to find a—"

"Leeza!" Artie cried, slapping her cheeks again.

"Get out! GET OUT!" he yelled at Sammie, shoving her again, this time onto a shard of glass. She rolled onto her side, then held up her forearm, revealing bright red blood flowing from a deep cut on her wrist. She squeezed the wound with her other hand as crimson streaks flowed off her elbow. She stared at Artie crouched over Leeza on the ground in front of her.

Artie frantically lifted Leeza into his arms and carried her into the house, leaving Sammie on the garage floor, surrounded by shattered glass, blood pulsing from her wrist and flowing across her palm and between her fingers. The red SUV stood a few feet away, its engine still running, the frantic windshield wipers fighting to clear the glass.

"SHE CALLED ME!" Sammie screamed from the garage as the door shut behind them.

Artie lowered Leeza to the couch and fumbled for his cell phone. "It's okay, it's okay," he repeated desperately. "It's going to be okay."

Leeza watched him make the call and press the phone to his ear. Her body was fused to the couch; her hands and feet were sandbags. She tried to blink, but her eyes wouldn't close. She watched Artie yell into the phone.

"My wife passed out! We need an ambulance!"

Leeza strained to make out what he was telling the operator. Her brain instructed her hands to wipe her eyes, but they refused. She thought she heard Sammie yelling from the garage, but the rain and brain fog drowned out what might have been a frenzied cry. A strange sense of relief washed over her; her mind was as listless as her body. *Is everybody safe?* The question was directed at no one in particular. *Is everybody safe?*

She couldn't tell how long she had been lying there—ten minutes? Ten hours? Men's voices hovered above her. The couch disappeared below her as she was lifted onto a stretcher and wheeled out the front door to the waiting ambulance with its flashing red lights—its own self-contained world of chaos. She heard the clanging of metal as the stretcher's legs retracted. As she slid into the rescue unit, she saw Sammie disappearing into a cab. Their eyes met for a brief moment through the downpour before Leeza heard the doors slam just beyond her feet. *Why is her arm red?*

Part II

10

Who Plays Rachmaninoff when They're Drunk?

L ate autumn weather in the Deep South was fickle at best and rarely followed through with its own forecasts. The morning greeted temperatures in the teens, but the sky was clear and promising. Local meteorologists predicted an unseasonable snowstorm to rival those on the eastern Antarctic plateau, and Grant was on the lookout for wayward polar bears and a pair of gay penguins.

Artie stared out the window as he washed dishes. His dissociated mind was free of any inner voice, confirmed by the emptiness in his eyes, and the way he pushed the soapy water over the dishes without looking. The months since the incident in the garage had been an emotional blur, a constant bounce between anger and disappointment over Leeza, and rage and disgust for Sammie. *How could Leeza have done that? How could she allow that woman back into her life? OUR lives? How could she squander all that progress? How could she betray her own family like that, for chrissakes!* Miranda had all the ammunition she needed, and Artie got an earful when he spent a few nights in his childhood bedroom. *If that bitch comes near us again, we will destroy her world.* And by "we," he meant the Byrons.

Leeza appeared in the doorway. "Let me help." She watched as he robotically rinsed the dishes and put them in the strainer with the suds still clinging to them.

"I'm good," he said.

She lingered for a moment. Then headed down the hall to her office.

A wine glass crashed against the edge of the sink, shattering in his hand and leaving a shard embedded in his palm. He held his hand up to the window and turned it slowly, estimating the depth of the wound by how much of the shard was sticking out. Blood was running down to his elbow and dripping into the suds. He pinched the exposed segment and slowly dislodged the arrow-shaped piece of glass, then lowered his hand into the dishwater, watching as the blood mingled with the tiny bubbles. He stared out at the unseasonably cold late-autumn day, watching dark red and burnt-orange oak leaves twist down onto the frosted grass.

L eeza contemplated the black-and-white piano keys. A glass of whiskey and the yellow binder stood at the ready on the bench next to her. She'd been more protective of the binder since Artie found it and threatened to destroy it if she didn't stop self-diagnosing and self-prescribing. But she couldn't let the setback in the garage derail her mission; her experiments were essential for her survival. Why couldn't he just see that? Why wouldn't he listen to reason? She took a stack of sheet music from the top of the piano and flipped through the pages. She settled on a Rachmaninoff piece, *Prelude in G Minor, Op. 23, No. 5,* and spread the pages in front of her.

Her thoughts drifted to the cold, white halls of The Juilliard School—both intimidating and exhilarating for a thirteen-year-old from Beaufort, South Carolina.

The audition had felt like a million years away, but it was finally here. "You have just as much right to be there as anybody else," Mama had told her a thousand times. The twenty-year-old

Steinway was a worn but beautiful workhorse that stood alone in the middle of an echoey practice hall, with wood floors, soaring ceilings, and walls covered in decades-old layers of off-white paint. A semi-circle of folding chairs with judges, complete with clipboards, pens, and poker faces, sat a few feet away.

Leeza emerged from the audition to find her mama waiting anxiously. Catherine could hear the music as Leeza played, and she cried the whole time.

"You did it, baby," Mama whispered as they embraced and rocked back and forth. "I got this for you," she said, holding up a silver chain and pendant.

"What is it, Mama?" The pendant was a grand piano engraved with the name 'Leeza.'

Leeza reached under her shirt and pulled out the grand piano necklace, rubbing it between her fingers. She kissed the pendant and returned it next to her heart. She finished the drink and tried to focus on the sheet music, which was becoming a little blurry thanks to Mr. Daniel's. In through the nose, out through the mouth.

Her fingers hovered above the keys, then descended to begin the Prelude. A few measures in, she hit a wrong note and stopped. She gathered herself and started over. After a few more measures, she made another mistake. She stopped, took another breath—in through the nose, out through the mouth—wiped her sleeve across her face, and started again. Two measures in—two sour notes. She stretched her arms over her head, then took a break to refill her glass. She turned the page of the sheet music and started again.

She didn't stop for mistakes this time, playing faster and louder. She hit several wrong notes, messing up full passages, playing faster and louder through the mistakes, through the carnage she was creating of the dead composer's masterpiece. She started banging on the keys with both fists. "FUCK!" she cried as tears streamed down her face. "FUCK!"

Artie and the kids appeared in the doorway—three solemn figures helplessly observing the spectacle. He had decided to let them watch.

Leeza gritted her teeth so hard her jaw ached—the words were forced out as she slammed her fists into the keyboard. "FUCK! FUCK! FUCK! FUCK!" she raged. Each "FUCK" landed a fierce blow on the defenseless instrument and was met with the tormented bark of discordant notes striking hammers against strings. Her head fell back, and the rage gradually dissolved into sobbing.

"Leesie?" Grant said carefully, staring at his mama, his eyes glistening.

She rested her elbows on the keyboard, cupping her face in her hands. Her sobs were replaced with a quiet, anguished cry, like a baby animal searching for its mother. She gently caressed the keys as if apologizing after the undeserved beating.

Grant joined his mama at the piano and lay his cheek on her shoulder. He patted her head with the tender touch of a distraught child, tears streaming down his face. "Leesie? It's okay," his voice cracked. "It's okay. I can turn the pages for you." She wrapped an arm around him. "I can turn the pages for you."

Artie touched Grant's head, then gently pulled him away and ushered the kids out of the room, pushing the door closed behind them.

Leeza suddenly threw the sheet music across the room. "You always were a bitch to me!" she yelled as the pages fluttered down.

"Who plays Rachmaninoff when they're drunk?" Artie said. He watched as she smudged her tears into her palms. "Maybe it just needs a good tuning," he added.

Leeza's laugh was sharp and brittle. "Let's go with that."

She cleared her throat, filled her lungs, and threaded her mind back from the breakdown to the inevitable adult conversation.

"Did you know Rachmaninoff had stage fright?" Leeza looked up at Artie and tried to speak through the whiskey and grief. "Sweet pea," she whispered. Then she noticed the bloody bandage. "What the hell?"

Artie crossed his arms and leaned against the door. "How's it going?"

She scoffed at the question, then asked with a tinge of sarcasm: "Why do you ask?" She wiped her face again and tried to focus on the blurry, red bandage. She knew she would stumble if she stood up, but she wanted to see his injury. "I should look at that."

Artie gathered the sheet music from the floor. "This piece has been tortured enough," he said. "You never could play after a cocktail... or five." He put the stack of music on the piano before going back to the door. "I thought we'd talk."

"Now? You wanna talk now?" she said incredulously. "You haven't said a dozen words to me in weeks, and *now* you wanna talk?"

"Unless you and Monsieur Daniels have an encore planned."

He got the sarcasm from his mother. *Screw you, Miranda.* She turned on the bench to face him. "Good a time as any."

"You spend so much time in here."

"At least you know where to find me. When I'm anywhere else in the house, you always find something to do in another room, like we're playing hide-and-seek. Gettin' old."

"Why do you have to lock the door?" he asked.

She didn't know he had tried the door. "Me time?"

"I'm taking the kids to Mama's house for a while. She said she wants to see them."

"That's a lie," said Leeza. "She's got no use for those kids, and you know it."

"I told you she'd come around."

"And you trust her? I'm really not okay with that."

"I wasn't asking permission."

"It's not up to you," she said.

"Sure as hell isn't up to you."

Leeza's tears returned. "Y'all are the only reason I'm even here right now."

"Don't use us like that, Leeza."

"This isn't you. You wouldn't act this way. And you sure as hell wouldn't say that." Leeza took her drink, stumbled to her feet, and joined him next to the door. "Don't let that woman get in your head. Everything's riding on this." Artie recoiled from the smell of alcohol on her breath. "You gotta talk to me, Artie." She waited, but he was still. "You wanna spend time with Mommy? The kids stay here."

Artie reached for the door handle. "You are certifiable."

Leeza slammed her palm against the door, blocking his path. She handed him her drink and motioned for him to sit. "You're upset about an incident you won't even let me explain! How long are you gonna mope around here before you're ready to talk like an adult?" She waited again. Silence. "You wanted to talk, remember? Talk!"

Resigned that he was trapped, he took a sip of the whiskey and sat on the piano bench.

"Why is the cocktail table turned backward?"

"Front is scratched." She'd practiced that answer.

"You're living in a bubble," Artie said.

An awkward pause settled between them.

Leeza went first, but it was irrelevant. "Sergei's Symphony No. 1 bombed so badly that he went into a deep depression. Disappeared for four years."

"You're risking our future on some fantasy you've concocted in your head. One promise after the other," Artie glared at the half-empty bottle, "but nothing changes."

"But he came back. Spent most of his adult life touring and performing piano concerts. He summered at his villa in Switzerland."

"I found your notebook."

"Died in Beverly Hills."

"Are you listening to me?" Artie stretched out the words, as if he'd said it a hundred times: "You're not listening."

"I can't give up just because you don't get it. I wouldn't have a future—not worth living, anyway." Leeza's eyes seemed to be focused on something halfway across the room, but halfway across the room there was only empty space.

Artie closed the cover over the keyboard, crossed his legs, and leaned back against the piano. "I found your notebook," he said again. "I looked through it while you were recovering. It reminded me of the crazy mathematics professor I saw in a movie once."

"A Beautiful Mind," said Leeza. "You think I'm a paranoid schizophrenic?"

Artie set the drink on the cocktail table. "Why did you have heroin in your system?"

"It was a false positive."

"Is that a thing?" he asked.

"It was diazepam and alcohol."

Artie laughed. "I saw the toxicology report, sooo..." No response. "Stephen told you to take some time off."

"Because the E.R. doctor told Stephen what happened, and he 'offered' me a short sabbatical. I could sue them for the HIPAA violation. There's this thing called patient privacy."

"That would be career-ending, and not for the one who broke the law." Artie stood up, pulled back the sheers, and stared out the window. "Are you seeing Sammie?"

She didn't see that one coming. "Have you lost your mind?"

"It would explain a lot."

"That's why you won't talk to me?" A look of dread and disbelief crossed her face. "Because you think I'm cheating on you?"

"It's on the list," he answered. "And I *will* find out."

Leeza scoffed, waving away the idea as she opened the door. "Go spend some time with your mama. The kids will stay with me. We'll have a serious talk when you get back." She steadied herself with a hand on the doorframe.

"Isn't it against the rules to drink when you're in therapy?" Artie said.

"This isn't the problem." She took Artie's hand as he moved by her. "This is a team exercise. We're *all* in it, the whole platoon. Do or die." She loosened her grip. "It's just... I love you so much."

"I believe you," Artie said. "It's the trust I'm working through."

11

Neurosurgery to Ingrown Toenails

The OR underwent extensive renovations while Leeza was deployed, and the operating suites now felt modern and clean. For years, senior leadership had peddled the "not in the budget" talking point until post-op infections, failing surgical equipment, and the exodus of scrub techs and circulating nurses left them with no alternatives. But it was probably the ceiling-mounted procedure light that fell on a patient during open-heart surgery that set the multimillion-dollar project in motion and led to the scapegoating of the career nurse-turned-CEO.

The deep brain stimulator case actually lined up for an on-time start and Dr. Randall and Leeza were scrubbing outside of suite fifteen.

"You've been preoccupied," Dr. Randall said.

"Why do you say that?"

He chuckled. "Observational impression. How was your time off?"

"Still adjusting to all the civilian comforts."

"If you need more time, we can reschedule appointments another week out. Just considering the optics."

You're suddenly worried about optics? "It's better if I work." Leeza was amazed—and disgusted—at how easy it was for surgeons to reschedule appointments that patients had waited months to get. Stephen would rather close the office than see outpatients himself. She could never imagine herself or Tana treating people that way. *I'll try not to tarnish your reputation—considering the optics.*

"My dad used to tell me that marriage was for suckers," he continued. "Took me three tries to get it right, but that poor bastard never did."

"What the hell, Stephen?"

"Wouldn't be the end of the world. And you wouldn't have to put up with that mother-in-law of yours anymore."

Leeza scrubbed her forearms and elbows vigorously as her agitation grew. The tiny plastic fingers of the chlorhexidine-soaked brush felt like a Brillo pad scraping across her skin.

"The thing about Miranda is that she always has something to say. Unfortunately for her, people couldn't be less interested in what she has to say. Bless her little heart." He scoffed. "No wonder Arthur was a grumpy old asshole. Poor bastard couldn't catch a break."

What started this? Why change the subject? What was she telling him? "He left us for a bigger practice," Leeza said. "You'll never get over that."

"We started this practice together, and I assumed we'd end together. Those assholes from New York said they only had one position and courted him like a virgin on a Greek freighter, so when he asked me how I felt about it, I told him I didn't give a shit. He called my bluff."

The chlorhexidine suds oozed in a circle around the drain as they rinsed their forearms.

"That's why you wouldn't change the sign. You hoped he would come running back."

"Wouldn't have mattered, turns out."

"Sorry for your loss."

"Back 'atcha."

"Honestly, Stephen, I don't feel it, sorry. You had to know there was a problem."

He gave the kind of shrug that said *Could be, could be not.*

Leeza hated that work had become so awkward before Arthur left, and she often wondered if any of it was her own fault.

"It's obvious you're getting an earful. You need to take what you hear from Miranda with a grain of salt. My family is going through a clunky phase, and it's no one's business but ours."

"Clunky. That's seriously glass-half-full. I like it. She's suddenly decided we should stay in touch, says she's planning to see the grandkids. Sounds nice."

Leeza counted to herself.

"Have you thought about what you'll do when I retire?"

"Maybe a sabbatical, or urgent care part-time," she lied. She wasn't going anywhere when he retired—the idea that he thought she would pack up her office just because he decided to quit spoke volumes.

"Urgent care? You?" Dr. Randall howled at the thought. "From neuro to ingrown toenails?" He considered neurosurgery the top of the food chain in medical practice and expected everyone to acknowledge it. And don't get him started on the chasm between MD and RN. Some of the biggest arguments between him and Dr. B. revolved around the idea of hiring a nurse practitioner until they realized how much less time they would actually have to spend with patients if they did.

"You'd go crazy," he added. "But maybe you could spend more time on your 'projects.'" He raised his hands in front of his chest, letting the water drip from his elbows, then opened the automatic door with the footpad. "The sky is not falling, my friend," he said as he disappeared into the OR.

Leeza's lips tightened. "I know that!" she called after him. "And we're not in high school, you pompous ass," she added, a bit quieter.

A rtie was backing out of the driveway as Leeza pulled up. The kids peered from the back seat as she pulled alongside the SUV. "Where are you going?" Leeza demanded.

"I told you where we're going," said Artie.

"And I told you the kids were staying with me."

"You don't outrank me, Leeza."

"Please let them out of the car."

"Please get out of the way."

"I need to talk to you before you go over there. It's about your mother," said Leeza. Artie continued down the driveway. "What is she telling Stephen?" she yelled as he backed onto the street. "Artie!" She stood at the edge of the lawn until they disappeared.

"W hat's wrong, Daddy?" asked Grant.

"Nothing's wrong."

Artie looked at his wedding ring and tuned the radio to 95.5 K-LOVE, a Christian music station.

"Jimmy Norlander's mama and daddy are getting divorced," said Grant.

"I thought you were over him," said Charlotte.

"I feel bad," he said, fidgeting with his friendship bracelets.

"Daddy?" said Grant.

"What is it, Grant?"

"Are you and Leesie getting a divorce?"

There is nothing his mother would like more. Artie looked at his ring again as they pulled onto the Mark Clark Expressway toward Beresford Hall. "Well, if we are, she hasn't told *me* yet," he said—half laughing—as he turned up the volume on K-LOVE.

"He's still picking fights," Grant said to Charlotte. The Christian music drowned out any chance he had of talking to his daddy from the back seat.

"I know, we're all in the same grade, dude," said Charlotte.

"This girl in American History told me she likes him, and I better stay away 'cause if she tells him I like him, he'll beat me up."

Charlotte rolled her eyes and put her hand on his. "And what's the Jezebel's name?"

"Don't do anything," he said.

Artie glanced at them in the rearview mirror.

"Don't worry about it, I just need a name."

The SUV pulled up the snaking cobblestone drive toward the Byron estate. Grant stared out the window and rubbed his twisted friendship bracelets as Artie caressed his wedding band, and Charlotte clenched her jaw at the idea of some zit-faced bully getting away with terrorizing kids because his daddy always lied for him.

Miranda had asked for some "catching up time" with the kids and pointed Arthur toward his father's study. The walls of the room were lined with floor-to-ceiling bookcases filled with a lifetime collection of signed first editions and antique encyclopedias. He watched from the window as his mother played catch-up. Charlotte and Grant sat across from her at the table next to the pool, drinking sweet tea and telling Gramma all about school. Every few minutes, Miranda handed them each a chocolate chip cookie and asked a question about Leeza and Artie. *Are Mama and Daddy doing good?* he could just imagine her asking in her sweet-as-pie southern voice.

Artie's mind wandered as he watched the trio from the study. He struggled to make sense of how someone born into a wealthy family could be so crass and indifferent, even downright cruel, when it came to people with "reduced circumstances." Shouldn't they be the opposite? Shouldn't they be motivated to help and share and to campaign for change?

When he was very young, he heard his grandfather use the "N-word" at the dinner table as casually as if he had said "pass the potatoes." It felt wrong, even as a kid. But it took years to realize how deeply rooted the class system was, and getting angry at the old man wouldn't change anything. He felt sorry for him. But he didn't have to let his mother off so easily. "Entitlement" was a four-letter word to the heir of the entitled.

He watched from the window, torn between allowing his kids to have a relationship with their grandmother and rushing out and sweeping them away from the jaws of deceit, manipulation, and conniving that was the very essence of Miranda Byron, matriarch of the Charleston Gazette and Charleston National News.

"Tell me again why we're here," Sammie said.

Across the street from the tent city under the Arthur Ravenel Bridge, Leeza leaned against the parked motorcycle while Sammie lay stretched out on the grassy shoulder, enjoying her new cherry cola flavored vape cartridge.

"Behavioral Science."

"Sorry I asked." She held her arm in the air so Leeza could see the two-inch pink line with tiny dots where the stitches had been. "Still hurts."

"I've told him over and over again it was my idea, it was just an experiment, and you had nothing to do with it."

"Let's just all meet up and talk about it," said Sammie.

"That'll take time; for now, I need some things from you."

Sammie put her wrist next to her ear and pretended to listen. "What's that, mister scar? You're still waiting for an apology?"

"I can't apologize enough, Sammie. I never thought you would get hurt."

Sammie scoffed. "Why can't I say no to you?"

"'Cause, you love me," Leeza said with a flirtatious smile.

That much was true—Sammie was very much in love with her. But she had actually fallen for Artie first. He was the only guy in high school who gave her the time of day, the kind boy who didn't care what the popular kids thought. Homely, unpopular girls flocked to Artie. But Sammie wasn't homely—she was a loner who didn't make friends easily. She had never known attention like that: not at school, not with her foster family, and certainly not at Congressman Dickface's house after he and his wife adopted her and separated her from her siblings for the first time. When Artie introduced her to Leeza in their first year of college, Sammie was convinced something life-altering was forming between the three of them. She made sure they knew about her feelings before she dropped out.

"I may be an idiot, but I'm not stupid," Sammie said.

Leeza nodded. They both knew Sammie had made many poor choices.

"It feels weird to say this, but I think you need me more than I need you," said Sammie.

You have no idea.

12

Neo's Choice

A sudden knock startled Leeza. She gasped as her hand jerked, sending the chart across the room, barely missing the patient.

Tana leaned in. "Holy crap, I am so sorry." She cringed at Leeza's expression as they both watched the patient pick up the chart.

"I'm so sorry," Tana repeated.

Leeza wasn't just mortified by her panic responses—there was the humiliation she felt when strangers witnessed them. And now, having a patient see it: this was a new level of real-life horror show.

"Sorry about that," Leeza said. "These new plastic clipboards are crazy slippery."

"Artie's on the phone," Tana said softly.

"I'll call him back."

"He says it's urgent."

"Got it," Leeza said, closing the door and trying to shake off the scare. A few minutes later, she found Tana in her office.

Tana sat in a barrel chair, deeply engrossed in Maya Angelou's poems when Leeza arrived.

Leeza dropped the patient's chart into the outbox on her desk; a hint of irritation swirled around her. "Is something the matter?"

"No," Tana replied.

"Really, girl?" Leeza turned down the classical music.

Tana propped Maya back in her display and took the chart from the outbox. She returned to the chair and tapped her fingernails on the chart in her lap.

"Thinkin' of gettin' back in the game."

In a knee-jerk response, Leeza cried, "Dealing?"

"No!" Tana scoffed. "Seriously? Jesus! Really?"

"Scared the shit out of me."

"That's the first thing you thought after all this time?"

"It's just... We all have skeletons."

"My skeletons are in the gutter, where they're gonna stay," Tana said. She sucked in a breath through her teeth before adding, "I met somebody."

A slow smile spread across Leeza's face as Tana's words sank in. She pulled Tana to her feet.

"Oh my God, Tana!" cried Leeza. "You know everybody from one end of this town to the other—"

"Some I'd rather not."

"Who is he? Have I met him? Must be real upper crust to wear you down," Leeza said, grinning. "What happened to 'I don't need no man?'"

"Just between you and me, I ain't gettin' my hopes up. He's a little rough."

"Rough as in..."

"Maybe I'm just what he needs."

"Like you're gonna *fix* somebody?" Leeza scoffed. "What you need to do is protect your peace, sis. And don't leave out any details!"

"We have visitations Sundays at 2:00," Tana said.

Time stopped. Leeza repeated the words in her head before finally asking, "He's in jail? Are you serious?"

"Gotcha!" Tana roared with laughter. "I've been waitin' all day to say that."

"Jesus Christ!" cried Leeza. "Don't you mess with me. You've been known to play with fire."

"He got out two months ago," Tana said as she closed the door behind her.

Leeza had come to appreciate Tana's sense of humor, but she could never tell when she was joking—something Tana loved to take advantage of. *You better watch your step, girl.*

She texted Artie.

> You rang?

> Hey

It wasn't the answer she'd hoped for.

> Tana said it was urgent

> *And yet you didn't come to the phone*

> I'm seeing patients. Sorry

> *Meet me at the playground*

Artie waited on the park bench, a somber figure in the drizzling rain, wrapped in a long raincoat, with a black leather Panama hat and driving gloves. Leeza loved the way he looked in hats, but unless there was a good reason for one, the hair got top billing. Children played while parents huddled under umbrellas and kept guard. Leeza shared hers with Artie and sat in the stillness for a moment, taking in the rainbow from end to end.

"Beautiful," she said softly.

"Fleeting," Artie replied.

Leeza glanced down at the mud puddle in front of the bench. "Your mother is next-level precious," she said. "All privilege and no grace. That woman has never heard a wood door slam."

Artie remained still, his hands folded in his lap as he looked ahead, gazing downward.

"Why does Stephen know more about this than I do?" Leeza asked. "I deserve to know what's being said behind my back."

In the few arguments they'd had over the years, he would always sit silently in the beginning, pretending to listen to his opponent's point of view before firing back with both barrels like a gunfighter in an old Western. It was a signature move he had undoubtedly inherited from Miranda.

"The sooner you acknowledge that what I'm working on is a permanent solution, the sooner we can move on from this," Leeza said. Silence. She gazed at the oblivious children playing beneath the towering rainbow.

"You think I don't understand what you've been through, and you know what? You would be right," Artie said.

"But?"

"You were my world. From the first time I saw you, I was like, I have to get next to that. I was so nervous when I asked you out; I remember the look on your face. I used to wonder what I did to deserve you."

He paused for several moments, as if he might end it there.

"We were on cloud nine back in the day," Artie continued. "Until the kids came home." His eyes traced the length of the rainbow from end to end and back. "That was a challenge, but we found our groove, and it was fine. Then there was post-grad. And then you were deployed, and weeks would pass without me hearing from you." He closed his eyes. "And when you came home, you were never really home. Then there were the pills, and the alcohol, the nightmares, the flashbacks, the relapses. The lies."

"I never lied."

"Withholding the truth is the same as lying."

There was no comeback for that.

"You have to be a mental gymnast to keep up with you on a good day. I feel like all my energy goes into talking you down, making excuses for you, or pretending that it's not getting worse—always pretending. It's a lie." Artie wiped his face with a gloved hand. "You don't even remember what happened."

"I remember you weren't supposed to be home for two more days," said Leeza.

"She could've killed you."

"Sammie had nothing to do with it," she insisted for the hundredth time.

He looked at Leeza. "I'm nobody's fool, baby. I know what I saw. And by the way, karma really is a bitch."

"You don't wanna mess with that."

"I'm not afraid of her. She's a damn swamp rat compared to us."

Such vicious words were unlike him. Artie could find the good in the guy who robbed the convenience store, stole the car, then threw the puppy out the window during the getaway. But he had clearly developed a deep hatred for Sammie.

"Do you have any idea how embarrassing it was that you showed up in the E.R. with a drug overdose, and then you were asked to take time off?"

"Embarrassing for who?" Leeza scoffed. "I see your mother's on your shoulder again."

"I'm the one living with it."

"I swear to God, if she talks about me to anybody..." Leeza's lips tightened. "You should never have called an ambulance in the first place."

"You were literally unconscious!" The decibels tripled. "Jesus Christ! What is wrong with you? What if the kids had found you? Did you even think about that?!"

"I could still hear what was going on. And I wouldn't have let anything—"

"You'd been clean for less than six months! Apparently, alcohol doesn't count."

Neither of them noticed the parents glaring side-eyed in their direction.

"It was an experiment; I've explained it! It's part of a much bigger—"

"I wanted this to work more than anything in the world," he said, his voice suddenly cracking. "But I didn't sign up for this."

"Cliché much?" Leeza winced as the words left her lips. "Sorry."

"You don't have to be cruel," he said softly, "on top of everything else."

"I said I'm sorry."

Artie took a deliberate breath and said, "I'm losing myself here, Leeza."

"Do you even hear yourself?" Leeza took his hand. "It just feels very abrupt."

"Abrupt?" Artie scoffed. "I've absorbed a lot. There's nothing abrupt about it. The ambulance ride was a turning point."

Leeza's eyes narrowed. "Your mother feels humiliated because of something that happened to me. And you're allowing her to get in your head."

Artie let the comment wash over him, but he didn't respond.

"We were happy back in the day; you said it yourself. I'm working through some shit, I'll admit that, but I'm going to fix this. I can't just give up."

Artie retreated to silent mode.

Leeza measured her words. "My experiments are based on years of research conducted by universities around the world. We're on the verge of something huge here. They are building on measurable and sustainable paradigm shifts in the human psyche. Mental illness remission. Everything could change if—" She gave him an opening. Nothing.

They stared at opposite ends of the rainbow.

"Look, just think about when we're old," Leeza continued. "We'll spoil the hell out of our grandkids—well, Charlotte's kids. We'll get there, I swear." She waited some more. "Like I told Stephen, it's a clunky phase—"

Artie broke his silence: "This relationship is in transition."

Her next heartbeat was a detonation. Her body shuddered in the wake of his words. Her face was numb. "No," she stammered, her chin trembling.

"Do you think this is easy for me?" Artie said, gritting his teeth. "It's killing me. This relationship is toxic."

"Give yourself permission to stop, Artie," she said calmly, slowly, softly, her own breath fluttering. "Let's breathe together."

"I'm just waiting for..." Artie wiped his forehead with the back of his glove. "I've never felt so helpless. I feel like I'm stuck in a theater watching a horror movie that never ends, and I can't get out."

"*Your* life is a horror movie?!" Leeza was dismayed. "YOUR life?!"

She had witnessed atrocities that he and his family could never imagine, yet *his* life was a horror movie—and *she* was obviously the villain.

Artie took a handkerchief from his pocket and wiped his nose.

"I guess I need you to tell me exactly what I can do to help you feel less helpless," said Leeza, forcing patience.

"Twenty-three hours and fifty-seven minutes," he said.

She knew exactly what he was talking about. She'd read the report.

"Twenty-three hours and fifty-seven minutes. That's how long we were in the E.R." Artie looked at the rainbow again, his voice somber as he relived that night. "You scared me to death."

They sat in the sprinkling rain as the arching colors in front of them seemed to intensify.

"I'm sorry," Leeza whispered. "It's a process; I didn't think it would... I just—"

"The red pill or the blue pill," he said softly. "The yellow note-book or the marriage."

"Neo's choice," said Leeza. "Brilliant. A little misguided, maybe, but—"

Artie bolted upright and spun around, facing her. "Not every-thing is about you!" he screamed. "The world does not revolve around Captain Leeza Allen-Byron! You obsess about every-thing!" Parents turned toward the sudden outburst, umbrellas spinning. "Why can't you be happy for once in your life? Why can't you just be content? What exactly is it that you're trying to achieve, Leeza?" Some of the staring faces had pressed cell phones to their ears as they watched the public argument. "You had everything!"

Artie turned his back and took a breath, then turned back around, measuring his words more carefully. "You used to be ob-sessed with your recovery, but then you decided you would try to figure out how to rewrite decades of research and thumb your nose at the accepted standards of care. You honestly think you know more about how to treat flashbacks and addiction than your doctors? I spent twenty minutes on Google, Leeza. Your research is utterly unsubstantiated."

Some of the umbrella-shielded parents had started corralling their kids.

"Here's a suggestion for you," Artie went on. "Why don't you put some of that energy into taking care of your family?"

"My family?" Leeza shot back. "Keeping MY family together is my only mission. And your OTHER family can go straight to hell!"

"Your priorities are a little blurred, Captain," Artie seethed. "I've been trying to wrap my head around it. Lots of people survive the same things you did. We know people who were in Afghanistan at the same time you were. Why are you still so affected by it? What happened to you?!" His eyes were on hers; hers were on the ground. "Whatever your excuse is for sneaking around and hiding liquor and drugs and God knows what else, just tell me what it is!"

"Fine," said Leeza, reaching for his hand. "Couples counseling. Whatever it takes. Let's stop talking about it and just do it. It's toxic, I get it. But we can fix it—if you just trust me."

"You are seriously unwell," he said, beginning to choke up. "And we can't fix this."

"I'm working on a treatment, Artie," Leeza pleaded. "I know it's possible; please just let me explain it to you. I've done all the research. I just need to conduct some experiments. And it's not just me working on this; there are studies, actual studies—"

"ENOUGH!" Artie screamed. "Enough with the fucking paradigm-shifting fucking whatever!"

He started walking away; the umbrella-cloaked parents were at full attention.

"Artie!" Leeza's voice cracked as she rushed after him, tightening her grip on the umbrella. "Slow down!" The distance between them was closing. "Do you really want to know what happened to me in Afghanistan?"

He stopped in his tracks. Leeza caught up to him.

"Do you want to know?"

He turned to face her. She lowered her umbrella and moved closer, rain mixing with tears on their faces. She said it again, slower. "Do you want to know what happened to me in Afghanistan?" She could see the exhaustion in his eyes. He hesitated. Then he said: "No."

Another explosion ripped through her chest—but this one was muffled, less catastrophic. Less surprising?

"I need space," he said.

Her face softened with resignation. She did this.

"Take your experiments or whatever and go." As he turned and walked away into the rain, he added, "Please."

A rtie pulled up the cobblestone driveway of his enormous childhood home where his mother still lived. Miranda and a petite woman with olive-toned skin appeared in the doorway; the woman was dressed in a familiar light blue maid's outfit and white apron. Miranda snapped an order at the new maid before walking alone toward the SUV as Artie parked. She wrapped her arms around her son as he cried in her arms.

13

You Know What They Say about Opinions

The mariachi band, Los Chicos Errantes, blared from inside Rancho Lewis restaurant all the way to King Street on Saturday nights. The popular Mexican joint was a hotspot for date nights, celebrations, and families, thanks to its huge portions and robust kids' menu. But the real crowd-pleaser was the ridiculous margarita menu—three pages of specialty margaritas and forty hand-selected tequilas. From shots to the fifty-two-ounce Naughty Maria served with up to six straws—and everything in between—there was something for everyone. The dining room and bar were colorful and loud, making it a great place to get sufficiently lubricated before driving all the full tummies back home.

Several tables had been pushed together for a large group of rambunctious kids celebrating a birthday. A helicopter mom had reserved the tables closest to the five-member band to entertain little Preston, but the swarm of seven- and eight-year-old besties was much more interested in playing duck-duck-goose around the entire dining room than pretending to appreciate live entertainment.

Leeza was too preoccupied replaying the conversation with Artie to worry about how other people failed miserably at teaching their children to behave in public. *Why is he hell-bent on screwing this up? Everything will be back to normal in a few months; why can't he trust me?*

A text from Sammie popped up:

checkin in u ok?

Leeza put her phone in her pocket.

A rotund Mexican waitress with a heavy Spanish accent swooped in, her arms loaded with steaming plates of food.

"Lil' Juan's chicken tenders and French fries?" Grant raised his hand and watched the plate hover in the air before it plopped down in front of him.

"Because that's what you do in a Mexican restaurant," Charlotte said as Grant's chicken and fries landed. Her cheese quesadilla followed closely behind. Leeza had her usual fish taco and side salad with a squeeze of lime.

Grant glanced at Leeza between bites. "Leesie?"

"Grant."

"What does promiscuous mean?"

"What?" Dread crept into Leeza's voice.

"He means precocious," Charlotte said, stretching what looked like a rubber band made of cheese into the air.

"Where did you hear that?" Leeza asked.

"Daddy's friend."

"Daddy has weird friends."

"You can say that again," said Charlotte.

"How long is Daddy gonna stay gone this time?" Grant asked.

"Do you know why he went to see Gramma?"

"'Cause she's sad Grampa passed."

"She just needs some company for a while," said Leeza. "He calls you every day."

"It's not a big deal when he's not around," Charlotte said. "You do everything anyways."

"Anyway," said Leeza.

"Anyway," repeated Charlotte. "Piano. Homework."

"Eating at restaurants," said Grant.

"Tell me all about school, don't leave anything out."

"Good," said Charlotte.

"Jimmy Norlander got a black eye," said Grant.

"How?" Leeza asked. Grant shrugged.

Leeza thought she saw a sly smile as she watched Charlotte take a bite of her quesadilla.

"Charlotte?" said Leeza.

Charlotte shrugged. "How am I supposed to know?"

"For homework, we have to think of a word that describes ourselves to others," said Grant. "But it can only be one word and not a verb."

"Interesting," said Leeza. "One word to describe yourself?"

"We have till Friday, but I already know my word," Grant said.

"The suspense is killing me," said Charlotte, with a trademark eye roll.

"Sketch," said Grant, decisively.

"Genius," said Charlotte, with back-to-back eye rolls.

"You'll have to explain that one," said Leeza.

"Cause before you can paint a picture, you have to sketch a drawing," said Grant.

"Hmmm... Because it's like a work in progress?"

Grant held up a thumb and grinned with every tooth in his head.

Leeza looked at Charlotte. "Kind of *is* genius, huh?"

"Preach, Shaniqua!" cried Grant.

"Except you used it as a verb, Einstein," said Charlotte.

A loud explosion ripped through the air at the center of the dining room. Leeza saw a burst of bright red filling the room. In a full-on panic response, she felt her body drop to the floor. She scrambled under the table, hands covering her ears, eyes shut. Her body shuddered with violent tremors. *The unrelenting, deafening sound of artillery and bombs exploded all around. The air was thick with smoke and the sounds of men yelling, chaos, and cries of agony. Two soldiers rushed into the medic tent with a stretcher carrying a wounded soldier in his early twenties and placed him on a cot in front of Leeza. She saw the blood-soaked gauze dressings just as he grabbed her hand!*

The waitress approached with the check. She looked at Leeza, still cowering under the table, chest heaving.

"Ma'am? You okay, ma'am?" she asked.

Leeza's consciousness resurfaced slowly, like being dragged out of an ocean across a sandy beach. The room felt padded and distant—unnaturally silent. It was the same silence that followed the artillery, before the screaming began. She looked around at the shocked expressions and wide eyes staring at her, diagnosing her.

"You need help up, ma'am?" asked the waitress, reaching for Leeza's hand. Leeza cautiously pulled herself up and sat in her chair.

"I dropped something. Thank you." She looked at the birthday table and saw colorful confetti and foil streamers. Another noise-maker exploded, and she flinched as the young children screamed with delight. The mariachi music started again; some of the musicians were still staring at her.

"Leesie?" said Grant.

"What, Grant?"

"I'll pay for dinner."

Leeza took a credit card from her wallet and handed it to Grant. He attached the card to the check and set it on the edge of the table.

"Thank you, sir." She rubbed her shoulders and neck, taking slow breaths, in through the nose and out through the mouth.

"Are you okay?" Charlotte asked, tentatively.

"Workin' it out, baby girl," she said. "What's your word, Charlotte?"

"Saturated," she answered.

O utside Dairy Queen after dinner, Grant devoured his Oreo cookie blizzard treat while Charlotte took her time. A few tables away, Leeza texted on her phone. Normal people don't eat ice cream when it's fifty degrees outside, which is exactly why she liked it there.

"Last time we came here, Mama told us she was going to Afghanistan," said Charlotte.

"She said she's home for good," said Grant, with a sudden look of dread.

Leeza joined the kids and helped herself to a taste of Charlotte's blizzard. "Family meeting. Huddle up."

"We *knew* it!" cried Grant, his voice cracking. They stood in front of her like she was their little league coach. "You said we were stuck with you forever!"

"I'm not going back in the Army."

"Is this about the adoption?" Charlotte asked.

"We're not supposed to talk about that." said Grant. "You promised."

"Actually, we *are* supposed to talk about that."

"When you're a teenager, remember?" said Leeza.

"God in heaven, please don't tell us you're having a baby," said Charlotte.

Leeza shot a cross-eyed look at Charlotte. "Yeah, right."

Grant grew anxious at the suggestion of anything that involved change, and he knew she wouldn't bring them to Dairy Queen to eat ice cream outside in the cold if something big wasn't about to happen.

"It's not a big deal," Leeza began. "When grownups have been together for a long time, sometimes they decide they need to take a little break for a while." She fed the information in small bites. "Just long enough to figure things out. And then they can get back together, and things can get back to normal."

"Isn't that what they call divorce?" asked Grant.

"It's what they call separation," said Charlotte.

Leeza rubbed Grant's forehead. "It's a separation, baby. Not a divorce. Where did you hear that word?" she asked Charlotte.

"Half my friends in school."

Tears burst from Grant's eyes. Leeza put her arms around him and kissed the top of his head. "Is it 'cause I like boys?" His voice trembled as he whispered, "Gramma said Jesus hates the sin but not the sinner, but she looked grossed out when she said it." He cupped his face in his hands as the cry escaped.

I will kill that damned bitch, Leeza thought. "Well, you know what they say about opinions—"

"They're like assholes; everybody has one," said Charlotte.

"Okay, that was my fault," said Leeza. "Here's the deal: I'm going to get an apartment for a little while, and Daddy will stay at the house, and you guys can come spend time with me anytime you want. And you can call me anytime. Understand?" Fighting tears, Leeza pulled the kids in for a hug.

"How long?" asked Charlotte.

"Two or three months, tops."

Leeza loaded the last suitcase into the back seat and closed the door. The motorcycle was strapped into the bed of her truck. Artie watched from an upstairs window as she pulled away; their eyes met as she passed.

The sound of a sobbing child echoed through the house. Tears streamed down Charlotte's face as she lay on the floor by her bed. Her pain would be inconsolable if anyone tried to comfort her. In the other room, Grant stared out the window, watching as Leeza disappeared. Trance-like, the young boy painted his face with lipstick, making random strokes across his cheeks, around his mouth, and across his forehead. He leaned into the glass, smearing a red imprint of his cheeks and nose. His blank stare reflected the confusion of a child struggling to comprehend something beyond his understanding.

14

Your Move, Chica

There was a text from Sammie.

> *I am not the enemy*

With a full schedule of patients, a steady stream of consults, the yellow binder growing thicker by the day, and hammering out the logistics of the experiments, Leeza had been able to keep her mind busy.

> *It's not you. I'll be in touch*

She stared across the room at her Doctor of Nursing Practice diploma, her hand resting on the open yellow binder. Tana knocked lightly and peered in before tiptoeing toward her.

"Consult in ICU. Male, eighty-two, C.V.A., high-grade stenosis, right carotid," Tana reported. "There's an addendum to the radiologist's report that says the ultrasound images are mislabeled. It's right not left, and the ICA and ECA annotations were X'd out by the tech on some of the images. You might wanna drop by the reading room first and have a chat with the radiologist before Dr. Randall gets wind of it. You know the battle cry…

"…blame radiology," they said in unison.

"After the damage is done, of course," Leeza added. "It's all good—as long as they snapped some images of the plaque while they were at it."

Tana handed Leeza the census with the patients' demographics highlighted in yellow; the affirmation was written across the top.

"How you holdin' up?" Tana asked.

Leeza read the affirmation aloud.

> "He will cover you with his feathers. He will shelter you with his wings. His faithful promises are your armor and protection."

Tana smiled at her friend and mentor. Years of supporting each other through harsh challenges had forged an unbreakable bond.

Leeza looked up at Tana. "You know it's temporary, right?"

"Of course. But a little faith never hurt anybody."

That's debatable, Leeza thought.

Leeza flashed a side-eyed smile in Tana's direction. "Sooo...?" she prodded.

"His name is Dante."

"Let me guess... bad boy."

"He's paid his dues," Tana assured her.

"Um-hmm."

"Besides, everybody's got a bad side."

"Keep the focus, girl. Dante is one lucky brother."

"Oh, ain't nobody draggin' me back down," said Tana. "Come too far. And still too much left to do."

"How serious?"

"On a serious scale... I'd say somewhere between a joke and a heart attack." Tana slapped the side of her thigh as she cracked herself up. "In other words, who the hell knows!"

"The power is in your hands, girl," said Leeza, "and you know where I am if anything goes sideways."

L eeza was in the "cozy" living room of her apartment at Willow Glen in North Charleston. She had taken over the lease from an Air Force pilot with orders to Joint Base Andrews. The commute wasn't ideal, but it was furnished, and it was available for short-term rental. The 1971 brick facade was tired but classic lowland Southern, and the manager seemed very helpful once she found out the person interested in the remainder of the lease was a nurse with an actual steady job. Leeza wasn't bothered by the fact that the Norfolk Southern line ran right by the apartments; she could hear the train coming from a mile away.

The yellow binder lay open in her lap, a pen in hand. The soothing classical music was abruptly assaulted by her phone.

"Artie!" she gasped, shocked to see his face on the screen. She started talking as soon as she hit the answer button. "Look, I've been thinking about everything you said, and I know you're confused, and I understand why. I get it, I swear I get it."

"Leeza," he interrupted.

"Just hear me out, please. I know what I've done to you, and I've been working on some ideas that'll help both of us; I just need to tell you—"

"Leeza."

"We need a change of scenery, let's get out of town, just the two of us. Do you remember that restaurant in Dupont Circle? Let's go back; we'll start there," she said, struggling to get the words out fast enough. "I promise I'll stop talking about your mother."

"Could you please just—"

"We both needed some time, Artie. I get it. It's all good."

"I have an attorney," he said. Her brain begged for a moment to process the words, but he kept going. *"I set up mediation for next Tuesday at three o'clock. It's preliminary. I'll text you the address."* Each heartbeat in her chest felt distinct from the previous, and she

realized she had arrived at the edge of the cliff. Her phone buzzed with a text from Sammie.

> *update por favor*

"You're not serious," Leeza finally managed to say, her voice barely audible.

> *Your move chica*

"The separation's been good. We've had time to process."
"It's been a week, Artie," she knew she was going to cry but she fought hard to hold it in.

> *Here for you*

"What about the counseling?" Leeza asked.
"I never agreed to counseling."
"You said you wanted this to work! This isn't you. This isn't you talking!" Leeza's chin was trembling.
"We're reliving the same chapters, Leeza." Artie ended the call.

> *Lets make it work*

"You bitch," Leeza seethed. She could imagine all the crap Miranda was telling her husband and kids.

Sammie's face appeared on the screen as the phone rang. Sammie was her lifeline now, and she couldn't risk pushing her away too. She took a breath, exhaled through pursed lips, then relaxed her face.

"Hey girl."
"You owe me," said Sammie.
"I got you."

15

Everything is Between a Church and a Tavern around Here

O n Broad Street, a block and a half from the Charleston
County Court, there was a brownstone walk-up with rent-
ed office space in the basement. The words etched in the glass of
the front door read:

Kit & Caboodle Professional Mediators ~ By appointment only

A tiny, paneled waiting area with four clear plastic stackable
chairs and a small table with a collection of *Game & Fish* magazines
preceded the main conference room. A shadow-box display of
game-bird feathers hung on a brown wall.

Inside, the mediator sat at the head of a clownishly large table,
the chipped oak veneer top covered in a network of countless
scratches. On the far wall hung a calendar with a photo of adorable,
cuddly puppies, happily representing the month of August—in
October. An espresso-brown IKEA bookcase completed the eclec-
tic Deep South design. Leeza sat to the mediator's left, across from
empty chairs, as they waited for Artie.

"Punctuality is a virtue, no?" asked the mediator, sorting
through a stack of documents. She had deep wrinkles and clearly
hadn't sacrificed a minute of her morning routine on makeup. Cat
hair littered the front of her black turtleneck. A crucifix hung from
a long chain around her neck, suspending the tortured Christ between her asymmetric breasts and on top of a second necklace—an
American flag. Her voice was patient and measured, like a yoga

instructor or a youth pastor. Jesus slid back and forth across the flag with each breath she took.

The door flung open, and all eyes turned to the woman bursting into the conference room, dressed in a sharp business suit, dripping with jewelry. A second later, *Victoria Beckham Beauty Portofino '97* followed, so strong she must have spilled it on herself. Leeza's eyes widened at the caricature in front of her. She looked like she had just stomped off the set of *Real Housewives of New York*, having slapped the shit out of her bestie for accusing her of stealing her earrings. She thrust a business card toward the mediator and yanked back chairs for herself and Artie. "This place isn't exactly easy to find," she said, glaring at her watch.

"Right between the church and the tavern, just like it says on the website," replied the mediator, still rifling through documents.

"Everything is between a church and a damn tavern around here," she hissed.

The mediator read the woman's card. "Victoria Langley. And you must be Arthur. Are we waiting for one more?" she asked, looking at Leeza.

"No," said Leeza.

"Very good. Good afternoon, I'm Marjorie Parker. I'll be mediating the pre-divorce proceedings of Arthur Charles Preston Nigel Byron the Third and Leeza Jamila Allen-Byron. Feel free to call me Ms. Marjorie. Both parties have chosen voluntary mediation. Do you both affirm that you are here willingly?"

"Yes," said Artie.

"Ms. Allen?"

"Mrs. Allen-Byron," said Leeza.

"Mrs. Allen-Byron," repeated Ms. Marjorie as she scribbled a note.

"Okie dokie," said Victoria. She had a permanent scowl on her face that said, *Get me out of this hellhole.*

"Mediation will include custody determination of the two minor children, Grant Lee Allen-Byron and Charlotte Lee Allen-Byron. All final declarations will be filed with the South Carolina state court and enforced by the court. Mr. Byron has invited counsel. Shall we begin?"

Victoria cleared her throat. "As the primary caregiver of the two children, both while Ms. Allen was deployed and—"

"Mrs. Allen-Byron," Leeza interjected.

Victoria glared at Leeza before continuing. "As the primary caregiver of the two children, both while *Mrs.* Allen-Byron was deployed and since her return, my client is requesting that—"

"Excuse me," Leeza interrupted.

"You'll have your turn," Victoria said.

"I just need to interject for a second."

"And there will be time for that. *Mr.* Byron is requesting that—"

"I'm sorry, but you stated that he was the primary caregiver, even after my return, so I just wanted to make a clarification."

"Are you communication-challenged, Ms. Allen?" asked Victoria. "Adults listen first, then speak." Artie shot a surprised look at Victoria.

Leeza leaned in, locking eyes with Victoria. With a voice measured and clear, she said, "Communication is a process by which information is exchanged between individuals. What part of that concept is kicking your ass? And it's Mrs. Allen-Byron."

The room seemed to hold its breath.

Ms. Marjorie raised a hand in the air as if she were going to throw a penalty flag. "Okay, okay, Mrs. Allen-Byron, you can ask your question."

Victoria retreated, shooting daggers at her opponent.

"You said my husband was the primary caregiver of our children, both while I was deployed and since my return. The truth is, when I was deployed, they had a Monday-through-Friday nanny, and we shared that expense. And since my return, we have shared equally in raising our children."

"Is that so?" asked Victoria.

"Why would you think otherwise?"

"Are you sure you want to go there?" Artie averted Leeza's glance. "I see this going one of two ways," said Victoria directly to Leeza, "and if you choose to challenge every proposal we bring, I assure you it won't end well for you."

"I'd like to talk to my husband alone for a moment," said Leeza.

"We need to move forward," said Victoria.

Artie started to stand, then paused, shooting a look at Victoria that was less of a question and more of an order. "It's okay," he told her.

Victoria made a show of gathering her pen and pad, dragging the moment out. Marjorie got up and opened the door. Victoria begrudgingly followed, her heels clicking on the hard floor. "You have five minutes," she said as the door closed behind them.

Leeza walked around the table toward Artie.

"Let's get out of here. We don't need this," said Leeza. "Let's just leave."

"We've been through this," Artie replied.

"Who's 'we' Artie? You know as well as I do this is not what you want."

"What's your problem?"

"My problem is you brought that feminazi cunt with you, and she's questioning my involvement in raising our kids. Am I supposed to just sit there and let that happen? That's never been what this is about."

"Victoria just wants to make sure—"

"Oh, 'Victoria wants to make sure?'" Leeza's voice was rising. "You never had any problems thinking for yourself. And where exactly did you find her by the way?" Artie avoided her eyes, and the answer snapped into place. "Your mother has been involved in this all along, hasn't she?" She watched his body slouch. "Bitch."

Even as the door was opening, Victoria plopped back down in her chair and glared at Leeza.

Artie leaned in and lowered his voice. "How is calling my mother a bitch helping you?"

"You thought that was for her?"

Ms. Marjorie was in youth pastor mode: "Mrs. Allen, if mediation is compromised—"

"Byron!" cried Leeza. "It's Allen-Byron!"

"Mrs. Allen-Byron, if any of these sessions are compromised, your divorce will have to be handled by the court, starting from the beginning. Let's 'parking lot' custody for now, shall we?"

As the others moved back to their chairs, Artie whispered in Victoria's ear. "Watch your tone, please." Leeza barely heard him.

16

Gotcha

Leeza sat in her chaise and faced Dr. Singh, who was settled in her matching chair. Specks of dust filled the sunbeam, swarming the back of Leeza's hand like aphids in a fantasy forest. It felt different from the underwater "lake dust" she remembered from her childhood in Beaufort. The candle had apparently been retired.

"Shall we talk about the mediation?" asked Dr. Singh.

"Roadside bomb comes to mind."

The doctor raised her eyebrows.

"It's amazing how attorneys seem like normal human beings from a distance," said Leeza. "He showed up with this freak of nature, referred to him by his own mother, mind you, and they came at me with both barrels."

"I would imagine you felt cornered."

"They got to him. I would give him anything he wanted. Still." Leeza glanced at the ray of sun on the back of her arm and imagined it would burn her skin off if she held still long enough. "The more he listens to them, the less chance I have."

"You expressed a desire to enter couples counseling?"

"Shot down," said Leeza.

"I want to preface my next statement by emphasizing that I'm not suggesting anything to you, I'm simply asking if it's something you have considered. Your answer may help steer our future conversations."

"Okay?" said Leeza tentatively.

"Staying in a relationship that fundamentally can't meet your needs is not a net positive. Many of us carry a lot of shame around relationship endings, but not all breakups are failures. Sometimes, staying comes at a greater cost than leaving."

Leeza's lips tightened. *What the hell? Why would a psychiatrist suggest such a thing and preface it by saying she's not suggesting anything when she clearly is?* Then it hit her like a full-on Oprah "Aha" moment: *You get a car! You get a car! Everybody gets a car!* Leeza just realized two things—two revelations that would prove very cathartic.

"Give me a sec," she said, taking time to process. *Dr. Singh's father was friends with Drs. Randall and Byron—they had a dubious 'referral understanding' for years. Dr. Singh inherited her father's practice after he resigned following an investigation into his 'experiments' in the psych ward at the hospital, and she's been in his old office ever since.* Leeza's arm burned in the sunbeam, but she left it. *When Dr. Byron gave her Dr. Singh's card, he said "let's keep it in the family."* The truth was obvious: *Revelation number one: Miranda strikes again. Revelation number two: Kashvi Singh is a quack just like her father.*

Leeza moved her arm to her lap and rubbed the burning skin as Kashvi stared at her clenched fists. "Maybe there are better ways we could fill our sessions," Leeza said.

"The barge is full of containers," Dr. Singh replied. "Each container represents a problem, a diagnosis, and a challenge we've recognized, each with potential treatments we need to sort. All of the containers are interlinked, which is why it is crucial they each remain on the barge. We must steer bravely and unflinchingly toward measurable and manageable outcomes. Trust me to pilot the barge, Leeza."

"Does the barge have a motor or are we relying on the current?" asked Leeza.

Dr. Singh was taken aback by the barb. "If you're dissatisfied with the pace, Leeza..."

I am not some ten-year-old who sets neighborhood cats on fire.
The relentless barge analogy forced Leeza to admit what she already knew: this kind of therapy couldn't help her. Only she could treat her condition, and only the formula lurking inside the yellow binder offered her any chance. Her research and experiments would eventually prove it. She also knew the tension between doctor and patient was ultimately counterproductive.

"I'm Sisyphus, pushing the boulder up the hill every day, and every day, I have to start all over because I wake up at the bottom of the hill with the boulder on my lap. I'm losing. The pep talks, the analogies, and the psychedelics aren't helping."

"Our suffering becomes encoded in our DNA and inevitably has some influence on decisions we make," Dr. Singh pivoted. "We're at a crucial turning point. Victory is not elusive for everyone. That's why you're still in the game—you know it to be true. Oftentimes, we're closer than we allow ourselves to realize. This internal state is not the truth of what's happening around us but simply a moment's interpretation."

It sounded like she was reading from index cards for a book report in a community college psychology class. "I feel like we're spinning our wheels here," Leeza said. "You want to talk about me walking away from my marriage because you think I will somehow be stronger once it's over?"

"I wasn't suggesting anything of the sort, and as I said—"

"Any issues I might be having within my family are not the reason I'm here."

Dr. Singh plopped her pad forcefully onto the table between them. "No more spinning our wheels," she said, with an intensity Leeza hadn't seen before. "I'm left with the sense that you're leaving something out. We've discussed a dozen traumas, each of which would explain the PTSD. But there's something else." Her composure gave way to a stoney stare; a Jekyll and Hyde-like shift that took Leeza by surprise. "What happened to you in Afghanistan?"

Did she actually just say that? Wow, even a broken clock is right twice a day—something the radiologists loved to say about the E.R. docs and PAs. Of course, there were things she wouldn't tell a psychiatrist, especially this one. It would be like Lyle and Erik telling Dr. Oziel they shot their parents. *Idiots.*

"This was your father's office, correct?" Leeza asked.

Dr. Singh's eyes narrowed. She *knew* there was something else. Leeza's problem was more than PTSD from losing a parent or working as a nurse in a war zone. She was hiding something much more serious, and Singh was onto her. "He founded the department of psychiatry at Southern General. He was a pioneer in the field," she said.

"I read he was sanctioned by the state board for unwarranted experimentation after a couple of lawsuits. I assume that's what led to the early retirement."

Dr. Singh sank further into the freakishly large, tufted leather chair as a sly smile formed on one side of her mouth. "You would have gotten along well," she said.

Gotcha. It was true. Artie told Miranda about the experiments and the night in the garage, and Miranda had blabbed everything to Singh. The two women sat in silence, relishing the cat-and-mouse game like two mafia dons savoring a Gurkha Maharaja cigar. But Leeza knew the physician would never win against this practitioner.

"Thank you," said Leeza. "I appreciate the perspective you've given me. I apologize if I came across as contradictory; it wasn't my intention. I'm working through a lot, and I know I'm lucky to have you." She got through the bullshit with a straight face because she knew Miranda would get the CliffsNotes.

"Pain is the price we pay for loving and having been loved," said Dr. Singh.

Jesus Christ, now she's quoting Queen Elizabeth. "Queenie Lilibet," Leeza said as she stood to leave.

"Excuse me?"

"Lilibet was the queen's nickname. She's the one credited for saying, 'pain is the price we pay for loving and having been loved.'" Leeza grabbed her helmet. "I think I have it on a Post-it note somewhere," she added on her way out.

Outside, Leeza started the bike and pulled on her helmet. "Tell me 'bout the barge, George," she said with her best Lennie Small impression.

17

"You Are Seriously Unwell," She Remembered Him Saying

The Willow Glen apartments were quiet on Sunday mornings. The God-fearing neighbors attended church, followed by brunch at The Golden Corral Buffet for an all-you-can-eat, post-bible-study fellowship with cousins, a wheelchair-bound grandparent or two, and every three-year-old in the county.

The yellow binder lay open on Leeza's kitchen table among a collection of medical journals, a dictionary, and Remington: The Science and Practice of Pharmacy, 23rd edition. A digital Physician's Desk Reference was pulled up on the laptop. Leeza worked on the formula for most of the morning, with only a single interruption: a flashback triggered by the sound of a car door slamming just outside her unit. That necessitated a shot of whiskey and an IPA from Revelry Brewing on Conway Street at 9:00 a.m.

Sammie had been texting all morning, but Leeza needed to focus. Sammie could suck the energy out of a room full of Charleston RiverDog fans celebrating a Southern Division Championship title. She poured a Jack and finished reading an article about a patient with recurrent rhabdomyolysis from drinking grapefruit juice while taking atorvastatin, and the PA who insisted he up his colostrum, *"because until your gut is healthy, nothing else can be healthy."* It was important to keep her mind focused on the research and to monitor the effects of the ever-evolving drug cocktails she was prescribing for herself: a milligram of heroin cut with powdered milk and Ritalin, with whiskey and Beethoven. Clonazepam with epinephrine, Sauvignon Blanc and Vivaldi. Cocaine with Red Bull, haloperidol, and Haydn, and a long list of others. If only she could use regression therapy on herself at the same time. *"What if I could convince you that all your phobias and childhood traumas and scary memories were nothing more than cartoon characters?"* she'd told Sammie. *"It's the controlled distraction that facilitates opening your mind to the catharsis,"* she told herself.

Each combination was intended to be paired with a walk down memory lane into the most hellish experiences of your lifetime, whether it was rape or torture, childhood PTSD or sex trafficking, deployment in a war zone, or whatever happened that got you on Effexor or Cymbalta or Xanax, Klonopin, Seroquel, Ativan, Elavil, Paxil, Lithium, Zoloft, Prozac, Jack Daniel's, Hennessy, or two bottles of Two-Buck Chuck every night. With a therapist in tow, the patient would begin during a lucid or baseline phase, then alter their consciousness with the formula, then they would be "guided to" a safe distance mentally. There, they would observe the impetus of mental derangement like an out-of-body experience. They would learn to put it in perspective objectively and figure out how to control *its* control over them: the reprogramming paradigm shift. Finally, they would practice motivation and goal-directed behaviors before chemical weaning. Of course, the coaching would come from specially trained professionals, such as experimental psychologists or apostatized Buddhists, but Leeza had to achieve some degree of success before any substantive trials could legally take place. And she didn't have any mice.

She found herself daydreaming as she stared at the sunbeam coming from the front windows. The lake dust was thick in the tall, narrow beam that aimed at the sofa on the far side of the room. She felt the Jack and IPA as she relived the conversation with Victoria at Kit & Caboodle: Professional Mediators. What was the point of being so aggressive and disrespectful? She remembered senior enlisted soldiers yelling at the privates and specialists, who cowered in fear. She imagined Victoria wearing Army fatigues with a general's insignia, barking orders at everyone in the room.

"Are you communication-challenged, Ms. Allen?" she said aloud, mimicking Victoria. "Adults listen first, then speak." She grew more agitated as she thought about the bitch with the jewelry and expensive perfume but no class. "Everything is between a church and a damn tavern around here," she mocked. And all Artie could muster was, "Watch your tone, please."

Leeza went to the bathroom at the end of the hall across from the only bedroom in the "cozy cottage." *"You'll have your turn, Ms. Allen,"* she heard Victoria say. Leeza turned on the shower then opened the medicine cabinet. The shelves were packed with prescription bottles, including several that had expired—dropped off by the families of also-expired patients. She ran her fingers along the lineup, picked one, emptied a few pills into her hand, and swallowed them with an IPA chaser. *"Make sure you're monitoring the small victories!"* The hot water was already steaming up the small bathroom. *"Are you sure you wanna go there?"* Leeza undressed as thoughts of Victoria filled her head. *"I see this going one of two ways."* She stripped to her bra and panties and went into the bedroom. *"We need to move forward! You have five minutes!"*

Leeza reached under the bed and pulled out a metal case. She took out a Sig Sauer P320 9mm handgun, just like the Army-issued weapon she carried during active duty. She slept with the loaded handgun in the officer's tent in Afghanistan on the few occasions she actually slept. She bought this one when she got back to the States because she was used to its grip and weight. She checked the chamber and inserted a magazine with a familiar click. "Are you sure you wanna go there?" she mumbled, mimicking Victoria.

She wrapped the belly band with the holster around her waist and shoved in the semiautomatic weapon. The steam from the shower started slinking down the hallway toward the living room like fog in a black-and-white Dracula movie. She opened the closet and took a military hat with a captain's insignia. *"How is calling my mother a bitch helping your case?"* she remembered Artie saying as she positioned the hat. She put on a camouflage shirt and went to the living room for another Jack, followed by the rest of the beer and a small line of coke.

She started marching up and down the hallway, making an about-face at the end, then marching back. Her right hand rested on the handgun; the Jack was in her left. The brim of the hat obscured her eyes as the steam filled the hallway and began to invade the living room.

"Left! Left! Left, right, left!" she called out as she marched, knees rising to waist height with each step.

"Sir, yessir!"

"Your decisions will be enforced by the court!" she mimicked the mediator.

"As the primary caregiver of two young children..." she said in Victoria's voice again.

"But I just want to ask a question," she responded in her own.

"About face!" Leeza's voice grew louder.

"But you were in Afghanistan!" Victoria's voice went on. "How could you possibly be a good mother to your children when you were in Afghanistan? You were in fucking Afghanistan!"

"About face!"

"Are you communication challenged?!" she yelled.

"What does that even mean?"

"Adults listen first!"

She saluted, "Sir, yessir!"

"About face!"

"Get away from her!" Victoria protested.

The steam filled the apartment. She was barely visible as she marched down the hallway.

"Sir, yessir!" she yelled, saluting again.

"This is a team exercise! There can be no dissension in the ranks! NO DISSENSION IN THE RANKS!" she yelled louder, marching with her hand on the gun between salutes. The Jack left puddles of eighty-proof alcohol on the floor as it sloshed out of the glass.

She went to the bathroom and stood in front of the mirror, shrouded by an opaque veil of condensation. She rubbed a circle on the glass to expose her reflection, looking past herself—

The soldier grabbed Leeza's hand as he struggled to breathe. His face was covered in blood, some dried to a dirty rust, some still crimson as he pleaded. Leeza put her free hand on the soldier's neck and stared at his face—so young—with full cheeks that his mama used to pinch between her thumb and index fingers, followed by a kiss on the forehead. Her thumb encircled his Adam's apple. She could feel the air gurgling back and forth under her fingers as he fought for each breath. She leaned in, forcing her thumb into the soldier's neck with all her might, cutting off his airway. His grip tightened as his eye widened. Finally, the gurgling sound stopped, as did time. She stood over him, staring. Her mind was too exhausted to think. Then, very slowly, his hand fell from hers. His body went limp as he let go of what was left of his fight for survival. Tears gushed from her eyes.

The steam moved like smoke in the war zone and Leeza was a shadow in the thickness. She resumed marching.

"About face!" she yelled.

"There's something else! What is it?!" mimicking Singh now. "What happened to you?!"

There was a frantic knock on the door.

"What happened to you?! They would hate me if they knew what I did!"

The knocking grew more forceful; several voices came from the other side.

"They would hate me if they knew what I did!"

More knocking, more frantic voices.

"You are seriously unwell," she remembered Artie saying. "And we can't fix this," she whispered. "They would hate me if they knew what I did."

Leeza dropped to her knees, wailing, pounding her head with closed fists. She fell to the floor and curled up in the fetal position as wretched sobs tore themselves from her body. "And we can't fix this... And we can't fix this... And we can't fix this."

The loud knocking on the door continued.

"Is everything okay in there? HELLO?!"

Leeza lay on the floor, crying and rocking herself. "They would hate me if they knew what I did." The steam was gone as the water, now running cold, continued in the shower. "Pain is the price we pay for loving and having been loved," she said softly. "Pain is the price we pay for love. Pain is the price we pay for love."

The voices continued from outside, *"Everything ok in there? HELLO?"* The neighbors banged louder. "OPEN THE DOOR!"

18

Saffron and Horizon

The Nomad Club was hopping as Josh and his tight jeans performed an upbeat country song about being in love with another man's wife who drove a '69 Mustang and drank too much, or ran over her dog, or was actually a guy, or something like that. The crowd was soaking up the performance while two bartenders worked frantically behind the bar like they were the last two contestants on a Japanese game show. Josh winked at Leeza as she came through the door. He changed the name of the femme fatale to *Leeza* mid-song.

Leeza heard someone calling her name over the music and laughter as Josh belted out another verse. She caught Tana from the corner of her eye, motioning wildly for her to join the table. Tana grabbed Leeza's hand. "Leeza, this is Dante," she announced proudly.

Dante extended his long, thin arms to greet her, flashing a toothy grin with a gold veneer on a front tooth. Tall and slim, he sported a jacket that was a size too big. Leeza tried to imagine where his shoulders ended under all that fabric. His tattoos extended to his fingertips. Self-possessed, he spoke perfect English with a subtle Spanish accent.

"Pleasure," he said as he gripped her hands emphatically.

"Likewise," Leeza replied. "Welcome to Charleston."

"Welcome *back* to Charleston," said Tana.

"Welcome *back* to Charleston," Leeza repeated.

The crowd erupted with applause at the end of Josh's set as he made a beeline for Leeza. "Your regular?" he asked.

"Did you actually just use my name in a country song?" Leeza laughed.

"I like puttin' a face with the name," said Josh, with a playful shrug. He noticed the two people with Leeza. "Tana, right?"

"Hey, Josh," Tana said. She got up, wrapped her arms around him, and whispered, "Good to see you." She savored his face for a moment before turning to Dante. "This is my friend, Dante." Josh shook Dante's hand, but his gaze lingered on Tana. "I'll be back," he said.

When Tana suggested The Nomad, Leeza assumed it was some place she had heard about and wanted to check out. She had no idea she and Josh knew each other. "You've been here?" Leeza asked.

"Used to come inside to get out of the cold," she said. "Josh let me be."

Tana was very candid about her struggle with drugs, and Leeza was often shocked by her stories about living on the streets, but she had no idea that Josh had been so kind to her over a decade ago in this very place. It was a sobering moment, and she was glad she had finally agreed to join them for a night out.

"Your work sounds fascinating," said Dante. "I can't get enough of the stories."

"Usually when we talk about work, people run for the exits," said Leeza. Dante let out a laugh that reminded her of the comic character Skeletor. Tana had mentioned that he was nervous about meeting her, but he seemed pretty relaxed. *I don't think anybody could make this dude nervous.*

Josh returned with a round of drinks.

"To the lucky couple," Leeza toasted. *He's the lucky one.* She didn't usually talk shop in social settings, but this time it might be appropriate, if for no other reason than to find out what Dante's aspirations were after prison. "What are you doing with yourself these days?" It seemed innocuous enough.

"Accepting the blessings bestowed upon me," he answered, lifting his glass.

In other words, mind your own fucking business. Fair enough.

Out of nowhere, two hands landed on Leeza's face from behind, covering her eyes. She felt her entire body shoot upward, knocking over her chair and sending her drink across the room, shattering as it hit the floor. *The deafening sound of artillery and bombs exploded all around her as the earth rumbled. The air was thick with smoke, the sounds of men yelling, chaos, and cries of agony.*

Leeza lunged, fists clenched, toward the source of the hands behind her. Terror filled Sammie's eyes as Leeza's fist stopped an inch from her face. A scream tore through the crowd in the same instant. Shocked customers spun toward the sudden commotion. "Fight!" someone yelled before the room went deathly silent. Leeza's disorientation was surreal. She gradually recovered, scanning the room nervously—the room that was watching her.

"I'm sorry! I'm sorry!" Sammie managed to blurt out, reeling from almost getting punched in the face. Leeza's chest heaved. Anger and raw humiliation replaced the terror from a moment ago. As quickly as Sammie reached out to touch her, Leeza jerked away.

"I said I'm sorry!"

Leeza felt the stares as she ran out of the club.

Josh grabbed the microphone. "Different floorshow every night, folks!" he said to nervous laughter and whispers.

Time slowed as Sammie and Dante locked eyes for a brief moment. His narrowed to a sliver, while hers widened in shock. A look of pure disbelief crossed Sammie's face, as if she were silently screaming, *"What the fuck is he doing here?"* Dante, on the other hand, gave nothing away.

Sammie rushed outside and found Leeza rocking back and forth with her head in her hands.

"**W**hat the hell, dude?!" Sammie exclaimed.

"I could've killed you!" Leeza screamed. "Are you even serious?"

Sammie lit a cigarette as she watched Leeza pace.

"What the holy hell did they do to you?"

"Do you get it yet? Huh?!" Leeza was still shaking as she opened a storage compartment on the motorcycle. She pulled out the yellow binder and waved it in Sammie's face. "This is why I need the formula! I need *you*, goddammit!"

Sammie let out a slow plume of smoke. "Dude, I would follow you to the ends of the earth, but what you're asking me for right now... I don't know what you need, but you obviously need *something*."

Leeza leaned against the bike as Sammie sat on the curb and took another deep drag. "Did you know I was in the hospital when you were gone?" Sammie asked. "They locked me up in behavioral health. 'For my own good.'"

"What?" Leeza scoffed. "So, we're back to you already."

"Artie made it clear he didn't want me around when you were gone, and you were gone forever." She rolled the cigarette nervously between her fingers. "I told myself it was just a bad fight. All relationships go through bad shit now and then, but I thought we had something; I thought we could work it out." Sammie reached up and walked her fingers softly up Leeza's thigh.

"We all agreed, all or nothing," said Leeza, stopping Sammie's fingers in their tracks. "When you guys had the falling out, that ended the relationship for everybody."

"It's always been about Prince Arthur." Sammie took a calmer drag from the cigarette, then flicked the butt into the street, chasing it with its own smoke. "That year y'all showed up at my place on New Year's Eve," she continued. "We played truth or dare. Artie dared us to kiss in front of him. One thing led to another, and you spent the whole night with me. I fell in love with a couple. And I was stupid enough to believe..." Sammie's words trailed off as she relived that night.

The night sky was clear and black as the partiers started swarming up and down King Street. There was a line forming in front of the club. It was still early, but Sammie had already ruined Leeza's night.

"Did you ever tell Artie about us?" Sammie asked.

"It was a one-off. It wasn't planned."

"He never did that to you, by the way. Not for lack of trying on my part."

"You said you were suicidal. I was worried about you."

"Works every time."

That's messed up.

"I know what you're thinking. Yes, that was messed up, I'm sorry. I wasn't ready to let go. One day we're a family, and the next thing I know, Artie's threatening me with a restraining order. So yeah, all of it was messed up."

"His family is a big deal in this town. You freaked him out."

"If I remember correctly, you said his mama's a bitch and his daddy treated you like shit."

"That's not exactly what I said."

Sammie's phone rang. She looked at the screen and ignored the call.

"Can I ask you a question?" Sammie asked.

"As if I would say no?"

"Why did you fall for me? You obviously liked me, or we wouldn't have ended up almost living together like some sister-wives thing."

Sammie had replaced the cigarette with her vape. Leeza gazed at her profile and watched as she took another drag before blowing the cola-flavored mist across the street.

"You have something I'll never have," Leeza said. "You're fearless; always have been. I love that about you."

Sammie scoffed, then peered up at Leeza. "I haven't changed."

"But things have." Leeza wasn't in the mood to rehash it.

"So, what about you?" Sammie asked.

"What *about* me?"

"I understand I pissed Artie off. But you and me..."

Sammie's phone rang again.

"You gonna answer that?" Leeza asked.

Sammie waited for Leeza to answer the question.

"I'm married," said Leeza.

Sammie answered the call and listened to the frantic voice on the other end, then hung up. "I know this ain't a great time, but I need to get home... like now."

T wo police cars were a glaring obstacle in front of Sammie's apartment building. An officer was talking to a large woman on the front steps. Sammie handed Leeza the helmet as they watched from across the street.

"That's my roomie, Saffron," said Sammie.

"What do they want with her?"

"You know it ain't her." As the last officer finally drove away, Sammie and Leeza crossed the street to the building.

Saffron was a rotund and animated woman with spiked white hair and too much ostentatious jewelry. She spoke with a contrived British accent, wore a large, colorful nightgown, and looked like a one-woman Broadway show. She greeted Sammie with outstretched arms.

"Sammie, doll." They did the two-cheek air kiss like proper royals before heading inside.

A young boy sat on the couch, totally immersed in a video game; the sound of car crashes lurched from the TV.

Sammie inspected the mess. Cabinets were open, drawers had been yanked out and scattered across the small apartment. The floor was strewn with clothing, knickknacks, and framed photos.

"They wouldn't listen to me," said Saffron.

"What did they want?" Sammie asked.

"They wanted to talk to you, love."

"About?"

"They wouldn't say, Duckie. They gave me a terrible fright, they did."

"They were looking for *something*," said Leeza.

Saffron demurely extended her hand.

"Leeza, this is Saffron," Sammie said. "That's Horizon."

"Nice to meet you," said Leeza.

"Pleasure's all mine, to be sure." Saffron held Leeza's hand and leaned in for a double air kiss.

"Did they show you a warrant?" Leeza asked.

Saffron laughed and shook her head. Sammie scoffed. Horizon smiled.

Leeza looked at the little boy, probably around six years old. He was still engrossed in his game when Sammie headed down the hall to her bedroom. She pulled a large dresser away from the wall and forced the top up from the back with an upward thrust of her palm. Leeza watched from the doorway. Taped to the underside of the lid was a semiautomatic Glock. She ripped the gun from the tape and inspected it carefully. She grabbed a thick envelope that had been secured next to the gun and fanned through the cash inside. Satisfied, she tossed the gun and the envelope onto the bed. Leeza recognized the gun as a Glock 9x19mm semiautomatic with a seventeen-round magazine. *How did she get a law enforcement-issued Glock?* Sammie's drug business was an open secret, but it was never discussed in detail among the three of them. They had heard that she was shrewd and ruthless, but they decided they really didn't want to know any more than that.

They went back to the living room. Sammie stopped in front of Horizon and snapped her fingers; the boy stood up, still playing his game. *Not his first rodeo,* Leeza thought. Sammie reached under the cushion and pulled out another Glock with a slightly shorter barrel, same magazine. Leeza knew that if she inspected them, there would be no serial numbers. She watched as Sammie examined the gun, then put it back under the cushion and motioned for Horizon to sit back down.

"What just happened?" Leeza asked as Horizon sat back down on the couch with the loaded Glock under him.

"Two-point safety," replied Sammie as she headed toward the door.

"Duckie," Saffron said in a hushed voice. "I heard the cops talking, love. Someone told them 'It was here.'"

"What was here? And who told them?" Sammie asked. Saffron shrugged.

"I'll be back in a bit." They headed back to the bike.

"Sounds like she's from England," said Leeza.

"It's fake. She wants to be an actress. Don't ask."

"Her kid lives with you?"

"It's complicated," said Sammie, lighting a cigarette.

She took a drag, looking through the swaying leaves of the century-old oaks outside the building. The leaves were black against the overcast evening sky.

"I would think you'd be more upset," Leeza said.

"Part of the long game."

Leeza opened the compartment and grabbed her helmet.

"I moved out for a while. Thought you might wanna know."

"A *while*? Is that what Artie would say?"

"I took over a lease in North Charleston. It's temporary."

Sammie scoffed. Leeza knew that look: Sammie was weighing Artie's Southern money against Leeza's own Southern poverty. "Did he finally realize happiness ain't for sale?"

"It's just a bad chapter, seriously," said Leeza. "I've got some ideas on the formula. I'll call you."

Sammie did a double-take, expecting a joke but seeing resolve instead. "You cannot be serious right now. Leave. That. Shit. Alone."

"I don't have a choice. And you *will* help me. I know you will." Leeza started the motorcycle and pulled away.

Sammie flicked the cigarette butt and crushed it with a twist of her foot. "Fuck my life," she muttered. Of course she would help.

B ack at the Willow Glen apartments, Leeza pulled off her helmet and texted Tana.

> I am so sorry you had to see that.

> Never apologize. ain't i taught you anything?

> josh bought a round after you left

> See you at the office. Dante loved you LOL

19

Another Recital

C harlotte expressed interest in the piano at the age of six. Leeza, who had been wondering if she'd ever find a reason to play again, was astonished and thrilled to discover her own little protégée. Charlotte had incredible memory, perfect pitch, an amazing ability to focus, and a genuine interest in music theory and history. A year later, the seven-year-old's perfect rendition of the first two movements of *Für Elise* served as a wake-up call for Leeza: the teacher needed to step up her game to stay ahead of her gifted student.

Charlotte was enrolled in the advanced music program at The Matson Preparatory School on Halsey Boulevard in downtown Charleston and had been a teacher's assistant since fifth grade. Leeza found the notion of an "advanced" music program in middle school amusing, even for a prep school. Still, they had a music program, which was better than what her school had when she was a kid.

It was the annual end-of-year music recital, and Leeza had sworn an oath on the blood and body of Christ that she wouldn't miss it, no matter what. When the afternoon arrived, she barely made it, thanks to a surgery that started late because of Stephen's impromptu meeting with the assholes from New York over at University Neurosurgery.

The parking lot was full by the time Leeza arrived, and she rushed inside to find Charlotte on stage, just two measures into Beethoven's *Minuet in G Major*. The audience was filled with

proud, beaming parents. Leeza watched from the back of the auditorium as Charlotte delivered a flawless performance.

Charlotte had struggled with stage fright over the years but
decided it was worth the torture if she wanted to fit in with the
popular girls. The Minuet was no longer a challenge; she could
play it in her sleep, but her nerves made her play it safe when
performing in front of an audience.

From the back row, Leeza scanned the audience. She spotted
Artie a few rows from the front, with Grant to his left and a
woman sitting to his right. She could recognize that bouffant anywhere—Miranda. They had to be the only mother and son in the
world whose relation was evident from the backs of their heads:
perfectly coiffed, perfectly colored, and not a hair out of place. And
his mother's wasn't bad either.

As Charlotte raised her hands from the keyboard at the end of
the piece, the triumph was met with roaring applause. She stood
for her center-stage bow and looked at Artie as he clapped and
cheered, with Miranda applauding politely next to him. Leeza
thought she noticed subtle differences in Charlotte's appearance.
She wasn't sure at first, but then, as she focused, she saw it: the
exaggerated black eyeliner forming a cat-like extension at the upper
outer corners of those beautiful, innocent eyes. Her hair was...
different. *And those boots! Where did she get those fucking Army
boots?*

Charlotte scanned the room, searching for someone she didn't
find. Leeza resisted the urge to jump up and down and yell "I'm
over here!" Charlotte returned to the piano for her second and
final piece. They had practiced *Sonata in E Minor, 3rd Movement*
by Florence Price—the first Black female composer to have her
work performed by a major US orchestra in 1933 in Chicago. Leeza
waited for the familiar piece to begin, but what she heard was not
what she expected. Instead, Charlotte launched into a very lively,
faster-than-written version of Scott Joplin's *Fig Leaf Rag.*

Leeza heard snickering from a group of young tweens near her in the back of the audience as Charlotte pounded the hell out of that walnut Yamaha baby grand. Her right foot was pummeling the sustain pedal with her Army boot. Previously beaming parents looked around nervously, as if seeking reassurance from a guidance counselor that they would survive the insurrection, while the young students bounced in their seats.

"Why don't you spend the night?" Miranda asked as Artie pulled onto the Mark Clark Expressway toward Beresford Hall.

"School night," Charlotte replied.

Miranda turned to look at the children in the backseat. "Thank you for inviting me."

"You invited yourself," Charlotte whispered, just loud enough for Grant to hear.

"I wonder what kept your mama," said Miranda, feigning concern.

"She might've been there," Charlotte said. Artie glanced at her in the mirror. She was on the verge of tears, her elbow resting on the armrest and her chin cradled in her palm.

"We'll find out when we go to the restaurant," Grant said.

20

Self-Pity

L eeza stared at the hideous veneer tabletop. The scratches, from years of abuse, reminded her of tangled strands of hair from a dusty brown wig—maybe worn by an old woman who was unable to take care of herself. The thought was just as unpleasant as the visual. *We're better than this.*

"Just to reiterate," Ms. Marjorie began, "a divorce decree serves as the final judgment in a divorce, legally dissolving the marriage and defining the rights and responsibilities of each party. Once signed by a judge, it becomes a binding court order, enforceable by law. By the end of today's session, each section of the divorce decree will be finalized." She pulled a stack of documents from an accordion file. "I want to thank you all for entrusting Kit and Caboodle Professional Mediators with your mediation needs." She unclipped the first section of documents. "I'll read each section individually and then pass them around for signatures."

"Property. Mr. Byron will remain in the primary residence. Mrs. Allen-Byron will continue to pay the mortgage and fifty percent of the utilities until either (A): the house is sold by mutual consent, or (B): the youngest child turns eighteen." She passed the document to Victoria. "Mrs. Allen-Byron will pay the amount of fifteen hundred dollars per month, per child, until such time that each child reaches the age of eighteen. This amount will include medical insurance. Tuition at The Matson Preparatory School will be divided fifty-fifty as agreed." She passed the document to Victoria.

"Seven hundred," said Leeza.

"Excuse me?" Victoria replied, as if a rancid odor had just crawled up her nose.

"Half the mortgage. No utilities. Seven hundred per child."

"You're not serious." Even Victoria's laugh was dismissive. "You have been part of these discussions since the beginning. You sat in that chair as every proposal was presented, stone-faced, I might add. You've had ample opportunity to voice your objections, so I do hope you're joking, although—"

"I thought *you* were joking," Leeza interrupted. "A hundred percent of the mortgage? You had to know that wasn't going to happen."

"We're not playing Gin Rummy," Victoria said, passing the document to Artie. "She's had her chance."

"And your documents are missing an important detail. I will continue to pay into the kids' college funds, as I have done since the day they came home. You conveniently left that out when you were presenting your 'proposals.'" Leeza turned her attention to Artie, the king of blank stares when he didn't know what was about to happen. "Or I could cash out those accounts and use that money to pay for his Sapphire Preferred card, his gym membership, and the Jaguar lease. He's somehow managed the daddy daycare retreats at the oyster bar all by himself." She turned back to Victoria. "Those things add up to half of what you're asking for."

Victoria looked at Leeza as if she were the source of the bad smell.

"And surely you must know about his passive income," Leeza continued. "I believe here in the Deep South we call it a... what are the words I'm looking for? Oh yeah... a trust fund. He makes as much as I do without getting out of bed."

Ms. Marjorie's eyes shifted toward Artie. "There was no mention of the college—"

"You want to talk about documents, Mrs. Allen-Byron? Shall we talk about the yellow binder?" Leeza looked at Artie incredulously. "What are you building, an atom bomb? Or maybe you would prefer to discuss the night in the garage, huh?" Victoria leaned in. "With the kids in the house. I hope you had time to reflect on that decision during your sabbatical."

They actually went there.

Artie's complexion went a shade lighter. The only sound was the chatter from the tavern next door.

"Didn't think so. Shall we proceed?" Victoria slid the document from Artie to Leeza.

"Are we proceeding, Mrs. Allen-Byron?" Ms. Marjorie asked.

Leeza was deflated by the bitch in the Chanel jacket—and her puppet master Miranda. Ms. Marjorie moved on.

"The custody agreement is the only thing awaiting an addendum. Upon agreement by both parties, I will hand-write the details of this section, and we can still get signatures today."

"We believe that due to her current living situation—" Victoria started.

"That's none of your business," Leeza interjected.

"Well, actually—"

"We'll work that out between us."

"To ensure the safety of the children—" Victoria tried to continue.

"Really?" Leeza glared at Artie. "First the money, now this? Why don't you just bring your mama with you?"

Artie tilted his head toward Victoria. "Please," he said quietly.

"What exactly do you think is going to happen to our kids as a result of my living arrangements?" Tempering her anger was becoming a losing battle.

"I just don't want them spending the night there," Artie said.

"It was your idea! And you haven't even been there!"

"It's not you. It's just that... North Charleston is—"

"It's not four thousand square feet on half an acre, so it's not good enough?"

Artie turned to Victoria. "Can we please stop?"

"Stop what, Arthur? I'm not here to coddle some addict."

Artie looked at Ms. Marjorie. "We're done for now," he said decisively as he pushed his chair back. "I need to process."

Ms. Marjorie's lips relaxed into a soft smile as she gazed at Arthur. She fondled her crucifix, temporarily separating Jesus from his flag. Both Victoria and Leeza were staring at him.

"For chrissakes," Victoria exclaimed. "Never again."

"Never again, what?" Leeza shot back. "Never again doing a favor for a friend? Going back to gold diggers and ex-wives fighting for a piece of some rich old asshole's estate?"

Victoria glared at Leeza with her Botox smirk. "You left Afghanistan toward the end of the skirmish, right?"

"Relevance?"

"Did any Americans actually *die* in Afghanistan the year you left?"

"Seventeen in combat, more with the suicides," said Leeza. *This poser is not really that stupid.* "Did you actually just say skirmish?"

"You're an educated woman, Mrs. Allen-Byron." She stared at Leeza with venomous contempt. "And allow me to thank you for your service. Still, this whole 'PTSD' thing feels awfully convenient."

Leeza shot a look at Artie as Victoria got up. "You're letting this happen?"

Artie saw the plea in Leeza's eyes and tilted his head toward Victoria again. "That's enough," he said, not firmly enough.

"All of this is a consequence of your own actions," she said to Leeza. "You're too wrapped up in self-pity to see it." She turned her disdain to Artie. "It's really not so hard, darlin'." She grabbed her bag and scarf. "I guess it's not just the left nut she's got in that tote, eh?"

Marjorie tightened her grip on the crucifix as if Jesus would flee the room.

Victoria's stilettos sounded like a flamenco dancer walking across the wood floor with the passion of Andalucía.

21

Don't Preach to Me about Choices

C lark's Coffee Company on Church Street was nestled in an upscale pocket of high-end shops and restaurants, located on the first floor of a bougie boutique hotel called 'Emilie.' The hotel rooms boasted names like 'Atelier Premier King,' 'Socialite Premier,' and 'Maisonette Superior Loft Suite.' Even Miranda might consider staying there without bringing her own sheets. It remained a mystery how the aroma of their famous croissants wafted all the way to the corner of Pinckney Street, but the buttery French delicacies were undoubtedly the first thing to greet you at the door—even before the Italian espresso.

Artie arrived thirty minutes before he told Leeza to meet him—partly because he wanted to mentally prepare for the conversation about the mediation, but also because Leeza was the type of person who would show up early to her own funeral. His mind wandered as he gazed out at the glowing streetlights, their brightness diminished by the encroaching fog. Fifteen minutes after he arrived, she spotted him from the door and took a seat at the table. A barista brought Artie's cortado, served with chilled sparkling water, as it should be.

"Did your mama enjoy the recital?" Leeza asked.

"We both did. Charlotte was incredible."

She regarded him carefully, drumming her fingernails on the table. "You stopped the inquisition."

"Paused it."

The drumming stopped. "Tell me what I need to do."

"First, I want to apologize for Victoria's comments about PTSD and the other stuff. She was out of line, and it wasn't fair to you."

"So she's fired?"

"We had a chat. She's not as cold as she comes across."

"I wouldn't bet the farm on that, sweet pea," said Leeza. "She's made a fortune shaking down rich assholes. She hands over a piece of the estate to their gold-digging girlfriends and keeps a chunk for herself. She could ruin a career with a phone call or some facetime on the six o'clock news. She sold her soul a long time ago. And you need to stop apologizing for other people."

Artie sipped his cortado, followed by a sip of sparkling water. The water was a palate cleanser intended for after the coffee was finished, but Artie liked the idea of coffee more than the taste. Leeza seemed edgy, but he couldn't really blame her. "Why are there so many things I don't know about you?"

A woman who looked like she could be the queen's lady-in-waiting presented herself. "Can I bring you anything?" asked the waitress in an airy voice. Leeza shook her head.

"What do you need from me?" she asked him as the lady floated away.

"I need you to see me, to acknowledge me."

Leeza scoffed. "As if—"

"You need to cop to the fact that there are consequences for your actions, regardless of all your excuses."

Leeza sat back and crossed her arms.

"For God's sake, open your eyes, Leeza. I honestly think you exacerbate your condition with the expectations you put on yourself; it's self-inflicted," he said. "You're never satisfied. It's not enough to be an amazing pianist. Are you really pissed off at the world because you never played Carnegie Hall?"

A thin smile graced the corner of Leeza's lips as the lecture continued.

"It's not enough to be a nurse; it's not enough to have a career that might actually allow you to spend time with your family. You wanted the master's, I get that. But you just had to go back and become a practitioner, and a doctorate, no less. Why in God's name?" He paused long enough for her to respond, but she waited. "You're always in the process of becoming. What do you have to prove? Your obsessions are pathological. If only you were as obsessed with your..." Artie thought better of finishing that sentence. "Your decisions impact everyone around you, not just you."

Leeza stared at the sparkling water, standing next to the fancy coffee like a chaperone. "Your obsessions are pathological," Leeza repeated, tapping her fingers again.

"You have to be the one calling the shots." Artie leaned in. "When you were in post-grad, you dumped your responsibilities on *me*."

"You and the nanny."

Artie's eyes narrowed at the remark. "We'll put a pin in that one," he seethed. "And whatever it is you're doing with your psychiatrist, you might want to get a second opinion."

"As you know, it's a requirement because of the prescriptions. I see a psychiatrist so I can say I'm seeing a psychiatrist. She's a quack."

The lady-in-waiting swooped in. "What's it gonna be, kids?"

"We'll share a croissant," said Artie.

"You got it," she said with a Cheshire-cat grin before gliding back.

"Are you done?" Leeza asked.

"It may be off topic, but since we're here, it still bothers me that you didn't go to my father's funeral. It felt awkward. I guess you needed to prove a point? He wasn't important enough for you to pay your respects? I realize you have a lot of anger, Leeza, but—"

Leeza leaned in, her eyes narrowed. "I live with the stress of mental trauma and the fear of uncertainty. It's not anger, sweetheart. And unlike the Byron family, I am not compelled to pretend to be sad for someone who treated me like dirt when he was alive."

Artie sipped his cortado, then reached for the sparkling water.

"If you really want to know, I stayed in school because it got me one step farther away from being treated like a bottom sucker by some prima donna in a white coat who thinks his shit don't stink." She locked her eyes on him. "Little did I know that getting a doctorate would just put me up there in a whole new stratosphere of prima donna. Your father told Stephen that a practitioner is just a nurse with a prescription pad." She gave it a second to land. "And nurses don't know which end of the scalpel is the sharp end. Stephen didn't say a word in my defense." Her chest rose and stopped.

Sounds like my dad. "He was an academic, not really a people person."

"I heard he was the life of the party," she said, finally exhaling. "As long as the party only included people with MD behind their names."

Tell me something I don't know.

"When I interviewed with Stephen and your daddy, I was working on my dissertation. The other candidate was a new grad. Your daddy was a little fidgety for some reason. When Stephen worked it into the conversation, reminding everybody that I was his partner's daughter-in-law, Arthur literally cringed."

The conversation paused for what felt like an afternoon. The clattering of dishes and the buzz of conversation filled the silence. Artie's neck shrank into his shoulders like a scolded puppy—there was nothing to say.

"Let me explain some things to you, starting with what it's like to be a nurse practitioner working for old generational-wealth white guys, including your daddy—God rest his soul. Stephen doesn't work overtime; he doesn't pull call or see patients pre-op or post-op. If he doesn't have a scalpel in his hand, he ain't got time for you. Tana and I run every bit of that practice except for the cutting."

That's a lot of baggage. "They don't know how lucky they were to have chosen you."

"And you... Mr. Arthur Charles Preston Nigel Byron the Third... I'm guessing they threw in Nigel because it didn't sound white enough. What have you worked for? The hardest thing you ever did was tell your mama and daddy about me. What does she hate most, huh? That I'm from the wrong side of the tracks? That Uncle Sam paid for my education? Or that I'm just a nurse? God knows I'll never be as white or as rich."

"She knew I was in love with you. Nothing she said could've changed that."

The lady-in-waiting stared from the counter. Leeza's lips tightened as she continued. "Imagine for a second what it feels like when you figure out that your mother-in-law referred a divorce attorney to her own son." A shuddering breath caught in her throat. "You sat right next to her when she said my kids deserved someone who was morally equipped to raise them, and you kept your goddamned mouth shut." Her jaw clenched tighter. "If anyone should have anger issues, I think I've earned it."

"I didn't keep my mouth shut." Artie fidgeted with his napkin. Miranda had him convinced that the only reason he needed Victoria was to ensure the kids' protection. What his mother actually meant was that they needed Victoria to make sure the trust fund and inheritance were protected. "I didn't know she was such a snake. It was uncalled for; I told you that."

Leeza stared at his profile as he contemplated the streetlights in the fog. "You said loved," she said.

"You know I love you." He swallowed, unable to bring his gaze back inside. "It's not easy, Leeza. I don't know what's worse: being alone or being with someone who makes me feel this way. I feel like I'm sacrificing a piece of my sanity—"

"If your FaceTime therapist told you that someone else can *make* you feel alone, you need to get a second opinion from somebody who ain't a thirty-year-old basement dweller squeezing you in between Call of Duty and Minecraft."

He felt the heat rising in his neck. "Being alone is better than feeling like this." He hated being talked down to; he'd dealt with it his entire life. "Talking with you is like having Sybil for a therapist."

The comment caught Leeza off guard. The idea of someone with multiple personality disorder as a therapist struck her as absolutely hilarious. She covered her mouth and looked away, struggling to control her laughter. She lowered her head onto the table, and her shoulders began bouncing up and down. Unamused, Artie stared at her.

Leeza fought to compose herself, pressing her hands tightly over her face as she snorted from the back of her throat. She pushed down the convulsive laughter that was determined to work its way out. She forced several slow, deep breaths and exhaled through pursed lips, then used the embroidered cream-colored cloth napkin to wipe her eyes. The royal baristas' heads tilted together as they whispered. She finally managed to regain her composure long enough to speak. "Well... this ain't a rom-com, sweet pea."

The queen's maid floated in and presented the plump, warm, buttered croissant between them. "Lively couple over here," she commented, chin lifted, and eyes lowered.

"Sorry," said Artie. "We're fine." And with that, she was off.

Leeza glared side-eyed at the back of the servant as she floated away.

"I was raised by two wealthy narcissists who had five miscarriages before I was born," Artie said.

"We're gonna talk about the miscarriages?"

"You asked if they threw in Nigel because my name wasn't already white enough."

"I shouldn't have—"

"So I'm going to explain it to you. Again."

"You don't have to. I'm sorry."

"And then I have some questions for you."

Leeza leaned back.

"They had a boy because that's what they asked God for, and I was an only child because that's what God chose for them. My names are the ones they'd picked for some of my brothers if we had had a big family."

She watched his chest rise.

"There were a lot of expectations, and I worked my ass off to meet them." He glanced at the streetlight again, still battling the fog of the dark autumn evening. "But I was a kid, and kids aren't perfect. And when you fail to live up to expectations, there are consequences—like being yelled at and locked in a closet, or being humiliated in front of your friend who was finally allowed to spend the night but never came back and never spoke to you again at school because your mother was a terrifying psychobitch from hell." He had told her about the awkward relationship with his mother, but he never mentioned the physical abuse. They both had their secrets.

"As for the part you didn't know, something happened to my father when I was around fifteen. He became withdrawn, but only at home. It was weird. I felt abandoned. And the more he ignored me, the more she disciplined me."

She watched him finish the cortado and the water.

"I was seeing a therapist throughout high school, even though Mama said depression was a congenital defect. She was convinced she must have done something wrong during the pregnancy. Regardless, I decided I didn't want to play in this sandbox anymore. I was still suicidal when I met you."

"Was I your rebellion?" she asked.

Artie felt the lump in his throat tighten like a fist. "You were my soulmate." He tried to swallow. "And you saved me."

"I'm sorry," said Leeza as she made a slow circular motion around the rim of her water glass. She drew a breath, and they took a much-needed break.

"You were one seriously damaged young'un," she said. "Explains a lot. At least I had fourteen good years. You didn't have a chance."

"Your turn," said Artie. "Tell me something I don't know."

There were a lot of things he still didn't know about her. She never talked about her teenage years. And it was quite a while after the wedding before he discovered that she enrolled in the ROTC program because she was broke and had run out of options.

Leeza was a pro at brushing off questions she didn't want to answer, and this time was no different. "You brought up the word sacrifice," she said. "What did you mean? I'm just curious what you think you've had to sacrifice."

"Are you even serious?" Artie replied incredulously. "You brought home two newborns like they were puppies you found on the side of the road. And I was not part of that conversation."

Leeza was jolted by his comment. "They were babies."

"And you went overseas just before they turned ten and left them with me for a year."

Leeza's lips tightened. "You wanted to be a father—"

Artie cut her off. "But I dealt with it. Because sometimes we take what we're given and just deal with it. Even if your story was contrived, to say the least."

Leeza slammed her fists on the table, piercing the room with the deafening crash of silverware and clattering coffee cups and water glasses jumping into the air and crashing back onto the reclaimed wood table an instant later. Startled customers spun around and stared as the attendant rushed over. This time, she didn't say a word, but she looked like a Rottweiler ready to rip an arm off.

"Those babies saw their nanny more than they saw you until they were four years old!" Leeza seethed.

"That's not true."

"They were taken away from their mama because she was struggling with her recovery! Were they supposed to just deal with it?!" Leeza screamed.

The barista hurriedly gathered the dishes from the table and wiped up the spilled water. "Settle down, missy," she said to Leeza with a nervous attempt at authority.

"Don't be ridiculous," Artie said. "There are processes for adopting kids, and you can't just—"

"It happened, didn't it?"

"Eventually," he scoffed.

A higher-ranking attendant was summoned. Her face was wrinkled, and she was much more serious, as if she were there for just such an incident. She signaled for the subordinate to clear the rest of the table, including the untouched croissant.

"While you were sittin' back here in your mama and daddy's mansion, bitchin' about wiping the asses of two Black babies, let me tell you what I was doin'. I was holding the hand of a boy with half his head blown off, staring at me with the one eye he had left. Dying! Not knowing why he was even there! How am I supposed to just DEAL WITH THAT?!"

The serious attendant was appalled by Leeza's words, her eyes suddenly widening like the gargoyle on the roof of the First National Bank on Broad Street. "I'm sorry, but y'all are gonna have to tamp down the commotion over here," she managed to say as customers stole nervous glances. The three of them took a brief pause together. The attendant's eyes returned to their old, weathered state. "We don't wanna be on a TikTok video, now do we?" she chuckled.

"Learned that in management school, did ya?" Leeza said, rolling her eyes.

"We're fine, thank you," Artie said. He leaned back and crossed his legs, suppressing the humiliation from the public display. He could feel every eye in the room on him. He wanted to leave Clark's Coffee Company and keep running, but he was determined to find out whether there was any reason to walk away from the mediation or if he should continue with the divorce. He needed to know, and he needed to know now.

"That explains the chip on your shoulder," said Leeza.

"Chip?" Artie's eyes narrowed. "I have no idea how to raise a teenage girl. And when I try to talk to you about it, you'd think

I was asking you to teach me how to tie my shoes. It's not that goddamned simple!"

"You need to have constant affirmation, don't you?" Leeza wiped her lips on the back of her hand.

Artie's body tensed. *Bring it down*, he told himself. Arguing with Leeza was a losing battle. She was so persuasive and intelligent that she could rewrite history just to prove a point, leaving one to question their own memories. But they were getting sidetracked, and he had asked her to come to Clark's Coffee for a reason.

"Yet another character flaw, my apologies," he said. He needed this night to end.

"You're an excellent father."

"That doesn't help," Artie snapped. He borrowed Charlotte's piano breathing exercises: in through the nose, out through the mouth, as he tried to steer the conversation back. "The direction our lives take is shaped by the choices we make. It's called destiny. And the choices we should be making together—"

"Choices?" Leeza scoffed.

Artie watched as her posture stretched upward; her chest swelled into a plate of armor as she pulled her shoulders back. He knew her well. She was weighing the next words very carefully.

"The day I found out I was accepted to Juilliard was the same day my mama found out about her breast cancer."

A hush gripped the room. Artie felt his jaw loosen as his eyes widened.

"When I was supposed to be spending all day practicing and going to classes and recitals in New York City, trying to become something that somebody might actually be proud of someday... instead, I stayed home and watched her die. The strongest woman I've ever known in my life, helpless as a dishrag." Leeza's chin trembled; her eyes were hollow. "The one person in my whole damn life who ever told me I could be anything I wanted; that I was actually worth a damn thing." Tears shimmered in her eyes. "Has it ever occurred to you... If she hadn't passed, we never would have met? And I would be on that stage right now in Europe or Asia or Africa. And she would be in that audience every goddamn time." She stared through Artie's soul. There was an extra second between each word: "Don't you ever preach to me about choices."

With the lump tightening in his throat, Artie looked at her, truly looked at her, in stunned silence. "You were accepted to Juilliard? Jesus Christ. How could you not have told me that? How could you just leave that out? You told me you applied, but you never told me... What the hell, Leeza?" His throat hurt as he tried desperately not to cry in the middle of Clark's Coffee Company on Church Street, surrounded by all those proper people. He might've been able to stifle the sound of crying, but he couldn't stop the tears. His eyes closed firmly, squeezing them from his eyes, then he tried to look at the streetlight again. The fog was winning.

Leeza stood up and reached into her pocket for some cash. "Couldn't do it alone, so..." she said, solemnly. "It was just one more failure. And the pile keeps getting deeper." She looked at the dollar bills in her hand, then slowly moved toward Artie. She turned and sat next to him quietly, side by side, with a glassy stare. The serious attendant couldn't look away; her eyes were full, like a character in the stage play who had forgotten her lines.

"When I left you and our family for a year, not knowing if I would ever see you guys again, or when the next half-dead body would be dropped in front of me," she said, placing her hand on top of his. "I knew you were thinking about me. I knew you missed me. I knew you were watchin' over me. I could feel you. I *felt* you." A tear raced down her cheek. "And I made it back, and here I am. And so what?" Her voice cracked. "So what?" She blinked tears away and looked into his eyes, then spoke softly, "You don't know what lonely is." She gave his hand a gentle squeeze, then dropped the cash on the table. As she stood to leave, she turned back slowly. "Oh, and uh, I don't do funerals."

Artie followed her with his eyes as captivated customers watched the drama come to an end. It felt like the final scene of a classic movie with a backdrop of streetlights consumed by fog. The serious attendant cupped her mouth and ran to the back room.

L eeza guided the motorcycle through the dreary streets to the edge of town, heading for the backroads of Charleston. The moon hung like a hazy white disk on the far side of what could have been a million miles of fog. She listened to *Claude Debussy's Arabesque No. 1* and remembered thinking, *This should be on everyone's bucket list.* The senses were consumed by a symphony that no amount of toxicity or fear or sadness or despair or post-traumatic stress disorder caused by putting young, innocent soldiers out of their misery could invade in the moment. Murder? Mercy killing? Death with dignity?

It was critical that she experience such transcendence as often as possible.

22

The Talk

The music from Teresita's radio was distant, yet distinctly Mexican pop, as it wafted upstairs, along with her cooking, from the kitchen to Artie's childhood bedroom. He was painfully aware of how sound traveled through the enormous home, like echoes in an empty warehouse. As a child, he felt oddly vulnerable if he spoke above a whisper. *Was that normal?* Because even whispers eventually found their way back to their source.

Artie left for college in the fall after his eighteenth birthday, having never slept on a bed larger than a twin. Sneaking a girl into his room would have been complicated, and even if he did, Miranda knew a twin bed would make any hanky-panky difficult at best. The room was just as he left it—a time capsule that Miranda would escape to when she felt moved to pray or hide from his father. It had served as his nursery and had been updated over the years as he grew into a young man. The walls were teeming with shelves full of trophies, plaques, ribbons, and framed certificates, all filling every inch. Artie hunched over the small desk where he had done homework and school projects for years, thumbing through folders filled with essays and exams, secret poems, and short stories.

His mother never knocked. "Discovering himself" as a teenager was a logistical challenge that had to be timed just right. Locks weren't allowed—unless your name was on the deed.

The door swung open. "Dinner is at eight," Miranda announced. "Teresita's been cooking all day, bless her heart." She opened a folded note: "She's made—uh—'Cha-loopas and pah -sole-leay-roe-hoe.'" She crumpled the paper and tossed it into the trash next to Artie's desk. "She's all excited you're here. Apparently, I should be more adventuresome when it comes to foreign food." She wrinkled her nose. "We'll eat on the veranda."

"Chalupas and pozole rojo," Artie corrected. "We chatted earlier. She's from Oaxaca. How's it working out?"

"She could've taught Yolanda a thing or two. Gotta get 'em young."

"She's actually well-traveled. And her English is flawless."

"How can you tell with that accent?"

"What accent?"

Miranda rolled her eyes. "Really?"

Artie inhaled. "You're in for a culinary treat, Mama." He glanced at her. "Be nice."

"Well, in any event, there's a meatloaf in the freezer," she said.

Artie could feel her staring at the papers in front of him. No doubt she had been through everything in his desk a hundred times.

"You could've been a writer."

The laugh slipped out before he could stop it. "That's hilarious, Mama. I wanted to be a writer, a musician, a journalist, an artist. I couldn't even talk about those things. You and Daddy had decided on my college and my career before I could walk."

She crossed her arms, her lips cinching into a pointed circle that Artie knew preceded either yelling or a dramatic exit.

"I suppose I could have double majored." He knew what she was thinking before she opened her mouth. "Before you say I'm being ungrateful, I'm not—it's just funny that you would say that now."

"Why would I think you're ungrateful?" she said with a sarcastic tinge.

"I need to ask you something." He moved to the bed, offering her the chair, but she stayed standing, arms crossed, poised for the inquisition. "I've been dealing with some things I was hoping you could shed some light on." He'd rehearsed this moment for years, never imagining it would actually happen. But since his dad passed, she might feel compelled to open up. "I wasn't a bad kid, Mama. You know that, right?"

"You think I'm wicked," said Miranda, as if she'd been rehearsing too.

"I don't think you're wicked, but I do think you and Daddy might've handled things differently." He took a deliberate breath as he considered whether to continue or drop it. "This wasn't a normal house; I get that now. I thought it was when I was a kid, but now I know it wasn't." He hesitated. "I see how my friends get on with their mothers. We never had that."

She was as still as an ancient statue, her gaze unwavering. She would not make this easy, and neither would he.

"You told me once that I was given the names of my brothers if they had lived. But you never told me anything else about you—or your family, for that matter."

She cleared her throat and glanced around the room, as if reliving all its memories. "We dreamed of having a big family," Miranda said. Artie watched her through the pause, unsure if she would continue.

"The first time I got pregnant, I was on top of the world. I couldn't wait to tell my mama." She sucked in a slow breath—he could only imagine the thoughts behind her eyes. "And when I found out it wasn't to be, I was devastated. I cried for weeks. She caught me crying and chastised me. She couldn't understand why I was upset. She told me there would be others."

Miranda scoffed. "Others? That's all you have to say? So, the next time, I waited a little longer to tell her, but that one wasn't to be either. That time when I cried, she actually laughed at me. She told me, 'This is the South, honey. Women have a dozen kids. Some have two or three at a time. If God intends for you to have a family, then you'll have a family.' That was the last time I told her I was pregnant until my third trimester with you. She passed away two weeks before you were born."

Miranda sat on the bed next to him. "Your father tried to be supportive, but I could tell the more we tried, the less interested he was in me. I was a failure in his eyes."

"I don't think he ever felt that way, Mama."

"Each pregnancy lasted a little bit longer: five weeks, nine weeks, twelve weeks, eighteen weeks. Your brother Nigel was stillborn."

She said it so matter-of-factly, but it hit Artie like a punch in the stomach. Emotion flooded his face as he reached out to touch his mother's shoulder. He noticed her hand rubbing in a slow circle on her belly.

"I felt so ashamed," she said.

Artie felt a lump growing like a fist in his throat.

"Your father insisted we try again right away. He said it would help me forget." She closed her eyes. "When I found out about you, I didn't bother with the nursery. Never even opened the door until you came home, and even then, I wasn't sure how much time we would get in here together. My mama never saw my one and only accomplishment." Miranda looked around the room. "I spent countless nights in this room, talking to her and to your brothers while I rocked you in my arms. But I'll tell you what, it took a long time before God was invited back." She wiped her nose. "But I came to understand... He wanted to get it right. But those who hope in the Lord will renew their strength. They will soar on wings like eagles; they will run and not grow weary; they will walk and not be faint." She blessed herself with the sign of the cross, then started pacing. "You can't imagine the humiliation of not being able to do something as simple as carrying a pregnancy." She stared at the shelf lined with trophies. "There you were... perfect. And I would have sold my soul to be the perfect mother."

"Mama, I'm sorry... you don't have to—"

"I wrote letters to your brothers while they were still with me. Some of them, I didn't know if they were boys, but I knew at least two of them were, so I imagined a house full of young men growing up to be strong, successful adults who would make a difference in the world. I wanted to raise a family that your daddy would be proud of. I kept the letters."

Artie cupped his mouth in his hand as the tears flowed, overwhelmed by a sudden surge of empathy and guilt. For a long time, he'd believed confronting his mother about his upbringing was necessary to move forward, but now he questioned whether his need for an explanation justified reopening old wounds. *Why did I have to bring it up? What was the point of confronting her after all this time? Am I that cruel?*

"How did you deal with—"

"Your father took me to see Kashvi."

"Singh?"

"She told me I had PTSD and was erratic, dissociating, disorganized attachment, or some bullshit. I was the one taking notes that day. She wanted to put me on some pills, light a damned candle, do a séance or something. I said, 'No, ma'am.'"

"Leeza sees Dr. Singh."

"I know. Her daddy and your daddy were friends for years. From what I hear, she and her daddy might have been better suited to a different calling."

Artie wiped his eyes and gazed at his wall of accomplishments. The torrent of emotions flooding over him showed in his face—confusion, sadness, remorse—but he knew he'd never have this opportunity again. He remembered how his father would often avoid eye contact with him and how awkward it made him feel. *Why won't he just tell me what I did wrong so I can fix it?* "What happened to Daddy? Something snapped when I was in high school."

"When you were fifteen, I told your father I started birth control after you were born. It slipped out in an argument. You would have thought I had masterminded 9/11. He never touched me again." She was eerily stoic, as if she were watching old reruns of her own life. "There's nothing quite like walking into a hospital nine months pregnant and leaving without your baby. After one live birth, I was done. But no amount of praying could make him forgive me." She stood in the doorway with her back to him. "I didn't sell my soul, and I wasn't perfect. God knows I was far from perfect. But did you really have it so bad, Arthur?"

"I'm not consumed by my childhood if that's what you're asking," he answered. "The problem is I suck at relationships. I'm told there's a direct correlation between that and—"

"You're thin-skinned, Arthur. Thank your father," she said, and walked out. The clicking of her shoes echoed down the stairway and across the entry hall, leaving him with a lingering ache deep in his belly. Jesus watched from the top of the double staircase as she vanished toward a remote corner of the palace.

23

She Always Plays Minuet in G

Los Chicos Errantes had the night off, giving the diners at Rancho Lewis a reprieve from the talented, albeit eardrum-shattering, trumpets. Equally important, there were no birthday parties, which meant the sugared-up herd of miniature humans stampeding around the dining room would be nowhere in sight. Leeza had taken a chance with the kids last time, but putting herself in the midst of a swarm of unrestrained seven-year-olds was dangerous enough for normal people, potentially catastrophic for those carrying souvenirs of war.

"Jimmy Norlander says Charleston is a gastro... somethin' somthin'," said Grant.

"Gastronomic paradise?" Leeza asked. "Gastronomes' destination?"

"Something like that."

"I highly doubt Norlander could say those words," said Charlotte. The popular girls had begun calling people by their last names; it just sounded sophisticated.

"We'll have to explore other options," said Leeza.

"Thank ya, Jaysus!" Charlotte exclaimed, looking toward heaven with praying hands before continuing, "I didn't see you at the recital."

Leeza's smile was mischievous. "You were amazing."

"What did I play?"

"I'm glad you asked. You played Minuet in G for your first piece."

"You *were* there."

"She always plays *Minuet in G*," Grant chimed in.

Minuet in G was a warm-up piece for Charlotte when she was in first grade. She could play it in her sleep. In fact, she *had* played it in her sleep because if she made even one mistake, she would lie awake obsessing about it.

"But you followed with a rousing encore of 'Fig Leaf Rag' by Scott Joplin, which was not in the program. Why?"

Charlotte shrugged. "It was a dare."

Leeza knew Charlotte was desperate to fit in, despite pretending not to care, so it was no surprise she'd have a hard time shrugging off a dare from the popular girls. Charlotte was gifted but struggled with self-doubt if someone looked at her the wrong way. She was constantly obsessing over the fact that she and Grant were adopted, and that their parents' identities had been kept secret. Leeza could only imagine what Charlotte had heard at school about why adopted kids weren't allowed to stay with their "real" parents when they were babies. Lately, Charlotte's quest to find out who her biological parents were had taken on a life of its own. *Was the black makeup a distraction, or a sign of rebellion?* Leeza had to mitigate the damage from a divorce that the kids had nothing to do with.

"You'll be happy to know it kicked my butt."

"What? It was faultless. Mr. Joplin would be proud. He probably couldn't have played it that fast, but he would be proud. It was a fitting encore." Leeza offered a fist bump, which was accepted.

"What's an encore?" Grant asked.

"That's when the audience begs for more," Leeza explained.

"Uhm, pretty sure it doesn't work that way," Grant said as he slurped his Mr. Pibb. "You know I can never eat skinny noodles again, right?"

"Jesus, take the wheel," Charlotte said with an exasperated eye roll. "Wanna hear something funny?"

"I would *love* to hear something funny right about now," Leeza replied.

"So, when they were making the program and they asked me what I would be playing, I said I had narrowed down my second piece to either Margaret Bonds' *Fugal Dance* or Florence Price's *Concerto in D Minor*. And they were like, uhm, maybe somebody that people have heard of? So, I said, 'I'm so sorry, what was I thinking? Florence Price was Mozart's mama, and Margaret Bonds was Beethoven's mama.'"

Leeza's eyes popped open as her jaw dropped.

"And they were like, 'Oh, yes, yes, absolutely, you're such a smart girl.'"

Leeza let out a belly laugh that shot straight to every corner of Rancho Lewis. "No, you did not!"

"Oh yes, I did," said Charlotte, rolling her neck in self-congratulatory circles.

"That's hysterical!" Leeza barely managed to say. "I'm gonna use that one!"

"Surprised you haven't."

Leeza dabbed her eyes as the laugh continued. "You need to warn me when you're gonna say stuff like that!" She rode the laughter for another minute or so. She could feel a dozen sets of eyes on her, but she didn't care this time. "Did you know Margaret Bonds went to Juilliard?"

"Yes, I did," Charlotte replied. "Did you know she went on tour with Mozart's mama?"

Leeza erupted again, waving a hand. "Stop it!" She pressed the napkin over her face to muffle the laughter.

Charlotte's neck rotated with even more self-satisfied confidence as she watched her mama laugh.

Grant side-eyed the two of them, then turned his back, feigning embarrassment in case anyone was watching.

Leeza took her time recovering. The laughter was a welcome relief, and she relished it. After the tears dried and she'd had a few bites of food, she turned the conversation back: "Question: What's with the boots and black eye makeup?"

Charlotte went still. "Didn't think you'd notice," she said.

"Because the Morticia thing doesn't work for you. No more makeup."

"You're not around, so…"

Mystery solved: It was her way of dealing with the separation. Leeza's immediate thought was how to get back on schedule with the experiments. She needed a formula that would dull her panic responses and manage her emotional challenges. It was the key to getting back together with Artie and making sure the kids had a stable life. There was too much at stake to quit now. *This is solvable. This is fixable.* Leeza and Sammie would need to focus their energy and shift into high gear.

"At least we have lessons on Tuesdays at five. I'll be with you two at the house while Daddy goes to his meetings. We can cook together, then warm-ups, then lessons," Leeza said.

"And you can tuck us in?" asked a wide-eyed Grant.

"And I can tuck you in." She leaned in and said with her best Bela Lugosi impression: "And you can tell me all your secrets."

"Lil' Juan's chicken tenders and French fries?" asked the Mexican waitress as she glided to the table, arms loaded with the same steaming plates of food as last time. Grant raised his hand. She plopped down the dishes and exchanged glances with Leeza. She was the waitress who had helped her up from the floor after the explosion at the urchins' table. "I'll be back to check on you," she said with a smile. She clearly remembered Leeza, and she must have also remembered that huge tip.

"I have a question," said Grant.

"Shocking," said Charlotte.

"Hit me," said Leeza.

"Why did you move out and not Daddy? Jimmy Norlander's daddy moved out."

That's a great question.

"I was wondering the same thing," said Charlotte.

"Jimmy said the only time the mama moves out is if she has a boyfriend," Grant offered.

Leeza laughed, but she knew she couldn't explain it to two twelve-year-olds. She couldn't even explain it to herself.

"It's not *who* moves out; it's how long they move out for," she said, hoping the gaslighting would suffice for now. "And like I told you, it's temporary."

"I have a question," said Leeza. The kids looked at each other. "For Dr. G."

Grant's eyes were as wide as saucers. It was never good when she started a question with "I have a question." "Yeeeaaahs?" he asked cautiously.

"Whatcha listenin' to these days?"

"Why?"

"Busted!" Charlotte laughed. The spotlight was off her!

"I haven't heard *Romeo and Juliet*, or *Shake It Off*, or *Should've Been Us*, or *Flowers*, or *Royals*, or *Halo*, not even a Shantay You Stay."

Grant's playlist had definitely changed lately. But he hated confrontation more than he hated change. The wheels were turning as he tried to figure out the perfect lie.

Leeza held out her hand, palm up. She could hear the hip-hop coming from his earbuds as he fumbled nervously. He needed a second to delete the playlist without her seeing, but it was too late. He was completely defeated as he handed over the phone in slow motion, as if she might change her mind before it finished its journey from his hand to hers. She put it on speaker and set the phone in front of her. The thumping, rhythmic bass burst out around them. Every other word was about bitches' booties, or sex, or cops, or drugs, or fights, or worse. Neighboring diners spun around with expressions ranging from shock to disgust, although some smiled and danced in their seats. *This is why you see those stickers with Parental Warning: Explicit Content.*

Leeza turned off the music and dropped Grant's phone into her backpack. She didn't have to say another word.

"It's just Ludacris," Grant whispered. "He's famous." He hated getting in trouble.

Grant wore his emotions on his sleeve; his moods were infectious. When he was happy, he lit up the room. And when he was down, the whole room wanted to hold him in its arms and cry with him. He was clearly upset that his mama didn't live at home anymore.

"Leesie," Grant said.

"Dr. G."

The words took longer when Grant was upset. "Why can't we stay with you when Daddy goes to Gramma's house?"

The real answer infuriated her. She would have to go with something else. "As soon as I have a big enough place for everybody."

The chlorine-blue sky hung like an enormous mirror over the pool of the Byron estate. The twins sat on the edge with their feet in the water next to the little bronze boy, who was perpetually peeing into his crystal-blue toilet. It was too cold for swimsuits, and kids weren't allowed in the hot tub, so they pulled up their pant legs and shed their shoes and socks. Miranda and Victoria sat across from Artie at the table on the covered veranda. Miranda left no room for confusion when it was "adult time" versus "kids' time"—and the rare occasions the boundary between parents and children was lifted.

"Jimmy told Miss White his daddy said his word to describe himself should be 'unplanned,'" said Grant. "It made her cry."

Charlotte studied the adults at the table across the pool. Victoria looked like one of the ladies on reruns of that show *Dallas*. She imagined Miranda shoving a finger in Victoria's face, then the two of them beating the hell out of each other, rolling around on the ground, and falling into the pool. That would be so awesome!

Teresita, wearing her white apron and light blue maid's outfit, appeared from the house with another lady in tow. She always answered the door when they visited and said things they didn't understand, even though Daddy swore it was English. Victoria and Artie got up as the new lady was presented to the trio as if it were her first day at a new school. Charlotte watched as the stranger gave her Daddy a really big hug and kept smiling even after she sat down next to him.

"You should go back to calling Mama Mama," Charlotte said.

Grant's bottom lip turned down as if he were being scolded. "She didn't hear me when I called her that," he said softly.

"That was when she first came home. She's better now."

"I like Leesie."

"I have a secret, and you're not allowed to tell anyone," Charlotte said.

Grant loved secrets, but he sucked at keeping them. "I swear," he promised.

"When I find out who my real parents are, I'm going to go live with them."

The foursome across the pool cackled as if somebody had told a dirty joke. Teresita brought four drinks in large silver cups that looked wet all the way from the top to the bottom, with some green leaves sticking out of the top.

"Why do you have to talk about that?" asked Grant.

"We're almost teenagers; we can do whatever we want," she assured him.

"I want us back together," said Grant, trying not to let her see him cry. She could make him cry so easily. The older he got, the more he hated it, but he still couldn't help it. "Just don't go away," he said, wiping his cheeks.

The new lady next to their daddy kept touching his arm, and she laughed more than anyone else. When he excused himself and went inside for a few minutes, she moved her chair closer to his. Then Miranda raised her frosty cup with the leaves on top, and the other ladies bumped theirs against hers. She looked side-eyed at the kids as she sipped from her tall, wet cup with the stupid green decorations on top.

24

Congressman Richard Tiberius Jordan, aka Dick

L eeza was washing her truck in the parking lot of the Willow Glen Apartments on a chilly but clear Sunday morning while the neighbors were out praying and grazing. The truck didn't have time to actually get dirty between washings, but that wasn't why she washed it. She used Mr. Miyagi's "wax on, wax off" method to clear her head. *The Karate Kid. Greatest movie ever.* Mundane, repetitive tasks helped take her mind off the realization that things were happening beyond her control, and that realization was tearing her apart.

She regretted losing control at Clark's Coffee Company, but Artie had said some things that pushed her buttons, and she snapped. They were so close to working things out and canceling the mediation; why else would he have stopped the assault and planned a meeting? But they just had to start sharing secrets. *Why can't I keep my mouth shut?*

She felt terrible for making light of his names—just thinking about her flippant comment made her chest ache. The idea of someone giving the names of her dead children to her one surviving child seemed bizarre and beautiful at the same time. Why hadn't he divulged that when he told her about the miscarriages in the past? *When did he find out about that?*

To end the separation, she needed a plan. She needed to convince Artie she was content, happy, and not obsessing. She needed to show him that she was following Dr. Singh's treatment plan and that she wasn't drinking. But most importantly, she needed to convince him that she had given up on the experiments and the formula—which was the toughest part because she had no intention of giving up on the experiments and the formula. She just had to be more careful and not get caught.

The crunch of tires on gravel at the far end of the lot pulled her attention. The car approached slowly, as if the driver were unsure where he was going. It eventually neared the building. Leeza dropped the sponge and watched the compact sedan—a Charleston Cab Company taxi—pull to a stop. Sammie climbed out and slapped some cash into the driver's hand. Leeza hadn't been expecting her, and she certainly hadn't given her the address.

Sammie waved as she walked toward Leeza. Her gait was unsteady and a little too wide. She flashed an animated grin and yelled *"Gurl!"* with the enthusiasm of a thirteen-year-old at her first concert after her third swig of Jägermeister.

Leeza knew Sammie's license had been suspended multiple times; the judge's ultimatum was never taken seriously until this last time. It was tough running a business from a cell, and Sammie was ambitious—she had high hopes of working her way up the food chain. She proudly waved her beer in the air like she was showing off a trophy for Woman of the Year—or maybe Drug Dealer of the Year, either way.

Leeza turned off the water and dropped the hose. "High or just drunk?"

"Nice to see you too," said Sammie. Her eyes looked heavy, and her words seemed deliberate, as if she had to think of each one carefully in order to construct a coherent sentence.

Leeza grabbed a lawn chair from in front of the building and placed it next to the truck. "Sit," she instructed. She added some water to the suds, then splashed the sponge onto the side panel.

"Remind me why you have a ginormous truck," Sammie slurred.

"You're high."

"Can I drive it?"

Leeza scoffed and shot a side-eyed glance at Sammie. "As if."

"What's with you and Artie and your spotless cars? You know, there's this new invention, it's called a car wash," she said, waving the beer above her head. "But they're for dirty cars, sooo... You're gonna scrub the paint off!" Sammie tilted the can straight up, chugged the beer, and let out a burp. "So you're a woman, you have a truck, and you have a motorcycle, and you're bisexual, but not like a full-on dyke or anything, just bi. Got it."

Leeza dropped the sponge into the suds and stood in front of Sammie. "What are you on?" she asked flatly. "You don't use. What happened?" Sammie knew the cardinal rule: never get high on your own supply. Leeza knew Sammie loved to drink, but she always swore she had been living the dealers' code—until now.

"Got a call from the Dick," she said, straining to focus.

"Your dad?"

"Congressman Richard Tiberius Jordan... Dick. Adopts a wet-back because he thinks it'll help his career, then makes her life hell."

"What did he want?"

"He says listening to Mexicans talk is like throwing two cats in a sack. *'I got nothin' against 'em, but I can't stand to hear 'em talk,'*" said Sammie, mimicking her adoptive father. "Now *that* is one evil motherfucker." She took a drag from her vape pen. "He called me Sammie because Rosario sounded too Mexican; did I ever tell you that?"

"What did he say to you?"

"He found out the cops paid me a visit. Told me to get out of Charleston." There was an ominous pause—"Or else."

"You're serious?" said Leeza. She needed Sammie to be clear-headed and available. Once the formula was perfected, she would go back home to Artie and the kids and tell Sammie it was time to go their separate ways forever. But until then, she was screwed without her.

"He knows all the cops," Sammie said. "Probably sent them himself."

A young child yelled from the far end of the parking lot, their excited voice growing closer. "But this is his creation," Sammie said, oblivious to the noise.

Grant was running toward Leeza. Artie and Charlotte were still getting out of the SUV.

"Leesie!" cried Grant, sprinting toward his mama.

"Grant! What are you doing here?" A tidal wave of emotion—grief, joy, shock—crashed over Leeza at the sight of all three of them. She waved frantically at Artie and Charlotte across the lot as she rushed to meet Grant. Artie remained by the SUV, arms crossed, watching. She met Grant halfway, wrapping him in a hug and kissing his forehead. "I didn't know you were coming."

Artie's stare was fixed on Sammie, sitting next to Leeza's truck.

"He thought a spot inspection would be a good idea," Charlotte said as she caught up with Leeza and Grant. "Like he's a fucking captain now."

Leeza was stunned. "What did you just say?"

"Nothing."

Leeza lifted Charlotte's chin. "You and I need to talk."

Grant walked toward Sammie with shy curiosity.

"You must be Grant," Sammie said as he approached. "Wow, you're getting big."

Artie yelled from the car, "Grant!"

"He just wanted to see where you live," said Charlotte.

"Tell him I'm looking for something closer to town."

"You can tell him. He wants to talk to you anyway." They headed across the lot to Artie.

He's here to get me, to tell me to come home! "Did I pass inspection, sir?" she said with a grin.

"Should have known you two couldn't stay away from each other." Artie was clearly not amused. Leeza looked back at Sammie, who lifted her beer and nodded with audacious confidence, like the whore at the end of the bar just before last call.

"She just needed to talk," said Leeza. Her excitement was dashed when Artie rushed the kids back into the SUV. "Charlotte said you wanted to talk."

Artie gestured the kids into the back seat, checked their seatbelts, and slammed the doors.

"I should be at the house with you and the kids. You know that."

"And leave your girlfriend all alone?"

"You know better." She hoped he did, but she'd worry too if the roles were reversed. She reached for his hand.

Artie glared at Sammie. "How is she not in jail?" His jaw locked as he suddenly stormed toward her. Leeza trailed close behind as Artie marched across the gravel lot and planted his feet just in front of Sammie.

"Seriously?! Tell me I'm not seeing this right now!" he seethed.

"¿Cuál es el problema, Príncipe Arturo? (*What's the problem, Prince Arthur?*) Looks like you could use a toke."

"Haven't you done enough?"

"Artie, listen to me," Leeza said.

"Christ, you've got a lot of nerve!" Artie's voice cracked, teetering between fury and disbelief. He thrust his finger toward Sammie. "It's not enough that you destroyed your own life? You wanna take everyone else down with you?"

"It's not what you think," said Leeza.

"What *does* he think?" Sammie asked, still slurring. "Let me guess, he thinks I forced you to get drunk and do drugs in the garage during a storm while your kids were sleeping upstairs and your husband was out of town. Am I close?"

"You're smarter than you look," said Artie.

"I remember a time when you would have been the first in line to a party like that and fucked us both on the garage floor. ¿Qué pasó? (*What happened?*)"

"You couldn't handle it, remember? You put all of us at risk." Artie turned his glare on Leeza. "Stupid move. I thought we could at least—never mind." He marched to the car with Leeza chasing after him.

"You thought we could what?" Leeza demanded. "Why did you really come here?"

Artie started the engine; his whole face was rigid. "You ignorant ass," he muttered to himself.

"You thought we could at least what, Artie?"

Artie stared forward, his chest heaving, as Leeza looked at him through the window.

"You're overreacting," she said. "We'll have to talk eventually."

"Yeah, well, it'll have to wait till we get back."

"Back?"

"Mama's taking us to D.C."

"Artie, for chrissakes, can we talk for a second, please?"

"We're done," said Artie as he put the SUV into gear.

"It's like you get some sort of pleasure out of seeing me upset," Leeza said.

He glared at Sammie again. "How does it feel?"

Leeza stood frozen, devastated, as he and the kids pulled away. She stormed straight back to Sammie.

"Kids are growing up. What's up Prince Arthur's ass?" Sammie asked.

"What the hell is wrong with you?!" Leeza yelled. The neighbors were returning home from the buffet fellowship and meandering toward their apartments. "He came here to talk to me!" She struggled to keep the volume down, careful not to draw attention since all the neighbors had undoubtedly heard about her 'nervous breakdown' last week. "You know we ended it with you because of shit like this!" She rolled up the hose and threw it into the bed of the truck before heading to her apartment and slamming the door.

S ammie curled up in the lawn chair and looked around the parking lot. It was true she was messed up, but she wasn't using. It was also true that her congressman father told her to get out of town. He knew every cop in Charleston because his daddy used to be one. He could have her locked up with a phone call and wouldn't hesitate to do it. She was pissed off, scared, and drunk, but she was clean. *You would know if I was using.*

She glanced across the lot where Artie and the kids had just been, then looked in the direction where Leeza had disappeared. "Where is everybody going?" she muttered to the dripping truck and bucket of suds. She twisted the empty beer can in her hands and leaned back.

The congressman would do whatever it took to climb the ranks within his party. He had his eye on a presidential run by the time he turned fifty-five. Once, during a debate, a white guy next to him started speaking Spanish while answering a question from a Hispanic audience member. Everyone seemed so impressed by the "gibberish." And apparently, one of the state senators had adopted a Black kid and somehow found a way to bring it up during every speech and interview. By the end of the same year, Rosario was the newest member of the Jordan family, joining her big sister Helene, who had blond hair and beauty-queen eyes.

Jordan used the fact that he and his wife had adopted a little Mexican girl to prove once and for all that "we couldn't possibly be racist." But he hated that she spoke with an accent, and he never trusted Mexicans anyway, thanks to all the stories his daddy would tell when he was a cop on nights in Charleston. "I'd take a Negra over a wetback any day," his father had said.

Sammie was never treated the same as Helene, and she cried a lot in the years after being separated from her brother and sister. Their foster parents had let them sleep in the same room and always tucked them in. But after the adoption, Sammie was alone even when she wasn't. By the time she turned thirteen, she was getting suspended from school for fighting and smoking. When she was fifteen, the secrets started. She finally told her mother that her father was making her pose for pictures and that it was supposed to be "their little secret." At first, it was with her clothes on. Then, he made her take off more clothes and pose in weird ways. But her mother wouldn't hear it, and she told the Dick.

The next time Sammie was sent to juvie for fighting, Congressman Jordan made sure she got the maximum sentence. A week after getting out, she ran away and never went back. There were no Amber alerts for Sammie, no flyers on phone poles, and no frantic pleas on television. She begged her foster parents to let her come back and live with them and her brother and sister. She swore she would do whatever they wanted her to do. She stayed out of serious trouble and was able to finish high school. She even tried college for a while. But the self-loathing, depression, and the alcohol held too much power. She took refuge with a tribe that didn't judge and became intimately acquainted with the streets. And she felt content.

Sammie let the crumpled beer can fall onto the crushed granite. She forced herself up from the lawn chair and took a deep drag from her vape pen. Her go-to flavors were Fantasi Cola Ice and Fizzy Cola Blast, but today, Fantasi was the clear winner. She stood facing Leeza's silver F-150 with the crazy aftermarket lift kit and enormous tires. A few drips of water clung to the surface as she stared at her distorted reflection.

"This machinery belongs with a dyke," she muttered, not caring who heard.

The twisted reflection in the shiny silver paint was abstract, yet recognizable. She leaned in and made faces, waving her arms above her head and laughing as the reflection mimicked her every move. She performed a soft-shoe routine on the gravel, turning in circles and miming the tipping of a top hat. Then she stopped, blew a kiss, and took a bow.

She walked toward the apartment where Leeza had gone. The door opened before she could knock. Leeza was texting as she motioned for Sammie to come inside.

"I need to take a wiz, then I'll leave you alone," Sammie announced.

By the time she returned from the bathroom, Leeza had opened two more beers.

"Guess I'm stayin'."

Leeza's eyes were bloodshot. Her face was swollen and streaked with wiped tears from convulsive sobbing since Artie left with the kids, and she was still dabbing her eyes.

"How did you find my apartment?" Leeza asked.

"You said North Charleston. I knew you wouldn't be on the sleazy side; this area has the most turnover because of the base, and the apartments open to the outside instead of a hallway. I know you can't handle being enclosed. Sooo..."

"You missed your calling," said Leeza.

"I get that a lot." She took a swig of the cold beer. "He really is uptight."

"Can you blame him?"

"We won't go there," Sammie said as she plopped onto the loveseat. "Remember when the three of us would go out to the bars? Everybody knew we were together. We were like royalty. Everybody wanted to know what it was like to be us."

"I've had a breakthrough with the research," Leeza said. "Turns out there have been similar studies; the only difference is I'm not a mouse. We're getting close."

Sammie had given up arguing with Leeza about the experiments. She knew they were happening with or without her, and if she OD'd again, it would be better if they were together. "We'll have to do it here for now," Leeza added as she handed Sammie a list.

"You owe me," Sammie said.

"I got you."

"There's something I need to tell you."

"If it's about sleeping with cops, I already know," said Leeza.

"That couple you were with at the club..."

"Tana and Dante."

"Yeah." Sammie was uneasy.

"She's my nurse, and he's her boyfriend."

"Do you know how she met him?"

"Let's just say they both have a colorful history."

"He's bad news," Sammie said.

"Tana can handle herself."

"It's not her I'm worried about." Sammie was respected on the streets, but she wasn't satisfied being a middleman, buying by the ounce and selling by the gram. She wanted her own turf and needed to be a supplier so she could control who was buying and selling, and for how much. It was the only way she would get enough money to leave Charleston forever. Her only obstacle was the guy already running that operation—Dante. If she could gain his trust and get close to him, then if he disappeared for some reason, she could take over his business, and she'd be set for life. After a few years, she would take the money and move to Hermosillo, only three and a half hours from the border and thirty minutes from La Herradura, where she was born.

La Herradura was poor and desolate compared to neighboring Hermosillo, and many people made the dangerous journey to the States in search of work so they could send money back to their families. Rosario's father decided he would take the whole family in search of "the promise." But only three of them made it, and they were three orphans under the age of five.

She would find her brother and sister, and they would all move to Hermosillo and visit their cousins and extended family in La Herradura. They would live a comfortable life, happy and safe, and the dick would never have to worry about her again, and vice versa.

"He seems harmless," said Leeza.

"Good," said Sammie. *He would put a bullet through your skull without blinking.*

She knew he was a three-strikes felon and assumed that if he was arrested again, he would go away for life. *So how did he get out? And why was he at the club? He can't do anything stupid; he's on probation.* She would just have to lay low and figure out how to get rid of him—again. And it would have to be before he figured out what she did.

25

Panties and Police Stations

L eeza stepped out of the shower, wrapping a towel around her chest. She took a sip of Jack before opening the binder. With a pen gripped between her teeth, she scanned the formulas, words, and compounds, instantly lost in the work. She had printed an article about dopamine receptor manipulation and paradigm reprogramming being tested in mice and had read it three times. She lay on the bed, resting the binder and the article on her chest. Her eyes were already half-closed. She felt more tired than usual these days, and she didn't resist as she dozed off.

"I Want to Know What Love Is" by Foreigner played on the portable CD player as Leeza and Artie enjoyed cocktails and popcorn, surrounded by boxes and packing supplies. They had been in the house for three days, and it seemed like they'd never get everything unpacked and put away. But tonight, they were taking a break and couldn't care less—they had their whole lives ahead of them. The doorbell rang. They smiled at each other and raced to the door.

"Wellness check!" cried Sammie, her arms full of goodies for the happy throuple. They pulled Sammie inside and Artie gave her a kiss as she came through the door. She presented him with a small wooden box containing a row of joints and some colorful pills.

"Yes!" He took one of the joints and kissed Sammie again.

Sammie handed Leeza a small plastic bag with white powder. She looked Leeza's body up and down and winked. "Hmm hmm hmm, you look good tonight."

Sammie emerged from under the sheets, landing between Leeza and Artie. They lay next to each other, recovering from the calisthenics-laden sex.

Artie rubbed his eyes. "Good Lord, you need to patent that technique." He nudged Sammie toward Leeza and watched them kiss. He grabbed Leeza's pink bikini panties and dropped them between their faces. Sammie pressed the panties to her face and took a deep breath.

Leeza's phone rang, jolting her awake. She took a deep, irritated breath through her teeth before reading the words on the screen: **Charleston County Jail.**

L eeza fidgeted as she took in her surroundings at the county jail on Leeds Avenue. The tiny, cinderblock waiting area was little more than a notch cut into the main hall. The fluorescent lights were harsh and ample. The clanking sounds of metal from doors, keys, cuffs, and chairs echoed with authority around the space. It occurred to her that this was the first time she'd ever seen the inside of a police station.

An officer escorted Sammie from the far end of a long hallway behind metal doors.

"What happened?" Leeza asked. Sammie stormed past her. "Three guesses."

Sammie stepped right into the street, the sound of screeching brakes and a blaring horn following her. She reached the sidewalk and spun around. "They didn't give up so easy this time!"

"What happened?" Leeza said again.

"Shit's about to get real!"

"What are you talking about?"

"I've been raided twice now! That shit doesn't just happen!"

"Do you know why?"

"How's Artie doin', huh? He say anything since he saw me at your place?"

"He wouldn't narc on you."

"Think! Saffron heard the cops talking. She heard them say that something was there!" Sammie waited.

"And?" Leeza shrugged.

"Somebody lied to the cops. He's always hated me! He's been waiting for this!"

"You know that's not true, Sammie."

"He's a user! You never could see that! He's a spoiled rich bitch!"

Leeza felt her fists tighten. *You are this close, bitch.*

"All that shit you're doing to yourself; he thinks it's me!"

"I told him."

"You're a liar!" Sammie started pacing again. "Artie goes to college, marries a Black chick to piss off his mama. Y'all can do no wrong, and everything I touch turns to shit!" Sammie stopped inches from Leeza's face. "The only time either one of you wanted me around was when you needed something from me!" She leaned a little closer. "I guess some things never change."

"We had a relationship with you! We were all happy! You're the one who—"

"Maybe if I had known it was conditional!" Sammie screamed. "He can take everything I have with a fuckin' phone call!" She stopped. Her voice caught with emotion as she tried to continue. "You were my family." She turned her back to Leeza and screamed into the night. "My FAMILY!" She wiped her face and cleared her throat as she walked away, disappearing into the darkness.

Leeza stood on the sidewalk and watched Sammie vanish. She found herself desperately trying to process the past few days. She needed to condense the events into something understandable—events that took her from the perfect home, kids, husband, dog, responsibilities and challenges and goals to this—this police station—this apartment—this lonely, tiny apartment that smells like socks and feels stifling and lonely. The garage. The experiment and the paralysis. Artie standing in the downpour. *Jesus Christ.*

A figure formed in the distance, slowly emerging from the darkness where Sammie had just disappeared. She was coming back, walking toward Leeza slowly—a look of resolve in her eyes, the look of unfinished business. She stopped within inches.

"Does this look like fearless to you?" Sammie said.

26

Calvin Klein & Versace

G rant begged Charlotte to play music "from this century" when it was just the two of them. While waiting for lessons to start, he would sit beside her at the piano, and they would belt out their own versions of contemporary songs. Charlotte wasn't the only one in the house with natural talent; Grant had a beautiful voice and sang extraordinary harmonies in their renditions. He had worked out his stage persona down to the smallest detail: performing original songs to packed arenas in a Catholic schoolgirl plaid skirt, a medieval warrior chainmail armor hoodie, and exaggerated eye makeup—only the eyes. *"Just gloss on the lips! These lips are money, honey!"*

Leeza stood across the room, leaning in the kitchen doorway as the kids performed their favorites—Sia's "Courage to Change," Celine Dion's "Power of Love," and Adele's "Someone Like You." Grant closed his eyes and rocked gently as Charlotte laid down the intro, and then they launched into American Idol-worthy performances.

Leeza knew they were good, but that song "Courage to Change..." Their performance touched her deeply. She watched the young siblings at the Steinway grand; their nuanced understanding of the lyrics and the control in their voices stirred something inside her. She wiped her eyes, imagining her mama sitting beside her before Mr. Brathwaite arrived for lessons. At home, the music was gospel, and her mama's harmonies reached the farthest corners of Leeza's soul. Now, she heard her as if she were the one next to Charlotte.

Charlotte's watch chimed five. Grant dragged himself to the floor under the piano, flipping through issues of *Posh Kids* and *Vogue* as Inspector Frisky sprawled out beside him. Charlotte opened *Czerny's Piano Exercises Op. 849.* In the kitchen, Leeza pressed both palms to her cheeks and cried.

Leeza joined Charlotte as she finished her first run-through of *Etude No. 28.* "I love this one," Leeza said, and began to play the exercise herself. Soon her hands were flying across the keys like tiny whirlwinds. Charlotte watched, studying every move. "Remember, legato in the left hand, staccato in the right, and easy on the pedal. The right wrist moves counterclockwise with the arpeggios."

Charlotte swayed back and forth and waved her hands as if conducting an orchestra. At exactly fifty-one seconds from beginning to end, Leeza's hands rose slowly into the air as if they were still connected to the fading last notes.

"My turn." Charlotte began the exercise again, and this time it sounded identical to her mother's. She finished with a melodramatic bow.

"Yes! One more time, then the concerto," said Leeza.

"Life would be so much easier if everything was in C Major," said Charlotte.

"Yeah, right, like Aunt Jemima pancakes without syrup, spring without the fall."

"I get it."

"A storm without a rainbow, a baby without crying."

"Really?"

"Cops without donuts."

Charlotte slapped her palm against her forehead, rolling her eyes.

"You were playing in F sharp minor when you were seven, and you never complained."

"I thought it was *supposed* to be hard."

"It's the pairing of the melody with the key that gives the piece its essence, its personality, its purpose," Leeza said. "You wouldn't dress a wrestler in a three-piece suit, or a swimmer in a ball gown. Mr. Brathwaite told me that the key gives us a glimpse into the composer's soul—it can even tell us what they were going through at the time. Once you hear the music speak its truth, it's like Wow—Just wow."

Leeza savored the memory of sitting next to her teacher in the house in Beaufort. With her mother silently observing from the kitchen table, Leeza felt purpose, pride, reason. Every lesson was a revelation, every corrected chord a victory. In those hours of disciplined focus, she felt her potential bloom, knowing she was doing exactly what she was meant to do. It was the best time of her life. "It's hard because it's beautiful. And it's beautiful because it's hard."

"That literally makes no sense," said Charlotte.

"You were learning *Adagio in D Minor* when you were six."

"*Adagio in D Minor* is slow. But then you gave me *Toccata and Fugue* like you were trying to kill me."

"Oh, you mean 'Carnage in D Minor?'"

"*Now* you tell me!"

"What's a tallywacker?" yelled Grant from under the piano.

"Where did you hear that?" Leeza asked.

"Norlander's daddy said the President is a tallywacker."

"Read your *Vogue*," she replied. "Takes one to know one," she whispered to Charlotte.

Leeza replaced the exercises with *La Campanella*. "It's this or *Nutcracker*."

"I have forever to learn *Nutcracker*," said Charlotte.

"You have two months before the ballet."

"Exactly."

"You can stop after the first three minutes; I don't want you to injure yourself." Liszt adapted *La Campanella* for piano and released his inner demons in the final minute of the third movement.

Leeza added Liszt to her practice rotation two weeks before her mama's diagnosis and never made it all the way through.

Charlotte's deep understanding of music allowed her to play with the agility and emotion of someone much older. Leeza listened as she nailed the first two minutes. At three minutes, her fingers were a blur, and her eyes were laser focused. Leeza expected her to stop at any moment, but Charlotte kept going. The arpeggios came more frequently and were more demanding. She kept going. Three and a half minutes, four minutes—done! Charlotte raised her hands from the keyboard and froze as the final notes dissolved.

"Can't argue with that," Leeza whispered. *Good Lord.* "Are you sure you want to study psychology?"

Charlotte scoffed. "Less competition. Did you know Condoleezza Rice played for the Queen? And she went into political science."

"I know everything about Condoleezza Rice," Leeza said matter-of-factly. "So, tell me about the other night."

"What are you talking about?"

"Really?"

"It was a while ago," said Charlotte.

"You were crying."

Charlotte knew she wasn't getting out of this. "I think he just doesn't like me."

"Who?" Leeza asked but figured it out just as quickly. "He's your father."

Charlotte rolled her eyes. "Technically."

"Technically?"

"On paper. I get reminded every day that he's not my real dad. Why do people even care?"

"I wish I could answer that."

"He's different when you're not here. He's always pissed about something."

"Pissed is a strong word. Preoccupied, maybe."

"He tells me something is wrong with me, then he changes the subject."

"He's doing his best, Charlotte."

"Ever since you left, he's always on his phone. God forbid you should ask who he's talking to."

"Sometimes, when adults are disappointed with the way things work out, they can have a hard time keeping their emotions in. Your daddy is struggling just like we all are."

"It was his idea." Charlotte lowered her head. "It totally feels like me and Grant are in the way." Her voice was cracking. "But that ain't nothin' new."

"I don't hear practicing!" Grant announced from under the piano. Leeza nudged Charlotte and winked. The two suddenly broke into a lively version of four-handed chopsticks in the style of Mozart.

"Good Lord," said an exasperated Grant. "Forget I said anything."

"One time, I told Grant to shut up, and he put me in time-out for three hours," Charlotte said.

Leeza took a deep breath. She was used to fixing things on the spot, but now, she felt as helpless as Charlotte looked. "It'll get better, baby."

Charlotte put her arm around her mama and leaned closer.

"Just so you know, you will have your own room at my new house," Leeza said.

"I want to live with you until…" Charlotte stopped herself.

"Until?"

"Until I'm older."

M eanwhile, across town, Artie had heard the same tired stories a million times at daddy daycare, and since he was
distracted anyway, he decided to call it a night. *What is it about
alcohol and short-term memory loss?* He drove around for forty-five
minutes, ultimately finding himself at Nordstrom Rack on Bow-
man Road in Mt. Pleasant.

He remembered Miranda talking about Nordstrom Rack as a
kid. *"At least there's a place for those with reduced circumstances."*
For years, he thought she was joking until he got older and realized
she had no sense of humor and was just being mean. He'd found
brand-name shoes there and didn't feel guilty about the great deals,
even if he was potentially depriving a shopper with 'reduced circumstances.' He would tell Miranda he found them in New York
or Milan.

Nordstrom was usually empty and library-quiet, just the way
rich people preferred. Its sidekick, the Rack, was where the action was. There were more associates roaming around, folding
one-size-too-small garments that had just been held up moments
earlier. They even had an employee whose full-time job was to
direct lines of customers with reduced circumstances in and out
of the dressing rooms.

Just past the men's belts were the men's underwear. He loved
the feel of brand-name underwear. For his birthday one year, Leeza
had given him gift cards, telling him he was only allowed to spend
them on underwear and had to model each and every new pair
for her. She finished off almost a whole bottle of Sauvignon Blanc
as he strutted down the make-believe catwalk in his new bikinis,
boxer-briefs with a five-inch inseam, and satin lounge shorts: Ba-
lenciaga, Versace, Equipo, Bamboo Cool, Papi, Calvin Klein.

He could see the women's lingerie a few rows over. He caught
himself looking around like a kid before stealing a candy bar. The
coast was clear as he slid down the racks to the women's section.
He stopped before a display of individually hung panties: silk with
lace, tiny sewn flowers, fishnet, and even a blasphemous thong or

two. Pink, black, ivory, hearts, polka dots. He pushed each hanger down as he admired the artistry. He picked out a few pairs and laid them on top of the rack.

"Nice," a voice behind him said, scaring the shit out of him.

He spun around. "Jesus Christ!" he gasped.

"I see your taste has evolved," said Sammie.

"What the hell?!" cried Artie, clutching his chest.

"Language, Arthur," Sammie said. "You almost actually said a dirty word." She flipped through his collection of panties in front of them. "Scandalous," she added with a grin. "I heard you two were separated."

"What are you doing here?"

"You both wore new undies when I came over—Calvins, Equipo. Hmm... Equipo, damn, those were hot."

"What is *wrong* with you?" He felt himself ducking as his eyes darted frantically around the cavernous outlet.

"I thought we could chat. Is there a problem?"

"Yes, there's a fucking problem!" he hissed, somewhere between a yell and a whisper.

"I just need us to be on the same page, that's all."

"You followed me here to make sure we're on the same page?!"

"Well, the cab followed you; I was playing hangman, I thought you'd never stop."

"What part of 'leave us alone' is kicking your ass?"

"You used to get off watching us model for you. Kink much?"

"I'm dead serious, Sammie," he said, trying to find a blend of firm and calm. "Leave me alone."

"Seems like just yesterday you told me I was part of the family. You were *this* close to using the 'L' word."

"Family doesn't assault cops while getting arrested for selling pot to minors at a middle school!"

"Well, maybe not *your* family," she said.

"And you swore you wouldn't use!"

"Caught up in the moment. Anyways, here's the thing: your wife called and asked me for a favor. What you saw in the garage, she did to herself. And whatever you made up in that pretty little head of yours that night, it's a lie."

"I know what I saw."

"And so you called the cops, or was it your mama that did that?" Artie was silent. *What difference did it make who made the call?*

Sammie reached under her shirt. Artie caught a glimpse of the handgun as she pulled out a pair of pink bikini panties and held them up. "Remember?"

He forgot to breathe. *You've had Leeza's panties all this time?* "You are a sociopath." He started hanging his collection of panties back on the rack.

"You're out of your league." Sammie moved closer. He could feel her breath and smell her hair... that familiar hair. "Because *you* have more to lose," she whispered. He could feel the handgun through her clothes. "And because *you* have nowhere to hide."

He felt the blood drain from his face. "You psychotic bitch," he muttered. *Is this what they meant by ruthless?*

"Which is it, psychotic or sociopath?" Sammie asked. "Or is it the same thing?"

"Just leave us alone."

"Hard to leave you alone when your wife keeps texting me. I wouldn't wanna to be rude."

"You're a liar."

"Of course, I am." Sammie held up her phone and showed him the texts. He scanned the words as his jaw tightened. He hung up the last of the panties.

"Just because everything good fell into your lap all your life, that doesn't make you any better than me," said Sammie.

"You had choices, just like everybody else."

"That just rolls off your tongue, don't it?" Sammie put her forehead on his shoulder. "Maybe my choices would be different if my daddy was a rich doctor."

He could feel the blood returning, hotter. *You either have success in this life, or you have excuses.* "If your daddy was a rich doctor, you'd be a rich drug dealer."

"You guys were like a movie, like an actual fairytale. I was in love with the idea of being in love with the two of you. But you know what I feel now, Artie? I feel sorry for you. Your silver spoon and Leeza's big league job... But truth be told, y'all are tryin' to cover up some seriously dysfunctional shit."

"You want us to be on the same page? How's this..." He reached for his phone in his breast pocket with his right hand as his left arm nudged the gun under Sammie's shirt. His thumb hovered over the screen. He straightened, lifted his chin, and said, "One call, and you evaporate." They stood in motionless silence, with the phone, the gun, the women's lingerie. "And Leeza gets on with her life." He selected a pair from the rack and held them up. "They're for me."

Sammie watched as he turned and walked toward the cashier. She held Leeza's pink panties to her face and took a deep breath, then hung them on a hanger and placed them on the rack alongside the new ones. He looked at her from across the store as he handed the cashier a credit card. Even from that distance, she could see the subtle, confident grin as he made a kissing motion with his lips.

Leeza and Charlotte were at the piano when Artie came in with a shopping bag and his phone next to his ear. He gestured to the kids as he headed for the kitchen.

"Night, Leesie," said Grant, giving her a hug.

"Night, Dr. G."

Leeza kissed Charlotte on the forehead. "Night, baby."

Leeza was putting on her coat when Artie returned. "Your girlfriend is stalking me."

Tell me you're not serious. "What the hell are you talking about?"

"She wanted to make sure I knew you were the one who reached out," Artie said.

"I told you I asked her for a favor—"

"If I so much as hear her name or see her face, she *will* disappear." He pointed a finger in Leeza's face. "Don't push me."

"Not a problem," said Leeza. He spun around and went back to the kitchen as she let herself out.

A s Leeza drove into the night, a cab crept up the street and stopped in front of the house. Sammie handed the driver cash before stepping out. She stood in the darkness and pulled out a vape pen, then turned her baseball cap backward. She sat down in the middle of the street, staring across the lawn as she watched Leeza's family move around in the warm, yellow light of their beautiful home.

Evaporate, huh? she thought. *Interesting choice of words. Is that your superpower, Prince Arthur? You make people evaporate?* She took a drag from the vape pen. *But we're family, remember? Why would you do that to your family? Tengo una idea mejor. (I have a better idea.)*

Her thoughts were scattered as she sat on the pavement in the middle of the road in the affluent American neighborhood three days before Thanksgiving. She hated cold weather. The nights had been chilly, in the mid to low 50s, and normally she would be inside a warm house, or apartment, or closet—anywhere but where she was tonight. Humidity and summer heat didn't bother her, but she avoided the cold at all costs. But her mind was so preoccupied that she didn't feel her spine tightening like water slowly freezing into ice.

She wouldn't be invited for turkey this year, and she needed to decide how she felt about that. She used to love social gatherings, especially when Mexicans were involved. Latinos didn't need much of an excuse for a party—they genuinely relished the celebration: the music, dancing, drinking, talking, laughing, eating, more drinking, and more dancing. Sammie would pretend she was related to everyone there, whether it was her real family or not—and of course, it never was.

Her mind was at one of those celebrations when the cell rang. She rarely answered her phone. She preferred to wait and listen to the voicemail before deciding whether to call them back. This time, she didn't look to see who it was.

Celebrating with Americans was a different experience. Things like weddings, Thanksgiving, Christmas, birthdays... they were always served with a steaming side of drama, and the hostess couldn't wait for the meticulously planned obligation to end. But even those were memorable for Sammie. She was pretty good at leaving the drama with its creators. So how did her life turn into one big soap opera?

The phone chimed as the voicemail concluded. She looked at the caller ID—Saffron. She held up the cell and turned on the speaker. Saffron's tone fluttered between exasperation, anxiety, and resolve—all delivered in polished Cockney slang:

"Alright, love. Things have taken a turn, and I need to let you know. Don't know what to say, duckie, I'm sorry. The bobbies were back, love, this time with the housing supe. The supe left a notice with some properly nasty words. He warned us to heed the notice or else, yeah? See, they've evicted us. Well, not exactly 'us'—they've evicted you, darling. Horizon and I can only stay if you promise never to return. Even then, I reckon we're on thin ice. So, there's the long and short of it, love. I'm so sorry.

"But I did find out one thing: remember that last time I told you they said, 'it was here?' The one said to the other, 'they said it was

here.' Well, apparently, they were told you nicked a local business, and the goods were stashed here. I know it's a pony, sweetie—that's not our game. Someone fed them a lie, and they tore the place stem to stern.

"Oh, and uhm, the supe was whispering to the bobby not two feet from me, duckie. I pretended not to hear, but I was right there, for crying out loud. He said he gave the congressman his word. I'm sure that's what he said. Didn't you say your old man was a congressman, love? I'm sure I heard that once. But how could he have... Anyway, I don't need to tell you this, but Horizon and I are fresh out of housing ideas. I don't know what they'd do with him if we had to go too. I am utterly gutted right now, utterly. I'll do anything to help you get out, but I pray you'll understand, love, eh? Okay, love, bye for now."

Sammie stared at Leeza's house. The November cold had turned to desert heat around her. She felt every breath moving in and out of her face as she dialed the Charleston Cab Company.

27

Momma Bears vs. Bullies

T ana burst straight in and began pacing around the office, unaware she had just startled the hell out of Leeza. She went back to the door and looked both ways down the hall before closing it.

Leeza rode out the panic response in silence, gradually allowing the tension in her extremities, her neck, and her face to recede. The pounding of her heart would take a little longer. *Are we seriously doing this right now?* "What's the matter?" Leeza asked, steadying her voice.

"There was a phone call," Tana said, still pacing.

"What phone call?"

Tana sucked in the deepest breath she could manage.

"Somebody sayin' awful things about you."

"About me?" *Is this a joke?* "Like what? Who was it?"

"I don't know. I told them you weren't here."

"What did they sound like?"

"Some chick," said Tana.

"What exactly did she say?"

Starting with her pinky, Tana assigned a finger to each accusation. "She said you threatened her, she said you like pussy, she said you're a drug addict, she said you were trying to kill yourself, and she called Artie a pussy-whipped mama's boy."

"Tana, listen. It's got to be a patient, maybe someone from one of my therapy sessions." She paused to see if Tana was buying it.

"None of that is true," she said, knowing all of it was true, well, most of it—she wasn't trying to kill herself.

"How would she know Artie?"

"What number did she call from?"

"It was a burner; I checked."

You're gonna mess with me at work? That's your move?

"I'll tell Dante to follow you home."

"It's okay, I'll figure it out."

"This ain't no time for you to shut me out," Tana insisted.

"Sorry, it's just..." If anyone could help, it would be Tana. And if anyone could understand the predicament, it would be Tana. But it wasn't fair to drag her into it. "If I need anything, I'll let you know."

"You know I have resources."

"I am fully aware of that," said Leeza.

"You can't just sit on this, Missy. One more call like that... I'll figure it out and take care of that shit myself."

Leeza grabbed her keys. "If it happens again, keep her on the phone and find me."

The phone was clamped to the dashboard and Leeza glanced at it every few seconds as if it might detonate without warning. She checked on the kids in the rearview between watching the road and monitoring the cell.

"So much for trying a new restaurant," said Charlotte.

"Daddy has a girlfriend," said Grant.

Charlotte's mouth dropped open as she slapped his arm. "She's not his girlfriend!"

Leeza stared at him in the rearview.

Charlotte glared at him, mouthing "Shut up!"

"Why do you say that?" Leeza asked.

"She's not his girlfriend, don't worry, Mama."

"She keeps touching him when he's tryin' to eat."

"Really?!" cried Charlotte.

"I hate it when Gramma babysits."

Really, Artie? You take them to your mother's and then leave them with her so you can go out? What the hell are you thinking?

"I have an idea," said Leeza. "Let's play the quiet game. Five minutes of silence starting right now."

Grant tried his best, but five minutes was asking too much. "Leesie," he whispered, as if whispering was close enough.

Jesus, take the wheel.

"Jimmy Norlander gave me a note from his dad," said Grant. "He wants to talk to Daddy."

"Why did he pass a note through you guys?"

"He told his daddy what you said."

Leeza's mind raced. "What did I say?"

"You said it takes one to know one when I asked you what a tallywacker was. He told Jimmy he would beat Daddy's A.S.S. if he saw him."

"Give me the note."

"It's for Daddy."

"Give me the note!"

Grant reluctantly dug it out of his backpack and handed it over. The 'note' was just a phone number.

"Hey Google, call 8435551649." Leeza turned up the volume of the Bluetooth speaker. Charlotte and Grant looked nervously at each other.

"What is she doing?" Grant whispered.

"Hello?" a man's voice boomed through the truck as they headed down Main Street.

"Hey, how ya doin'? This is Mrs. Byron, Grant's mama. Is this Mr. Norlander?"

"This is me," said the senior Norlander.

"Grant gave me your number and said you wanted to talk, so I thought I'd follow up. Is this a good time?"

"I said give it to his daddy."

"Well, my understanding is you took issue with something I said, is that right?"

"It don't matter—"

Really, asshole? "And since I have you, I thought I would just take care of it. So here's the thing… My husband and I have listened to stories about your family around the dinner table for the past year. You are well within your rights to make excuses for your son's behavior, 'cause you do you, right? But you are setting that child up for a harsh lesson because one of these days he's gonna meet somebody a little bit bigger and a little cockier with a daddy who's just as big an asshole." Charlotte and Grant's jaws dropped. "And they're gonna beat the livin' shit outta that poor little boy." She glanced through the rearview mirror at the wide-eyed twins.

"*Now listen here!*" Jimmy's daddy attempted to interject.

"Uh-uh," she said over him. "I'm almost done. Now, little Jimmy is a bully, plain and simple; everybody knows it. The teachers know it, the students know it, hell, even the board knows it. Seems like the only people who don't know it are his mama and daddy."

Grant's eyes darted around the truck. "I'm dead," he whispered.

"You might think you're bein' a real man for takin' up for your boy when he pushes a little girl down on the playground or when he threatens to beat somebody up because they look different or talk different, but you are not doing him any favors. So, to be abundantly clear, the next time I hear from *anybody* that little Jimmy so much as looked at somebody cross-eyed, you and I will be having this conversation face to face in front of Principal Augustine and a lawyer. Do you understand what I just said?"

"You don't have to be a—"

"There is help for families in crisis, and I would be happy to provide you with references and all the contact information you need if you're interested. In the meantime, please remember to go through proper channels if you want to communicate with other parents because I would hate to add a felony charge of intimidation of a minor to your already long list of personal issues."

Charlotte's slack jaw closed to a timid grin as she fist-bumped Grant.

"As far as talking to *me*, you should be sure to keep this number handy, okay? And if you have anything you need to say or if any questions pop into your head, do not hesitate to give me a ringy dingy. I do wish you and yours a lovely evening."

Leeza tapped the red circle and disconnected the call. "Tell me you wanna talk to somebody's daddy when I'm the one you need to talk to? You're gonna talk to *me*, bitch!"

Leeza swerved into the pharmacy's parking lot and pulled into a parking spot. She grabbed the yellow binder from the passenger seat and shoved it into the glove compartment. "I'll be back," she said before slamming the door.

"**A**nd that's. How. Ya do it," said Charlotte, watching her mama walk away. "Any questions?"

Grant shook his head emphatically. "I'm glad she called that bitch Norlander's daddy a tallywacker."

Charlotte's mouth dropped open as she stared at her brother. "You did not just say that."

It was Grant's turn to swirl his neck in circles. "Um hmm!"

"I'm pretty sure she could kick his ass," Charlotte added.

Grant raised a dramatic finger in the air. "Next subject. I wonder if they have a Mexican restaurant where she lives."

"Why? In case they have skinny noodles on the kid's menu?"

"Leesie ruined skinny noodles for me, remember?"

"Yes, and it was epic."

"There she is!" cried Grant as Leeza headed for the truck but stopped to look at her phone. They watched as she stared at the screen.

S ammie was sending pictures—lots of pictures. Leeza flipped through images of Artie and the kids: Artie on a park bench as the kids played; the kids getting on the school bus in front of The Matson Preparatory School on Halsey Boulevard; the back of Artie's car at night; Artie at a department store; their house—at night! Then she remembered what Artie said: *"Your girlfriend is stalking me."*

She called Sammie's cell. *I am not playing this game with you,* she thought. "Damn it, Sammie!" she muttered to herself after several rings. She waited and left a message after the beep. "Hey girl, what's with the pictures? Call me."

She was startled by a vibration and a text alert. It was Tana:

> *Dante is here lets meet up*

She closed the text, redialed Sammie's number, and waited for the recording.

"I get it. You're pissed as hell, and you think you've figured it all out. Just meet me at the club. We'll have some drinks and talk." She hung up. Staring at the pictures Sammie had sent, she took a shaky breath and redialed, acutely aware of the kids watching. "Do not call my office again. We don't want to do this, Sammie. So let's not, alright?"

Leeza knew Sammie was hurt and pissed and maybe even embarrassed. She also knew that Artie, Miranda, and Congressman Dick weren't helping the situation.

She softened her tone. "I'm sorry. I should never have gotten you involved, and I am really sorry I did. Please talk to me." She had to convince Sammie to back off before it got further out of hand—and she had to make it very clear that there were certain lines you just don't cross. "You have to know that if you go anywhere near my family... I will find you."

Part III

28

BREAKING NEWS

L eeza pulled up to the apartments but stayed in the truck. The tired façade of the old building wasn't aging well, and the plastic planters filled with dusty fake annuals weren't helping. She remembered thinking, "Whoever came up with the name has no idea what a Glen is," the first time she saw it, and the whole place was starting to get on her nerves. The online pictures had looked so homey and inviting; the one-bedroom was even described as "cozy" with a "summer cottage feel." What they failed to mention was that the "cottage" smelled like a chemical accident involving Fabuloso and a hamper full of gym socks. The apartments had seen heavy tenant turnover through the years, and it was turning into a verifiable dump.

"If those walls could talk," she whispered. She flipped through the pictures from Sammie and texted again.

Just call me please.

She turned off the engine and grabbed the grocery bag and backpack. As she headed to the apartment, she gazed at the tilting aluminum mailbox. *Ghetto.* She reached for her keys as she approached the door, but it wasn't only unlocked; it was ajar. She froze, then leaned forward to look inside through the narrow opening.

"Hello?" She slowly pushed the door open and peered inside. Her heart raced as the grocery bag slipped to the ground. The lamp lay on its side, broken glass scattered across the linoleum. An empty Jack Daniel's bottle was under the table, and more glass was on the counter. The fridge and freezer doors were wide open. She spotted the yellow binder in the freezer. Swallowing hard and afraid to look, she thumbed through its wet but intact pages, then set it in the dish drainer and called the manager.

"This is Leeza," she said. "I've been broken into."

A police officer was walking through the apartment with the manager, while a second officer spoke with Leeza just outside the front door.

"Have you touched anything?" he asked, writing notes on a cartoonishly small flip pad.

"No," she replied.

"Any ideas as to who would do this?"

Leeza knew when she moved in that there were dealers and addicts in the area; the proximity to the base made it inevitable. But the building itself had seemed reasonably safe, she remembered thinking. There was a prostitute named Lily who worked the corner of the parking lot on Fridays and Saturdays, but only after dark, and never on Sundays.

"No."

He looked at her incredulously. "There was no sign of forced entry."

Two lanky teenage boys stood outside an apartment a few doors down from Leeza's, smoking joints and staring at her and the officer. She noticed amateur tattoos on their wrists and hands; their faces looked so young, like the half-dead soldiers.

"It's an old building; God knows how many keys are out there," Leeza said.

"You live here alone?" he asked, still scribbling on his pad.

"Temporarily."

"Call me if you think of something," he said, offering his card. "And get yourself a dog."

"Thanks," she said, feeling a mix of unease and frustration. *Charleston's finest right there, folks.*

Leeza dumped salad onto a tan Corelle plate. A sliced avocado and a lime waited nearby. Yo-Yo Ma's Prelude from Bach's *Cello Suite No. 1 in G Major* played as her mind raced.

The lamp was upright, and the broken glass had been swept up. The television was on but muted. The cello solo filled the apartment as a large man with a head-spinning plumber's crack worked diligently to replace the locks and doorknob, adding an additional deadbolt for good measure.

"You're all set," said the locksmith as he hoisted his wayward pants. "Here's your keys, your receipt, and a business card."

"Thanks for coming so soon."

Leeza tested the locks, then replaced the old keys on her keyring.

L eeza was spending a few hours a day on her research. Having the time to do it was the only positive in an otherwise painful chapter; time she would have otherwise spent with the kids—cooking, homework, bedtime—she could use to focus on the formula. But focusing wasn't that easy. She thought about how much she and Artie had loved each other's company before the deployment: movies, reading, sex, talking, traveling, sex. Their connection had grown deeper over time. She blamed Miranda for encouraging him to give up on the marriage so abruptly, so easily. Why did everything have to fall apart all at once? She was dwelling on regrets and decisions that couldn't be undone. *Enough*, she thought. *Focus!* she snapped at herself for getting so easily distracted. The more she was able to concentrate on the work, the less she thought about how lonely and miserable she felt. Was this the new normal—work as the only escape?

She set the binder on the coffee table and picked up her plate and fork. The room was dark, except for the reading light and the glow of the muted TV. She liked the idea of using the TV as a night light, but hated whatever noise was spewing from it. She knew it irritated Artie, but he never complained.

A sudden blast from outside rattled the building, sending her plate and fork crashing to the floor. She heard herself scream as she hit the ground, curling into a tight fetal position, forcefully covering her ears. *The deafening sound of artillery and bombs exploded all around. The air was thick with smoke, the sounds of men yelling, chaos, and cries of agony. Two soldiers rushed into the medic tent with a stretcher carrying a wounded soldier in his early twenties and placed him on a cot in front of Leeza. The soldier desperately grabbed Leeza's hand!*

She forced her eyes open and hugged her knees to her chest as she lay on her side—slowly wading through the mental hellscape of the full-body panic response like a panicked drowning victim swimming toward the surface.

The blast sounded like the illegal M-80s the neighbor kids would fire off on the Fourth of July when she was a kid. She hated them then, too. She clutched the binder to her chest.

A bold chyron flashed on the TV screen in bright white letters on a red background: BREAKING NEWS: Congressman Shot During Apparent Burglary.

Leeza watched from the safety of the floor, still curled in a ball on her side. In the newsroom, a Black woman with blond hair reported the story before cutting to on-scene footage of police cars and flashing red lights. An ambulance was parked in front of an affluent home, with neighbors in pajamas looking on. EMTs wheeled a stretcher out of the house, carrying the body of a man wearing blood-soaked pajamas. A paramedic held an IV bag above his head while an oxygen mask covered the man's face. A field reporter spoke to the camera before cutting back to the newsroom.

Leeza crawled to the door, turned the new deadbolt, then pulled it toward her and looked outside. She quickly retreated back, closed the door, and turned the deadbolt, locking herself in with a click. She didn't attempt to process the breaking news unfolding across the room. Instead, she pulled herself up and slid down the hallway to the waiting medicine cabinet, where a miniature Jack, a couple of Ativan, and a hydrocodone welcomed her. She slid into bed and slipped into unconsciousness.

Ten-year-old Leeza was warming up with Czerny's Piano Exercises Op. 849 in the living room in Beaufort as her teacher and her mama sat at the kitchen table. The beams of light from the kitchen window were filled with omnipresent dust, lingering in the air like that stuff floating in the lake when you opened your eyes underwater.

"She's going to outgrow me soon," said Mr. Brathwaite.

"Need to hold onto you as long as we can," said Catherine. "Next level means more money."

"I'll do my best, but she sure is special, Miss Catherine. There's no stoppin' that girl. She's goin' to the top, I can tell you that."

Catherine's face beamed with pride as she stared at her little girl at the piano.

"That baby girl is gonna save both of us. I don't know what I did to deserve her."

Mr. Brathwaite leaned in. "She has a surprise for you. She wrote an original piece that she wants to play for you. Shhh."

Catherine smiled. "You're right, no stoppin' us now."

29

"Step-Ball-Change the Fuck Back!"

A mist had developed on the way home, covering the helmet's shield with a thin opacity, like steam on a glass shower door, or a medicine cabinet before you wipe it and see your horrifying reflection.

Leeza parked the bike, walked toward the mailboxes, and noticed a small hole in the leaning aluminum structure. She rubbed her fingertip slowly across the damaged metal, thinking, *The gunshot from last night?* Something caught her eye at the edge of her vision. She looked up and saw her apartment door wide open, the wood around the handle splintered from having been kicked in.

It was far worse this time. Furniture was thrown around the room, and there were fist-sized holes in the drywall. *What the fuck?!* Her mind raced. *Assholes!*

Leeza ran to the unit where the two lanky boys had been smoking pot and staring at her and the cop. She banged on the door. "Hello! Hello!" she yelled. No answer.

She ran to the office. '**Closed for lunch**.' "Hello!" she yelled through the locked door. "Hello!" She pounded with both fists. "There is some ghetto bullshit going on here!"

Leeza stormed to her truck, glaring at the apartment door as she went. She started the truck with her foot hard on the gas. She spun it around, throwing gravel into the air as she backed up to the apartment door. *Not today, motherfuckers!* She imagined staying at a downtown hotel with security, private parking, and actual cops.

She took the metal case with the handgun to the truck, locked it in the glove compartment, and then returned inside. She went straight to the dresser, pulled everything out, and stuffed her suitcase full. She dumped the contents of the medicine cabinet into grocery bags. She carried the suitcase outside, dropped it into the bed of the truck, and threw the grocery bags into the back seat. She left the kitchen for last.

After a final peek into the bedroom and bathroom, she headed up the hall—and stopped dead. *What the hell?* She walked toward the kitchen, staring intently at the door of the old, white fridge. Photos were taped all over the front of the old appliance—snapshots of familiar things: her family, her belongings, and her life. Prints of old photos. Prints of new photos. She saw her hand move in slow motion toward the images in front of her; they hung on the refrigerator door like criminals hanging from a tree. There were prints of selfies she and Sammie had taken in bed together, a photo of Leeza and Artie in the shower, and one of Artie posing in black-and-white Dolce & Gabbana briefs.

Sammie.

There were photos of Artie sitting on a park bench as the kids played, and another of the kids coming out of school. She looked at the selfie of her and Sammie in bed. *Why?* She touched a photo of Artie with red crosshairs drawn over his face. Her knuckles turned white as she clenched her fist, the confusion evaporating and giving way to a cold anger born in the deepest parts of her soul.

Rung ten is rage. On rung ten, you are not able to rationalize what is happening, and you have lost control of de-escalation. But you can still see the tenth rung, all lit up; it's pulsating with bright, fiery flames. You know what you have to do. You can never let yourself stay above the first rung for long; you are always de-escalating in your mind to get off the ladder. Always aware of the ladder.

She grabbed the helmet and motorcycle keys; the truck with her suitcase, meds, and gun would have to wait.

Leeza shoved down the bike stand in front of Sammie's apartment building and ran up the steps. Taped to the front door was a pink piece of paper with the words:

NOTICE OF EVICTION

"Sammie!" Leeza yelled, banging on the door. "Sammie!" She pressed her ear against the door. "SAMMIE!" The instant Saffron cracked it open, Leeza forced her way in. Horizon was crouched on the sofa, playing a video game; the sound of loud screeching cars filled the room.

"Where is she?" she said through clenched teeth.

"Where is who, Duckie?"

"SAMMIE!"

"Calm yourself, lassie," Saffron said, clearing the remains of a McDonald's Happy Meal next to Horizon. The Pokémon cards and stickers were safely guarded between his knees.

Leeza followed Saffron into the galley kitchen, glancing over her shoulder for a split second to make sure Horizon was out of their line of sight. As Saffron dropped the red cardboard into the sink, Leeza grabbed her arm, spun her around, and pinned her against the counter with a knee between her legs and a forearm pressing across her neck.

"Tell me. Where. She. Is. Now." Leeza's voice was raw, her eyes demonic.

"What the hell, bitch?" Saffron snapped, dropping the phony accent. She yanked up her dress and produced a Glock semiautomatic from a holster around a pannus of superfluous white flesh. She leveled the gun at Leeza's head. "Step-ball-change the fuck back."

Leeza could feel the cold, hard metal between her eyes. She felt the nauseating metallic click as the safety released, vibrating through her skull.

"We're good. It's all good," said Leeza, arms raised.

Another law enforcement-issued firearm, what the hell?

"You've gone balls up, mate," Saffron said, accent restored. "Coulda got yourself wiped, ya know?" She pointed the weapon at Leeza's face. "So there's no confusion, I'll say it once, but I'll say it very clear—I see you again, and I'll maim ya. Nice and per-manent-like." Saffron leaned in, inches from her face. "Questions, Duckie?"

"Nope." Leeza crept backward toward the door as Saffron inched along with her.

"Yes!" cried Horizon, as his opponent's car crashed into some-thing awesome and disappeared into animated plumes of smoke and fire.

"Get some help, you psychotic bitch," Leeza seethed.

"What's that, sweetie?"

L eeza canvassed Charleston, searching for Sammie, cutting through afternoon traffic and past crowds of people. She passed a church where homeless outlines hunkered in sleeping bags on the front steps, and the police station where cops huddled in pairs. Her eyes darted and strained to catch a glimpse.

At The Nomad Club, she questioned a bartender who shook his head. She went to the back of the club and swept the women's restroom, then peered out to the patio before heading back to her bike. She passed the playground and the Pineapple Fountain and the tent city under the Ravenel Bridge. She pulled up to the house and parked in the driveway. She peeked through the windows and looked through the French doors on the back porch, checking and rechecking the locks. She looked into the garage and saw the Colonel stretched out on the cold cement floor in his own insu-lated world.

Back in midtown, the sudden blare of a car horn was followed by screams as Leeza ran a red light, barely missing an oncoming car. She laid the motorcycle down, crashing onto its side, and slid into the intersection. A second car slammed on its brakes, stopping just in front of her as she lay in the street.

"Jesus Christ!" yelled the old man who almost hit her.

Leeza was disoriented. Voices surrounded her.

"Call 911!"

"Help him up!"

"You okay?!"

"Don't move him!"

Her leg was on fire as blood soaked through her shredded pants. She gritted her teeth and jammed her heel into the asphalt. *Tibia's intact,* she reassured herself. She forced herself up and limped to the side of the road as a crowd gathered. She saw the trail of blood against the black street as she started the bike and raced away from the scene of yet another spectacle.

30

She Knows What You Did

The Phosphate Palms Motor Lodge, just two blocks from I-26 on the edge of town, was the perfect headquarters for dealers and hookers. Sammie knew the place well; she'd moved plenty of product there and even crashed there back in the day. It was the kind of place that would scare "lily-whites" to death, but she felt right at home. She paid in cash, slipped the dentally challenged receptionist an additional fifty, and checked in as Carmine Lupertazzi. For the next forty-eight hours, she'd retreat into a safe cocoon—a comfortable cushion between herself and earthly consciousness. Here, the chaos couldn't touch her.

She knew that the reason people overdosed on drugs was because they didn't know what they were doing, or became careless, or because they disregarded the fact that they might annihilate themselves. But she didn't have those problems; she was a pro. She knew how to use drugs as a tool, and she would be just fine, thank you very much. On the rare occasions she did use, it was for specific reasons: recentering, recharging, reorganizing, and reconnecting. Drugs were an instrument—used to create a brief diversion—not a coward's way out. *It's nobody's fuckin' business anyways.*

Dante's return had thrown a wrench in her plans. She'd spent years mapping out the perfect strategy and the perfect escape: build a thriving drug business, earn Dante's trust, get Dante thrown in prison, take over Dante's turf, open an offshore account, get rich, flee the country, and never look back. But now everything was screwed, and she wasn't handling it well.

On top of everything else, she found herself raging against Leeza and Artie. She couldn't stand feeling used. *"Better to be the user than the used,"* Dante had once told her. And she *really* couldn't stand feeling disposable. Daddy Dick made her feel disposable. Leeza and Artie made her feel disposable. But Dante wouldn't get away with it—not happening.

Calling the office and talking to Leeza's nurse should have been enough to send the message that she wasn't going to be fucked with. But after the eviction, she lost her mind—and she lost control, trashing Leeza's apartment not once, but twice. And there was the visit to Daddy Dick's house. *Jesus*. They wouldn't be able to pin that one on her—she was too smart for that. But for now, she needed to lie low before she got herself killed—or worse, arrested. It was the perfect time for a reboot. Just a little weed, some beer, and a little heroin. Never bring more heroin to the party than you need. Once your brain starts begging for another hit, it's too late for reasoning. You'll either enjoy the ride or kill yourself trying.

Time for the controlled descent. She popped open a can of Juicy Pale Ale from Holy City Brewing. *Nectar of the gods*. She lit a joint and filled her lungs with the benevolent cloud that would soon buffer her displeasure. She studied the smoke as it dissipated from her chest, watching as it saturated the musty air in the dank motel room.

She sat on the floor, laid the Glock next to her, and backed herself into the corner, welcoming the subtle wave of calm from the beer and the joint. She preferred to smoke heroin rather than shoot it. Soon, the trifecta would be complete.

Her peripheral vision began to dull as she hyper-focused on the moody texture of the far wall, noticing details on it she'd never seen before. *Is that blood?* The splatters had been scrubbed with Fabuloso or vinegar. She could vividly imagine the struggle that put them there but decided not to.

She remembered Daddy Dick telling her she was self-destructive. *He's a clueless idiot*. She was always in control in every situation, and she knew it. She knew how shit would end before it even started. She would be the last one standing in a bar fight, or a turf war, or a strategic decompression with heroin and weed, or pills and tequila. *Bring it on.*

Soon, she would succumb to the call of the Sirens—the half-bird sisters of Greek mythology. She loved reading those stories in middle school and had fallen asleep countless nights with a copy of The Odyssey on her chest. In her mind, she could see them clearly. There she was, at the Phosphate Palms, falling victim to their alluring song. In this case, the allure promised to dull her anguish.

As she thought about her master plan crumbling, her brain slogged through the stages of grief—from denial to acceptance—and back around again. The Sirens' song came in the form of a deliberate blend of weed and heroin and another can of Juicy Pale. The faded linoleum floor was cold at first, then it wasn't. In other words, she was comfortably numb—and beautifully blind.

Sammie stared blankly across the room with one hand on the Glock, her eyes in and out of focus. The orange and beige bedspread perfectly complemented the sixties macramé owl and brown paneling. *How can the cleaning people not notice that the lampshades are crooked? Do they even have cleaning people?*

The stage was set. The plan was in motion. Her body and mind were floating. The next twenty-four hours were hers to decompress and forget. The following twenty-four were hers to recover and remember—and to plan her next steps.

Unfortunately, the chemicals only briefly held their ground after the initial calming tide, failing to sedate her as her mind refused to cooperate. She couldn't relax and let the heroin, beer, and weed work their magic; instead, she was obsessed with Dante. The sight of him at the club was seared into her mind, and she could still see his face as if he were hovering over her. The more she thought about him, the more livid she became. Instead of calming her, the drugs peeled away every layer of restraint and reason, fueling her need for revenge.

It was that livid state of mind that made her pick up her phone and stare at her list of contacts—and make the call. *Don't do it.* The receptionist picked up. *Hang up the fuckin' phone.*

"*Neurosurgery Associates. How may I direct your call?*"

"Leeza," she said. The business name on the screen seemed to breathe, its letters expanding and contracting. *Holy shit.*

"*Leeza Allen-Byron's office,*" said Tana.

"Is the doctor with a patient?"

"*Excuse me?*"

Sammie rambled as she stared at the cell phone in front of her. She told Tana about the yellow binder, the formula, the night in the garage, and the fact that Artie caught them and blamed her. She told her that she had been Leeza and her husband's plaything back in the day when they still had use for her.

"*Where are you?*" Leeza demanded.

"Well, well, well, if it ain't doctor wannabe. Didn't know you finally joined the conversation. How did you manage to take time out of your busy day for little 'ol me?"

"*You need to get yourself together, Sammie. Listen to me—*"

"I think you need to worry about your own shit, not mine."

"*Tell me where you are!*"

"What's the matter, baby? Afraid your coworkers are gonna find out about your sexcapades and your drug addiction? Your kinky side?" Sammie scoffed. "You're a failure, and you know it. Why don't you move to Amsterdam? They've got all the drugs and pussy you can handle." She slid down the wall and lay on her back, resting the Glock on her belly. "You let him believe I was the reason you passed out in the garage."

Silence.

"WHY?!" Sammie screamed.

"*I swear to God, I told him you had nothing to do with it. I've told you that.*"

"All of a sudden, the dick tells me to disappear. You fuckin' believe that? Where exactly am I supposed to go, huh?" The words hung in the air until Sammie exploded: "WHERE AM I SUP-POSED TO GO?!"

Moments passed. Sammie scoffed, unsurprised by the silence.

"Cat got your tongue, baby?"

"With me," said Leeza.

A deep laugh erupted from within Sammie—then stopped. "I had everything figured out! It was *all* planned. Couple more years and I could get out of this godforsaken shithole. I even got Dante disappeared, then he had to show back up again, but he's gonna get got!" She flicked the joint across the room. "And Artie," she scoffed. "Told me he could make me evaporate with a phone call. Who talks like that anyways? Evaporate? Really? Did you know at his daddy's house there's a fake kid peein' in the pool? Is that what rich people spend their money on?"

The other end of the conversation was dead quiet.

"He ruined your life. He's ruining *my* life. Fuckin' idiot!" Sammie's rage was palpable; saliva sprayed from her mouth as she growled. "But Prince Arthur's gonna find out who makes the rules."

"Don't even think about it," Leeza said firmly.

Sammie ended the call and sat up, then slid back into the corner. She slowly traced the gun down the side of her face, then turned the barrel upward beneath her chin. She lingered there for a long moment without breathing, then, slowly, slid the gun down the front of her body, rested it on her lap, and allowed herself to exhale. She could hear distant sirens and the muffled sounds of arguing and slamming doors. But Carmine Lupertazzi was safe. And invisible.

T he parking lot of the Phosphate Palms Motor Lodge showed years of neglect, with broken asphalt and grass growing through cracks that resembled the atherosclerotic vessels on Freddy Krueger's face. A 2005 Cadillac DeVille DTS sedan in light cashmere idled alone in the far corner of the lot. "Let's Get It On" by Marvin Gaye crooned from the aftermarket speakers as occasional clouds of smoke escaped through a rolled-down window. Dante kept the old car in pristine condition and had pushed the dual-cam NorthStar V8 with 320 horses to its limit on several occasions. He enjoyed the herbal cigarettes with the gold-wrapped filter, which proved nearly impossible to get his hands on when he was locked up. Dante relished his freedom. He had been randomly tailing Sammie since he saw her at the club with Tana and Leeza, but he didn't know she was using, or that she was desperate, or that they were stalking each other.

L eeza pressed the phone to her chest, her heart racing.

"Oh no, she did not!" Tana exclaimed. "That bitch just said she's the one that got Dante locked up."

"She's been to Miranda's house," said Leeza. "Jesus Christ."

"This ain't good," Tana agreed. "We gotta find that bitch."

"There are a few places I can look for her."

Tana leaned over the desk and locked eyes with Leeza. "I know you heard the same thing I just heard," she said. "That tweaker just threatened your family *and* Dante, and you're just gonna go 'look for her?'" Leeza was still. "You need to remember your time in the Army, baby, 'cause you about to find yourself a war zone."

"I know her," said Leeza.

"And I know junkies!"

Leeza called Artie's cell as Tana watched. Voicemail.

"I need you to call me, okay? Or just have one of the kids call if you're busy; just need to hear from somebody." She redialed. Voicemail again. "Look, I need you to take the kids to your mama's house. I need you to get out of the house, okay?" She took a breath. *Calm and firm, calm and firm.* "She knows what you did, Artie. You or Miranda, whatever, it doesn't matter now. You really need to go. She knows what you did." Leeza disconnected.

"And she knows where his mama lives," Tana added.

Leeza took off her lab coat and was heading to the door when Dr. Randall appeared. He motioned for Tana to leave with a tilt of his head, waited for her to pass, and then closed the door.

"Got a second?"

"Actually, Stephen, I don't. I was just leaving; I have to—"

"It'll wait," he said, plopping down in the chair next to Maya Angelou and crossing his legs. "Can I see your prescription pad?"

"My prescription pad?"

"Yeah, where is it?"

"It's in my drawer. Why?" She checked the drawer. "It's always right here," she said, confused that it wasn't there. She checked the pockets of her lab coat.

Stephen pulled out a script and handed it to her. "Got a call from the pharmacist."

Leeza read the prescription. "That's not my signature."

"But it's your script. And I certainly hope it's not your signature," Stephen chuckled. "You could lose your license." He got up to leave. "Who the hell is Rosario Byron?" Leeza shrugged.

Stephen paused in the doorway. "Why are you limping?"

"It's nothing," said Leeza.

"Be more careful, huh?"

Leeza called Artie. Voicemail.

"Hey, I'm headed over to the house now. Call me when you get this." She ended the call and redialed. *Dammit!* She waited for the message. "I'm getting a little weirded out here. I need to hear from you guys, alright?"

Leeza pulled up to the house and ran to the front door. Her key didn't work. *Seriously?* She banged on the door and rang the doorbell. She went to the side of the garage and peered through the window. The garage was empty except for the napping Colonel. She went back to the truck and checked her phone. Nothing.

As Leeza backed out, Artie and the kids turned onto the street from the opposite direction.

"Is that Leesie's truck?" cried Grant.

"Where?" asked Charlotte.

"No," said Artie.

"Daddy?"

"What, Grant?"

"How do you know that lady?"

"Ummm... The one on the roof?"

"No!"

"The one on the cover of *Vogue*?"

"No!"

"The one on Mars?"

"No!"

"The one on the life raft with the shark chasing her?"

"Mother of God!" cried Charlotte.

"The one at Leesie's apartment," Grant said.

Yeah, he knew which one. "She went to our college a hundred years ago."

Grant thought about that for a second. "I think she was drunk."

The garage door opened as the SUV pulled into the driveway. "Inspector Frisky!" yelled Grant as the garage door closed behind them.

31

Inspector Frisky and the 9mm Glock

A cab crept up the street and stopped in front of Leeza and Artie's house. Sammie handed the driver cash and stepped into the humid night, her head twitching as she rubbed her nose and sniffed. Turning her baseball cap backward, she glided across the lawn and slid down the side of the house to the back porch.

She peered through the window into the dimly lit downstairs. She fought the thick haze inside her head as she picked the lock on the French doors and eased her way inside. A growl, followed by the sound of toenails tapping toward her on the hardwood floors caught her attention. She let Inspector Frisky sniff her, then pulled a treat from her pocket and held it in front of him. She patted his head as he chewed on the beef-flavored *Munchy Stick* dog chew with three Ativan tablets embedded in the shaft.

Struggling to focus, she wiped her nose on her sleeve and looked up from the bottom of the stairs. Reassuring herself the gun on her right hip was tight, she started up.

As she neared the top, she heard the shower running in Leeza and Artie's bedroom. Sliding down the wall toward the kids' bedrooms, she rested her palm firmly on the handle of the gun. She creaked open Grant's door, then walked over to his bed. His eyes were closed, the blanket pulled up to his chin. A rainbow-colored nightlight illuminated the *Vogue* magazine and the fedora on the nightstand. She lingered over him as he slept, staring at his perfect skin, smooth as black marble. There was a subtle twitch of his eyelids as he watched the dream inside his head.

Sammie went back to the hallway. The next bedroom door was ajar. She peered through the crack, then eased it open. Moonlight illuminated Charlotte's outline under her pink-and-white striped comforter. Her glasses lay on top of *The Nutcracker*. As Sammie crossed the room through the moonlight, her body cast a black shadow over Charlotte. Random thoughts flipped through her mind like a slideshow. She seized on the thought she was looking for: *I was never the enemy*. It brought a wave of anger as she recalled the events that got her here: Leeza had called her; Leeza had asked for help—illegal help; Artie caught her helping Leeza and blamed her for the overdose; he ran home and told his mommy; then her apartment was raided—twice! Dante got out and was probably putting two and two together by now. She felt her teeth grinding as she sifted through the recent memories. She suddenly realized she had removed the gun from her hip without noticing. Her eyes narrowed as she stared at the back of Charlotte's head. Her grip tightened on the Glock, which was rising slowly in front of her, of its own accord. Her mind felt strangely detached.

A sudden nudge at the back of Sammie's leg jolted her back to reality. She spun around to see the Corgi staring up at her with exposed front teeth, a throaty growl, and intense stare. Inspector Frisky was looking for answers, and his patience was wearing thin.

Shouldn't you be taking a fuckin' nap?

Voices came from the master bedroom. Sammie turned her back to the dog and slid out of Charlotte's room, pulling the door closed and securing him inside. She replaced the Glock on her hip and tiptoed toward the voices.

She peered inside the room. The voices were coming from the shower. A dress was draped over a chair in the corner. Artie's Tommy Hilfiger shorts and Equipo Brazilian low-rise briefs in black, with the bull logo, were in a pile on top of the dress. *Those look familiar.*

She grabbed Artie's cell phone from the nightstand. The passcode—still birthdays. *Pathetic.* There were missed calls and texts

from Leeza and an outgoing call to 'R Jordan.' Her teeth ground
together again. She looked at the ceiling, then stuck out her tongue
and slowly licked the entire screen before putting it back on the
nightstand. She pulled out her own phone and took a picture of
the woman's clothes and Artie's underwear. She noticed panties
on the floor next to the chair—the ones Artie bought at Nordstrom Rack. She wadded them into a tight ball, held them to her
face for a deep breath, and shoved them in her pocket.

She opened the nightstand and pulled out a taser. Leeza had
tried to convince Artie to keep a firearm in the bedroom, but he
wouldn't hear of it—the taser was the compromise. As she shoved
the taser far under the mattress, the shower turned off.

"DADDY!" Grant screamed. Sammie spun around to see him
standing between her and the doorway. "DADDY!" he squealed
louder. A ferocious bark erupted from behind Grant as Inspector
Frisky lunged toward Sammie, sinking his teeth into her calf, his
head shaking viciously in a blur of fur and rage. She grabbed the
gun and slammed the butt of the 9mm Glock into the side of the
dog's head. Inspector Frisky was unfazed. It wasn't enough. She
gripped the gun in both hands and swung from above her head,
landing the butt on his skull with a dull thud of metal against bone.
The Corgi let out an agonizing yelp, released his grip, and cowered
away, leaving a trail of blood on the wool rug. Grant pulled the
injured dog into his arms, staring in horror at the intruder.

Artie burst in, wet and naked, just as Charlotte appeared in the
doorway in blue flannel pajamas. Charlotte watched frantically:
her naked father, her crying brother, the bleeding dog, and the
gun-wielding intruder with blood on her leg—all in her parents'
room. Artie made a dash for the nightstand's hidden taser as Charlotte ran to her room and slammed the door.

Sammie ran down the stairs as Artie frantically dug around
for the taser before realizing it was gone. Naked and desperate,
he crawled over to Grant and Inspector Frisky, searching for the
source of the blood. The thud of a body falling down the last

few stairs reverberated through the upper floor, followed by the slamming of a door.

32

Praise Be!

The decision was made. Leeza would stay at the Willow Glen apartments and let the maintenance man fix the door again. The only way to end up in the same room with Sammie was to offer herself up. It felt like luring a starving feral cat from the underbrush—chances were good it would rip her arm off, but after what Sammie did at the house, and after all the threats, there were no options left.

Leeza could be out at a moment's notice; her packed suitcase stood in the corner. She pulled the metal case from under the bed and examined the semiautomatic. She checked the chamber and inserted a full magazine. Down the hall, the TV was on but muted. No classical music played that night; the place felt aseptic, anti-cottage. She called Sammie and listened to the recording.

"Hey, look, Artie and I have been talking, and we feel like we can work this out with you. I asked him to come over tonight," she lied, hoping Sammie would believe her. She didn't know who Sammie was more furious with, but it didn't really matter. "We'll both be here. It's not too late, Sammie. Try to make it, alright?" She disconnected. *You psychotic bitch.* She turned up the ringtone, even though it scared the hell out of her every time it rang.

Sammie was an expert at not being found, and now she was pissed off and unpredictable, so Leeza had to think fast. The phone vibrated and chirped with a text, startling her as usual. "CHRIST!"

There was a thumbs-up emoji from Sammie. Leeza stared at the text. *That was quick. We're gonna end this.* Now that she had

Sammie's attention, a barrage of emotions churned in her stomach—uncertainty, relief, dread—like heartburn on top of nausea
on top of a yeast infection. She separated the blinds and peered
into the darkness. *I got you.* A sudden beeping pierced the silence,
causing her to jump and lose her grip on the gun. "FUCK!" She
glared at the coffee pot, then snatched the gun off the floor, set it on
the counter, and poured a cup. Every time she poured coffee, she
remembered the drag queen at The Nomad who said, "*I like my
coffee like I like my women; nowhere near my dick.*" It was funnier
the first time.

She sat facing the door with the gun in one hand and the coffee
cup in the other. *None of this had to happen. It should have been
easy. If Artie hadn't gotten into it with his mother and come home
early without texting or calling... That was Miranda's fault. That
woman can stir up shit in her sleep.*

Time ticked by. Her eyes grew heavier and the caffeine wasn't
helping. *Where the hell are you?* She had no idea how it was gonna
go down with Sammie, but several scenarios swirled in her head.
What if she actually showed up? She wasn't just going to admit
that this was all an unfortunate misunderstanding and offer to
help with the formula—not after being evicted. Leeza thought
about the recent progress with the research and how encouraged
she'd been lately. Her mind wandered as she struggled against the
creeping waves of fatigue.

She had lost track of time when she heard a car door shut
somewhere in the parking lot. She set the empty coffee cup on
the floor and peered out the window. A cab headed out of the
lot, pulling onto Ward Avenue. She stared at the door and waited.
Silence. No footsteps, no voices, no neighbor's door. She reached
for the doorknob and wondered if the damaged frame would ever
be repainted.

Another text startled her—even when she was looking directly
at the phone, it always scared her.

Full moon

Leeza squeezed the grip of the gun.

I'm inside

Anticipation wrestled with dread as she waited. *Don't jump when she knocks on the door. Don't jump when she knocks on the door.* Time seemed to stop, no sound, no motion, just growing impatience. She knew she was going to jump.

Fifteen minutes.
She chickened out. She's probably halfway down the train tracks by now.
She parted the blinds and squinted into the darkness. Lampposts cast pools of light that pierced the dark parking lot like alien crop circles, but they were the only things out there. Even the lanky wastoids had called it a night. She glanced at the binder and the stack of prints she had pulled off the fridge. She looked at the door with its new set of locks and the splintered wood where Sammie had kicked it in. *That looks like some New York back-alley rat-infested hostel.* She slid the handgun into the belly holster and pulled her shirt down over it.

Her hand lingered against the gun as she scanned the sparse apartment. *No laughter, no piano practice, no smell of dinner cooking, no bickering twins, no farting dog.* Loneliness and loss tugged at her heart. *What the hell am I doing?* She took a long, deep breath. Her fingers were on the gun, but her gaze fell on the yellow binder, and lingered there.

She pulled the gun from its holster, emptied the full magazine, and dropped the rounds onto the kitchen table. She re-holstered the unloaded weapon and pulled her shirt down. *I can't go to prison because of you.*

She opened the door, peered out, and then stepped outside. She pulled the door shut until she heard the click.

Fifty yards to her right was Ward Avenue. A narrow line of trees separated the road from the train tracks. Sammie could have walked the tracks all the way from Willow Glen back to town. Leeza imagined Sammie as an actual werewolf or vampire, lurking through the woods at night without a trace of fear. Sammie had told her how she liked to walk the tracks when the moon was full to clear her head. *That skinny Latina bitch is more dangerous than anything crossing her path in the middle of the night.*

She took a few steps onto the worn blacktop and looked in both directions. It was unusually quiet at Willow Glen. She felt a churning ache in her stomach. *Where is everybody? Was it 'buy-one-get-three' pizza night at the bowling alley?* She scanned the trees lining Ward Avenue. *Maybe she's smoking a cigarette.* She remembered bivouacking in the Army—on a clear night, you could see the glow of a cigarette from a thousand yards away, or was it five hundred? *She's got to be in the woods.* Leeza moved toward the end of the building where the lampposts didn't reach. She stood at the corner and stared at the tree line, waiting for her eyes to adjust. Nothing. *She wants to play games.*

Around the corner, the side of the building was pitch black. The weeds were overgrown and probably invited snakes and other critters. The grass and weeds would be wet with dew by now. She would take a quick peek, then head back to the apartment and wait outside for a bit longer.

She leaned around the corner, looked to her right, and met the shadow of a face inches from hers. Her mouth flew open, but the terrified scream stayed trapped in her lungs. Every muscle in her neck froze as she fumbled for the gun. Sammie yanked her by the jacket, slammed her against the building, then drove her to the ground, knocking the breath out of her. Leeza felt herself dragged by the ankles into the black, wet weeds at the side of the building.

Pain crushed the back of her head as she was pulled across the rocky ground.

The retracting slide of a semiautomatic handgun clicked and echoed through Leeza's soul. Three long seconds passed before she felt the cold metal resting between her eyes. She struggled to catch her breath, but she could feel Sammie's. She sensed her essence and smelled her hair—that familiar scent.

The soldier and Leeza were holding hands. "How ya been, Captain? It's been a little while."

Leeza was dazed, but the throbbing pain on the back of her head was very real.

The soldier's voice echoed in her mind: *"How ya been, Captain?"*

She struggled to draw air into her lungs with Sammie's knee pressing down on her chest. The pressure of the metal against her forehead had her pinned to the damp gravel. *Am I dreaming?*

"It's been a little while."

She felt Sammie's mouth against her ear and her warm breath on the side of her face.

"I don't like being played," Sammie said. "I don't like being lied to. I don't like being dumped." She jammed the gun harder into Leeza's forehead. "I am not disposable!"

Leeza thought she heard the faint sound of car tires. *Somebody's coming.*

"I can't leave, and I can't stay," Sammie seethed. "Y'all fuckin' destroyed me!"

Leeza was disoriented. The nest of tall wet grass made her think of a fresh grave. *Is this where they'll find me?*

The tires crept nearer. There was another sound—also distant, but familiar. *Music.* "Please," Leeza pleaded.

Headlights crept toward the corner of the building. The tall weeds looked like witch's fingers, twisting and conniving in the breeze. *Let's Get It On* wafted in the distance, but the sound was getting close. Leeza squinted as the car approached the corner; she could tell the headlights were getting closer. Soon, the car would be in sight. It would come into view, and it would pull her inside and sweep her away. A red Jaguar SUV and a guy named Artie? Blond hair and a tweed newsboy cap and driving gloves? "*Did you miss me?*" he would say. "*Always,*" she would answer, just like every time he asked that question. But that was then, and this was now, in the wet weeds, with a gun to her head. She was content with these being her final thoughts. She wouldn't linger like the soldier on the cot with half his head blown off. No one would have to cut off her airway to put her out of her misery. A bullet to the head is instant.

"*How ya been, Captain?*"

As Marvin Gaye serenaded the parking lot, the pressure of the cold metal Glock continued against her forehead, causing the lump on the back of her head to throb. She was pinned, barely breathing, with Sammie's knee on her chest. Just before the lights reached the corner, she felt the metallic click of the gun. Her eyes blinked, even though they were closed. Sammie had released the slide, and the pressure on her forehead was gone. She heard footsteps running into the pitch-black night behind the building, toward the train tracks and away from Marvin's voice. The car reached the corner, but it didn't turn toward her and the tall grass. It kept going—toward Ward Avenue. "*I'm right here!*" she wanted to scream but couldn't.

That was her last memory until the first rays of morning sun filtered through her eyelids. Struggling to claw her way out of what felt like a coma, she lay hidden in the tall grass next to the apartment building. She was alone. She was alive.

S ammie ran through the narrow line of trees and climbed up to the train tracks. The light of the full moon made it easier to see the railroad ties, but it also made it easier to be seen. At this time of night, the only folks she would cross would be tweakers, or a clan of homeless, or possibly a couple of dudes doing the nasty in the woods. But the night was quiet as she made her way to the cutoff at the Ivey Creek Apartments, a route that would snake her toward the Phosphate Palms. She remembered spending entire nights on the tracks after she ran away from Daddy Dick's house. She relished the familiar smell of creosote beneath her feet.

Sammie was a force in her own right, having learned from the best—and the worst. Dante had shared countless words of wisdom as she was learning the ropes: "The only people you apologize to are the ones you intend to kill. Everyone else gets an explanation." Sammie had done some ruthless things in her lifetime—some for the fun of it, others not so much.

She had decided that she needed to get out of Charleston after all. There was the eviction, the heat from the cops, the trouble with Artie, and the dick. And, of course, her fucked-up plan to hibernate for two days at the Phosphate Palms.

Calling Leeza's office was dumb but calling Leeza's office while on heroin was next-level crazy. The more she tried to decompress, the more she thought about Dante and what he was planning. And she was pissed that Leeza and Artie were ganging up on her. Then came the plan to scare Artie at the house, but of course, the damn kids had to wake up. *What's up with that short little fuckin' dog?* Back to Dante. *Fuckin' Dante!* If he'd figured it out, he wouldn't stop until she was gone, and Dante didn't leave a mess. And, of course, there was tonight—Leeza and her stupid games. *Artie will be here too, let's work this out. Do I look that ignorant?* She hadn't intended to hurt her at the apartments; she just wanted to warn her to call off the Byrons. She waited for Leeza to come out, but then the damn car was getting too close, and they would see her as they came around the corner. So, she bolted.

Leeza lay on the bed with tears gushing out. The indentation from the gun barrel was throbbing, and the knot on the back of her head was growing. "I can't do this," she whispered. "I can't do this. I can't do this." She cradled the bottle of Jack Daniel's in her arms. The little wooden box with the bent spoon and white powder lay open on the nightstand. As she lost consciousness, the sound of *Barber's Adagio* followed her into her dreams.

In the medic tent, the only sound was haunting classical music. All seemed calm to the ears, but the chaos continued to unfold around them as the soldier and Leeza held hands. The top of his head and one eye were covered with blood-soaked bandages. He rubbed her hand in his as violins and cellos and oboes played softly.

"Captain, how ya been? It's been a little while. You're lookin' good, ma'am."

Leeza choked back tears as she stared at him.

"How's Rachael?" she asked.

"She's great. Today would have been our ten-year anniversary. She met a great guy. They have a son, Owen, after her grandfather. How are Charlotte and Grant?"

"Getting big."

"Beautiful, too. Hey, what was that saying your mom always said to you?"

"Try to be a rainbow in someone's cloud."

"Oh yeah, Maya Angelou. I remember now. It's in that book you have in your office. Your mama's so proud of you."

Leeza struggled to keep her emotions in check.

"You seem out of sorts, ma'am."

"Just life."

"Talk about your future again," said the soldier. Leeza tried to smile as tears soaked her cheeks. "Oh, you know, just spoiling the crap out of my grandkids someday."

"Can't wait to see that." Leeza nodded and let go of his hand.

"Captain... Don't be a stranger."

Leeza tried to avoid looking at the other cots with the bodies of young men, but she could see the blood-drenched sheets from the corner of her eye—and something was moving. She slowly turned toward them.

"Oh yeah, those are my buddies," said the soldier. "The ones you also killed."

"They were dead," she whispered.

"They'd like to talk to you," said the soldier.

"They were dead."

"They'd like to talk to you."

"They were dead."

"Kill the fucking enemy."

"They were dead."

"You will breathe fire."

"They were dead!"

"Your actions will be justified."

"THEY WERE DEAD!"

Sammie walked northbound on the shoulder of Stall Road toward Ashley Phosphate. It was still dark, and she thought about going back to the tracks until sunup, but she was only five minutes from the Phosphate Palms and decided to keep going. She could hear a car approaching from behind. She moved over, giving it room to pass, but it crawled much slower than the twenty-five miles per hour limit, and as it pulled up beside her, it came to a stop. She watched as the driver's window lowered and a Glock 9mm 19X leveled at her throat. The back door of the cashmere Cadillac DeVille opened... and waited. She wouldn't get a round off before they dropped her. She looked into the back seat. Whoever had opened the door had moved to the far side. She saw him in the shadows. Dante.

Variations of how things could go down raced through her mind. If she ran, they would shoot her in the back, and her body would be hidden in the brush on the side of Stall Road. If she got in the car and he knew what she did, she would end up in a pit somewhere thirty miles from the nearest Circle K. If she got in the car and he didn't know, the worst he could do would be to scare the hell out of her and remind her of her place. She stepped toward the car. The man with the gun held out his other hand, palm up. She pulled the Glock from its holster and handed it over before sliding into the back seat.

"You're out late," Dante said as the car continued north toward Ashley Phosphate Road.

"New clients."

The car smelled of herbal cigarettes, and the cream faux-leather seats were freakishly slippery. She noticed the driver's Hawaiian shirt as he reached to turn up the music. *You need a driver now?* Marvin Gaye crooned from the aftermarket sound system. *You've been following me. No surprise there.*

Sammie was always acutely aware of her surroundings. She memorized street signs and landmarks. When she took a cab, she would pretend to be blind; she knew which street they were on by how long it took between turns, the direction of the turns, and how the surface of the street felt. She stared out the window during the silence; they were obviously in no hurry. They passed the motor lodge as the driver turned onto Ashley Phosphate, then merged onto I-26 East just past the Cracker Barrel. She felt herself slide across the seats with every turn.

"Do we have someplace to be?" Sammie asked. Dante was silent. His smug poker face was infuriating.

I-26 East merged onto 526 West. They were heading toward the Westmoreland Bridge. *General William C. Westmoreland Bridge*, Sammie thought. *They couldn't name it the Tanya Tucker Bridge or somethin' easy.* If she jumped out when they were on the bridge, they wouldn't be able to turn around, and she would be able to make it back to town. The farther they drove, the harder it would be to find a way back—if she was alive enough to find her way back. Another ten minutes of silence. She heard the blinker. Exit 11B to Paul Cantrell Boulevard, then Glenn McConnell Parkway.

"Good to see you back in town," Sammie said. "I have to admit I was surprised to see you the other night."

Dante scoffed. "I could tell."

"What's your friend's name?"

"Tatiana," he said flatly as the driver turned right onto Bees Ferry Road, just past the Walmart Supercenter. Less than a mile farther, they turned right into a church parking lot.

"We're going to church?" Sammie asked.

"Never a bad idea," said Dante. The driver stopped near the back door of the large building, which looked more like a renovated movie theater than a house of worship. He unlocked the back door and entered a code into the alarm system. He waved them in and held the door. *This is next-level fucked up. A drug dealer and his chauffeur pull up to a church at five-thirty in the morning and let themselves in.* The driver locked the door behind them.

Sammie looked around the enormous room as she stood before the biggest stage she'd ever seen. Brightly colored neon tubes lined the walls. She had heard of mega churches and had even seen them on the news when the pastor got arrested or something, but she never had a reason to go inside one. A white grand piano with mirrored legs, a huge drum set, three keyboards, and a dozen guitars stood ready for some serious rock gospel. A set of bleachers for the choir completed the elaborate setup for the weekly pep rallies. *This is some Texas-sized bible-thumping shit right here.*

The driver gestured Sammie toward the stage. Confused, she glanced at Dante, who nodded—as if giving a toddler permission to have a cookie. She moved slowly to the stage's edge and looked back at the two men.

"You've been tortured in your lifetime," said Dante.

This motherfucker is gonna try to baptize me.

"The Lord tests the righteous, but His soul hates the wicked and the one who loves violence." He joined Sammie in front of the stage and placed his palm on her forehead. "From torture comes wisdom. It's inevitable. How do you choose to use your wisdom, Rosario?" The enormous room was deathly silent in the pre-dawn hours. Sammie's eyes were fixed on Dante's wrist, just above her nose. His palm was warm and felt like hand lotion, a simple touch that made her skin crawl. Dante finally stepped back and pointed at the lectern in the center of the huge stage.

"You want me to go to the preacher's desk?" Sammie asked.

"Lectern."

She could feel her heartbeat as she tried to figure out what the hell was going on. She was usually pretty good at remaining calm when all hell was breaking loose around her, but this was freaking her out. She preferred familiar surroundings, and she preferred to know where all the exits were. She climbed the four steps up to the stage and walked to the lectern. And there she stood, facing the empty, holy auditorium at five-thirty in the morning—with her nemesis and his bodyguard/fixer staring at her. *Holy shit.*

Sammie had been told as a kid that "the church" sponsored her and her siblings after they were found in the wreckage that killed their parents. It was "the church" that decided to put them with foster parents, and it was "the church" that encouraged the adoption. *Why didn't they just send us back to Mexico to live with cousins until we grew up?* She had always equated "the church" with Daddy Dick—and the abuse—and she preferred to distance herself from all of them.

Dante's voice erupted in a loud baritone, as if he were preaching in a Southern revival tent without a microphone. "The Word became flesh and made His dwelling among us. We have seen His glory, the glory of the one and only Son, who came from the Father, full of grace and truth."

I heard you could find Jesus in prison, but holy crap.

"What I say, you say back," Dante instructed.

A spotlight hit Sammie's face as a metallic click simultaneously echoed around the room. She raised the back of her hand to shield her eyes. Her heart rate ticked up a few more beats per minute.

"Now I know that you are a child of God, and that the word of the Lord from your mouth is the truth," his baritone voice resonated like thunder across the Grand Canyon. Sammie adjusted to the spotlight and looked at him. "What I say, you say back!" he yelled. "Now I know that you are a child of God."

Sammie repeated softly, "I know that you are a child of God." She let out a nervous chuckle. *I hope this is a joke, you sick fuck.*

"Louder!" Dante shouted.

"I know that you are a child of God," she said, raising her voice.

"Rosario! Look at the last row!"

Sammie looked across the cavernous house of the Lord to the last row. The spotlight created streaks in her vision, forcing her to wince.

"Now I know that you are a child of God!" Dante yelled.

"Now I know that you are a child of God!" Sammie shouted, hoping the deserted last row could hear her. What felt silly at first was quickly veering into batshit crazy territory, and she was getting worried. And scared.

"And that the word of the Lord from your mouth is the truth," Dante bellowed.

"And that the word—"

"Of the Lord from your mouth is the truth!"

"The word... of the Lord... from your mouth is the truth."

"We are from God, and whoever knows God listens to us," he yelled, channeling his best Jimmy Swaggart.

"We are from God, and whoever knows God listens to us!" Sammie echoed.

"But whoever is not from God does not listen to us!"

"But whoever is not from God does not listen to us!" Sammie shouted back.

"This is how we recognize the Spirit of truth and the spirit of falsehood!"

"This is how we recognize the Spirit of truth... and the spirit of falsehood!" Sammie's eyes glistened. *Don't you fuckin' cry*.

"You shall NOT give false testimony against your neighbor!"

"You shall not give false testimony against your neighbor!"

The words echoed off the farthest walls of the theater—converted into a house of worship—but still a theater.

Dante stood and began clapping. "I have no greater joy than to hear that my children are walking in the truth," he said, his normal volume restored. "¿Estás dispuesta a decir la verdad, Rosario? (*Are you ready to tell the truth, Rosario?*)"

Sammie's body was rigid. She couldn't feel her hands, but she could see them, white-knuckled as they gripped the lectern. The holy wood felt cold and empty, just like everything else in her life. She leaned into the frigid surface, as if to prove a point.

"Sí. (*Yes.*)" *You sick fuck*. A tear escaped. Dante had succeeded in scaring the hell out of her.

Another metallic click echoed from the back of the room as the spotlight vanished. The venue disappeared for a few seconds until Sammie's vision recovered. Dante and the driver were already walking up the aisle toward the back doors.

"So we're done?" Sammie said from the stage to an audience of silence. She rubbed her eyes and rushed behind them. Even if they didn't give her a ride, she wanted her gun back.

As they merged onto 526 toward Charleston, Sammie considered asking what the hell that was all about, but she figured she would find out eventually—she was sure he was setting something up. The driver stopped at the far side of the Phosphate Palms lot. Dante handed Sammie a small envelope. "Open Saturday, show up Saturday," he said. Hawaii 5-0 threw her gun out the window as they drove away.

L eeza woke up screaming, "THEY WERE DEAD! ALL OF THEM WERE DEAD!" She had no idea how long she had been out or what day it was as she frantically searched for her phone.

Sammie had texted her a picture of a woman's clothes draped over the chair in Artie and Leeza's bedroom.

Artie had texted:

> *Heading to mama's.*

Waves of relief and anger flooded Leeza's body. She had to wipe her eyes before she could read the next text from Artie.

> *she was here!*

> *did she think i was joking!!!!!*

> *dog at animal hospital*

> *blood everywhere!! WTF!!!*

She dropped to her knees with her face buried in her hands.

33

Pony Up, Soldier!

Physically and emotionally exhausted, Leeza slumped into the corner of her office. Leaning heavily against the wall, her body rocked numbly to Puccini's *Nessun Dorma*. The indentation on her forehead was a mottled patch of purple and rust. Clutching the yellow binder to her chest, she replayed the dreams in her mind. She could feel her thumb pressing the life out of that kid in the medic tent as if it were happening in the very moment; his last few breaths rasped beneath her thumb. They had spoken many times in her dreams—even daydreams—and he always asked her to talk about her future, but she had never seen the others before.

They'd like to talk to you... They were dead!... They'd like to talk to you... They were dead!... Your actions will be justified... They were dead!

Leeza was startled by Tana's knock. "Christ!" Her hands flew to her head as the binder hit the floor.

"I keep doing that. I'm so sorry," said Tana, putting an arm around Leeza's shoulders. "Shhh, sorry, sweetie."

"Not a good time," said Leeza.

Tana saw the indentation between Leeza's eyes. "Jesus holy H. Christ!" she cried, reaching out to touch it.

Leeza flinched. "Don't."

Tana's hand tightened on her own arm. "Sit down," she insisted. "Now."

Leeza slid into a barrel chair.

"First your leg, now *this*? And whatever *this* is, it ain't from no car accident." Leeza remained stoic. "I love you like a sister, but you are one stubborn bitch." Tana locked the door. "You weren't even gonna tell me about your leg till I saw the blood." No response. "You know who I am, where I come from, what I went through. You know every damn thing about me," she went on. "And you know if I catch the motherfucker who did this to you, I'll kill 'em with my own hands."

"I got this."

"You don't got shit!" Tana picked up the binder and dropped it next to the book of poems.

Leeza rocked herself, a look of defeat in her eyes. Her chin quivered, but she refused to cry. "It's my fault Artie left. I've done some fucked up things." She looked up at Tana. "Do I just give up? Lithium and a housecoat?"

Tana waved her arms above her head as if trying to get someone's attention. "Excuse me!" she cried. "I'm right over here! ¿Tengo que decirlo en lenguaje de señas? ¿Árabe? (*Do I have to say it in sign language? Arabic?*), I can roll an interpreter on an iPad in here, you know that! Why are you incapable of asking for help?" She shoved the other chair in front of Leeza and sat down. "Remember where we met?"

Total non sequitur, but okay. "Yes," she said in a tired whisper. "I crashed your NA meeting."

"Ten-and-a-half years ago, August the twenty-fifth. Hot as hell."

"How do you remember stuff like that?"

"Here comes this scrawny Black girl walkin' in. When you got up the nerve to talk and said you were doing research for your degree, I knew right then and there I wanted to know you."

"Psychology in nursing."

"You looked like a twelve-year-old Black girl with coke-bottle lenses. I couldn't look away," Tana said, still incredulous after all these years.

Leeza laughed. It felt good.

"And later on, when you told me about how your mama had breast cancer when you were barely in high school..." Leeza lowered her head. "You're the reason I went back to school. And you're the *only* reason I made it through that damn school. You're my best friend, Leeza."

"You always seemed so determined."

"Determined not to go backward. Determined not to end up back in the gutter. You helped me realize the one thing that changed everything: I don't need nobody but myself." She cupped Leeza's chin. "That was you."

"Look at you now."

"You go in the military to get an education, and they nearly killed you. Still tryin' looks like. And still, you're quick to help everyone else, but you put up a damn wall when you need somethin'."

"You don't understand—"

"That chick on the phone's out of her mind, and I know she's got somethin' to do with all this. Lord only knows what she's thinkin' to do." Tana leaned in. "You know who she is, and I got a damn good idea." She let that sink in. "You know I know you, Leeza," her voice lowered. "I've heard all the rumors, all the stories. Sorry, but it didn't take much to put two and two together."

You heard the stories because Sammie's a street urchin with a big mouth. That's why we dumped her. "Maybe you can help me."

Tana sat up straight. "When and where? We got some catchin' up to do."

"She doesn't play by the rules."

"Leeza, Dante knows her too, and if he gets to her before you do..."

Dante, a convicted felon. Four years at Edgewood for distribution. Murder charge dropped for lack of evidence. Leeza had researched that, too.

"When and where?" Tana repeated.

"She's everywhere and nowhere."

"Lord help me." Tana was exasperated. "You got the grace of a swan, the strength of a lion, and the venom of a snake."

You have no clue.

"Stop sitting there! It's time to pony up, soldier."

"Where did you hear that?"

"Documentaries."

The door handle rattled suddenly, followed by a loud knock. Tana unlocked the door and held it as Dr. Randall barged in.

"Give us a minute," he said abruptly. Tana knew that was her cue to get out. She squeezed past him, her Southern smile saying, *"Fuck you and the horse you rode in on."* She headed down the hall humming a country song about 'friends in low places.'

Leeza loved Tana's tenacity and knew she'd be back as soon as Stephen was done with whatever was so important that it couldn't wait.

He closed the door and immediately noticed Leeza's forehead. "Jesus Christ," he said. He paused for a second, but when Leeza didn't say anything, neither did he. "That little notebook you carry around, can I see it?"

"What are you talking about?" It was no use; the binder was on the table next to Maya. She reluctantly handed it over.

"Is this some kind of joke?" he said, flipping through the pages. "Heroin with amphetamines, whiskey and Beethoven... Barbiturates with epinephrine, Sauvignon Blanc and Vivaldi... Cocaine with Red Bull, haloperidol and Haydn—"

"You left out dopamine receptor manipulation. How do you know about it?"

"Caught my eye when I was walking past an exam room. You're the only other one in this office smart enough to know what a chemical compound looks like."

"It's research. There are psychiatrists out there who experiment on people with all kinds of combinations of drugs, meditation, regression—still throwing spaghetti at the wall. Then there's actual research on dopamine receptor manipulation and paradigm reprogramming for people with PTSD, addiction, non-organic mental imbalance. I'm thinking about a research grant, maybe a documentary eventually."

Dr. Randall flipped through the pages. "You do know that sounds like some voodoo, backwater shit, right?"

"Some of it's promising."

He dropped the binder on her desk. "Don't use my name."

"I wouldn't think of it," she mumbled.

He started for the door, but a strange quiet in Leeza's eyes caused him to hesitate. He knew she was a capable provider and a fierce patient advocate. She was also a dedicated colleague. Yet, there was a burden in her eyes that he hadn't seen before. Leeza was struggling.

"You've worked your ass off, Leeza," he said, his voice softening. "You've earned the privilege to diagnose and treat. That makes you a physician—and *that* makes you a scientist. A scientist is someone with exceptional critical thinking skills who embraces research and accepts when their hypotheses are proven wrong. Proving any-thing—right or wrong—is progress."

Leeza eyed Maya as Stephen spoke. He rarely took time to ac-tually have a conversation, and she wondered where he was going with this.

"Addiction has been studied for a hundred and fifty years. If it were as simple as reprogramming dopamine receptors, it would have gone the way of polio by now."

"It's only been in the last fifteen years that it was defined as a chronic brain disorder," Leeza stated. "And there's a lot more to mental illness than addiction."

Stephen nodded; there may have even been a fragment of an approving smile. "You're a fine nurse practitioner. Don't get your hopes up over this one. Many are the plans in a person's heart, but it is the Lord's purpose that prevails." And with that, he was gone.

"So much for critical thinking."

Tana curtsied behind him and closed the door. "If I treated somebody like that when I was comin' up, my daddy would've stomped a mudhole in me."

"Graphic," Leeza said.

"Got somethin' for ya." Tana slid her cell across the desk. There was a text under Dante's name. She squinted to make out his avatar, a close-up of a tooth with a gold veneer inscribed with the letters: DNR. *Do Not Resuscitate. Clever.*

The text was cryptic—an address and a time, maybe? *"rutlg 6 53 abb."*

"Uh…" Leeza shrugged.

"Find the Airbnb on Rutledge Avenue; it's on the website. 6 means Saturday, 53 means 5:30"

"You've got your own language and everything; that's adorable."

Tana shot her a confused look. "What, this? Plain as day."

"We're literally on Rutledge Avenue. A little close to home, don't ya think?"

"Never follow a rat into the gutter."

What the hell does that even mean? "An Airbnb? Really?"

"He's makin' her come to us," said Tana. "If she don't feel safe, she won't show."

Tried that once.

"Besides, he's got more aliases than Puff Daddy—and just as many credit cards. They'll never tie him to the scene."

Leeza didn't like the sound of that. *The scene? What does he plan on doing to her?* She knew Dante had a score to settle with Sammie, but she and Sammie needed each other now more than ever. They just needed to meet face-to-face—sober and unarmed—so they could call a truce and make a plan to work on the experiments and find the formula once and for all. She would have to go along with their plan for now. If there was anyone who could subdue Sammie, it was Dante, and at this point, subduing Sammie would be the only way Leeza would have a chance in hell of reasoning with her.

"Lock and load," Leeza whispered.

"His daddy's a preacher. Says he goes to church, but I don't know if I believe that." Tana looked at the indentation on Leeza's face and ran a finger across it. "That'll fade." Her gaze moved from Leeza's forehead to her eyes. "Did you ever have faith?"

Leeza looked around at the framed pianos and harpsichords, Puccini's *Nessun Dorma* still whispering in the background. "I think I buried it with my mama," she said softly.

Tana placed her palm on Leeza's head and bowed her head. "Blessed is the man who remains steadfast under trial, for when he has stood the test, he will receive the crown of life, which God has promised to those who love him." She kissed the indentation from the semiautomatic Glock, then cupped Leeza's chin. "It's okay to question. He's with us regardless."

34

Hawaiian Shirts and Paralysis

It was nearly dark at five-thirty, thanks to the end of daylight saving time. A gray and black compact sedan with a lighted TAXI sign and Charleston Cab Company stenciled on the doors pulled up to the Airbnb on Rutledge Avenue. The two-story brick end-unit townhome faced the street and sat next to an alley—perfect for a quick escape. The website promised an entire rental unit for six guests, with two bedrooms, a jack-knife sofa, and one-and-a-half baths. Sammie stepped out and dropped some cash on the seat next to the driver. She rechecked Dante's note before knocking.

Dante's driver/bodyguard/doorman/boogeyman wore his signature Hawaiian shirt; his Glock was strapped to the front of his chest. There was a mutual glare as she squeezed past. *How did you get fatter in one fuckin' week?* Sammie thought. The blood drained from her face when she saw the silencer. *That wasn't there before! Run, you stupid bitch!* He motioned for her to lift her arms and spread her legs, then patted her down before twitching his head toward the couch. *Code for sit your ass down.*

Dante coolly emerged from a back room and took his spot in the kitchen, separating them by an island. A set of kitchen knives sat next to a pink 'vintage' toaster behind him—high carbon stainless steel, one-piece, anti-slip handle, dishwasher safe, display block with a built-in sharpener—Sammie knew her knives as well as she knew her guns, and those bad boys could do some damage. The Hawaiian shirt blocked the door. Dante blocked the knives. They were strategically positioned.

Dante nodded. "You made it."

Here or some ditch, Sammie thought. She had been dreading this. Had he figured out she narc'd? No way—she'd called from the landline during one of the many times she broke into Daddy Dick's house when they were on "family vacation." There's no way he knew. And there was no way he was going to bluff a confession out of her. She had been obsessing over the church incident. *What kind of mind-fuck was that?* He wore the same oversized jacket with a different tie, both ugly as hell.

"You look good," Sammie said.

Dante inhaled like he was trying to suck all the air out of the room. "Who doesn't love being free in the South this time of the year?"

Or anywhere? Any time of year? Seriously?

"Ahhh, that Atlantic oceany air. Te voy a invitar a mi barco. Te gustaría, ¿no? (*I'm going to invite you out on my boat. You would like that, wouldn't you?*)"

Did he just say oceany? "Me encantaría. (*I would love it.*)"

"You're uptight, Rosario. Relax, relax."

She tried to breathe as naturally as possible, forcing herself not to let her gaze land on the knives or the door—both lifelines, and both out of reach. She just needed to stay alert for any sudden moves.

"Anything you want to tell me?"

"I don't think so."

"No?"

"No." She imagined shoving the gun between his eyes like she did Leeza's—only this time, she'd pull the trigger.

He tapped his fingers on the island. "Tell me what lessons you took from your experience in the Lord's house."

He's setting me up.

"What do you remember?"

"Umm, religious people like to tell the truth?"

Dante walked around the island and stood directly in front of Sammie. Leaning forward, he spoke in one of his deeper voices: "I'm going to let you in on a little secret."

His face was too close; she could feel his breath. He smelled like herbal cigarettes, gin, and Ricola lozenges.

"My daddy owns that church. I grew up in that church. I helped rebuild it. He used to say to me as a kid, "There is only one thing I got no use for in this world, and that's a liar." You stood at his lectern and professed to be truthful in the name of God."

Sammie paced her breathing, trying to look calm. She wasn't scared—she was pissed.

"Do you know what they say about the future?" Dante asked.

"I'm sure you'll tell me."

"Embrace it or become a victim of it."

"Sounds about right."

"The question is, how do you see your future, Rosario?" He suddenly channeled Martin Luther King Jr. with melodic assurance: "We must walk on in the days ahead with an audacious faith in the future."

Sammie didn't know who he was quoting, but she assumed it was taken out of context.

His vertebrae cracked as he straightened upright, like a kid cracking their fingers, except backbones shouldn't sound like that. He lingered before returning in slow motion to the far side of the island. "At Edgefield, I heard you might know something about how I got there."

Fuck. My. Life. To. Hell.

"Then I saw your face at the club..."

He's bluffing.

"You've been a busy little weasel."

"It wasn't me," she said calmly. *Just say it, asshole. But you can't, can you?*

"What wasn't you?" He tapped his fingers. "I had big plans for you, Rosario." He savored the dramatic pause, as if waiting for divine inspiration. Somehow, you knew it was a pause and not your turn to speak. "But here we are." He glanced at the doorman-chauffeur. "Okay. That's a discussion for another day. Today isn't about us."

Another day? What's happening?

"What went wrong, Rosario? What brought you here?" He sounded just like that detective in juvie who tried to get her to confess to something she didn't do. Well, something she actually *did* do, but he would never know that.

"Walking down the wrong road at the wrong time?"

Dante studied the clear-coat on his freshly manicured nails, turning them in the light as if looking for flaws. He had all the time in the world. "I'm not referring to three days ago."

Sammie was not about to dive down that rabbit hole. "It is what it is."

"You are motivated," Dante continued. "I know you aspire to accomplish more than you have, but comparison is the thief of joy."

I'm supposed to find joy in my life? Really?

"Business is good, would you agree?"

You are stone-cold insane. "Awesome."

"You know the vibe on the street. There's this new formula, some mix of street and prescription drugs. Have you heard of anything like that?"

Careful. "Doesn't sound familiar."

"I want you to meet an associate." Tana emerged from the back room where Dante had been hiding. "This is Tatiana. Miss Tana to you."

"Encantada de conocerte, (*Nice to meet you*)," said Tana. The sound of Tana's voice sent shock waves through Sammie's body.

"Parece que has visto un fantasma, (*You look like you've seen a ghost*)," said Dante. He opened a cupboard, chose a small porcelain teacup with purple pansies and hummingbirds, and set it in front of Tana. It could have been the highlight of a Victorian high tea.

"No nos hemos conocido, (*We haven't met*)," said Sammie.

Tana glared at Sammie as if she were looking at the school shooter who had just murdered her kids. She pulled a water bottle from her purse and poured an amber-tinged liquid into the teacup.

Sammie's face froze. *That's the shit that paralyzed Leeza.*

"Even comes in a liquid," said Dante. "I'm thinking of recycling miniatures like Hennessy or Johnnie Walker Black." He looked at his driver with the Glock. "Does Don Julio 1942 come in a miniature?" The fat man gave a thumbs-up and smiled. "That's it!" Dante exclaimed. "Blessed be."

Sammie glanced at each of them, then the knives, then the door—blocked by the man with the ridiculous shirt and the gun with the silencer. Tana took out a lemon, flicked open the blade, and sliced the lemon in half before squeezing it into the cup.

"It's probably not a good idea," Sammie finally managed. "Look, Tana, please."

"*Miss* Tana," said Dante.

"Miss Tana." Sammie's anger shifted, and her brain signaled it was time to get nervous. "It's just that I may have heard of something now that I think about it. It's not good. It's not good." She faked a laugh, "You don't wanna play around with that."

Tana slid the delicate porcelain teacup across the island toward Sammie.

"Wait! I didn't do anything!" Her anger was building.

"Bottoms up," said Dante.

"She knows! She knows I didn't do anything. Ask her!"

"Nobody said you did anything. Where is this coming from?" asked Dante, eerily calm.

Sammie glared at Tana. "This has nothing to do with me, and you know it."

"It's a tangled web, isn't it?" said Tana.

"You're blaming me? You know I couldn't make that!" Sammie pleaded. "That stuff will paralyze you!"

"You said you hadn't heard about it," said Dante.

A sudden banging rattled the front door. Tana and Sammie jumped as they looked toward the entrance, mostly obscured by the junglescaped billboard that was the fat man's shirt. He pressed the gun onto the center of the door, pointing toward the unsuspecting Gen Zers as he looked through the peephole. He aimed at the body closest to the door. Sammie weighed her options: she could scream for help to the voices just outside. But they were drunk. And they would laugh. And they would move on anyway. The doorman looked at Dante and shook his head, indicating there was no problem, then held up a finger to Tana. They all listened intently to the muffled conversation outside.

"Nah, man, this ain't it. I told you," slurred one of the young partiers. "Has to be," another dude answered back. "I need to go to the club!" a high-pitched, drunk girl insisted. "Whatever, dude," said the first one as his voice trailed off down the sidewalk. Hawaiian shirt man gave a subtle wave, a silent 'all clear.' Dante's lips curved into a quiet smile as he looked at Tana.

Tana drummed her nails softly on the counter beside the teacup as she turned her attention back to Sammie. They had reached the edge of an unspoken dare.

"Look, you want the truth." Sammie said.

Dante laughed his Skeletor laugh. "And nothing but."

"Miss Tana works with a girl named Leeza Byron. We used to be friends. She called me and asked me for help with some concoction—supposed to cure whatever makes people crazy. She wanted me to get her heroin and coke so she could mix them with whiskey and Advil or vitamins or whatever and listen to Mozart or Coldplay or whatever. She called me! That's who you should be talking to!"

Tana and Dante were as still as a pair of Dillard's mannequins when Sammie heard a sound from the back room. She watched as Leeza emerged, joining the other two mannequins to complete the display. *What. The. Actual*— There they were, the three of them, arms crossed and frozen in time, staring at her through glass eyeballs.

Sammie glared at Leeza. "You need to start talking."

Tana set the switchblade on the island and inched the teacup forward.

"How did you and Miss Leeza meet?" Dante asked.

"This ain't Jerry Springer, Dante." Sammie was done with this asshole.

"You're right." His face went rigid. "Niceties aside. Pick up the cup."

Sammie planned the next few seconds with surgical precision: she turned her head toward the Hawaiian shirt—she could feel their eyes follow hers—then, suddenly, she lunged across the island, grabbing the switchblade and Tana's shirt, pulling her forward, and pressing the blade against her neck.

The click of the Glock's slide filled the room for a split second as Sammie yelled at Leeza, "Move!"

Leeza backed away as Sammie forced herself around the island and behind Tana, holding her arm behind her back and the blade at her throat. Leeza stared helplessly as her friend cried out in pain. Sammie dragged Tana backward and pressed herself against the wall so she could see all three of them. Dante never flinched.

The fat driver dude calmly pointed the silencer at Sammie's head. He took a step closer, aiming between her eyes. Dante held up a finger. The driver waited for instructions.

Leeza was focused on the blade against Tana's throat; the slightest move and there would be blood. Dante also watched, but if there was a thought in his head, he didn't let on.

"Let her go," said Leeza.

"Tell them," Sammie said, her voice and hands were steady, calm, in control.

"I called you and asked you for help," said Leeza.

"It was all your idea."

"I asked you to bring me the ingredients."

Sammie glared at Dante. "I fuckin' TOLD YOU!"

Dante slid the teacup from the edge of the island back toward him. "You were right. I shouldn't have doubted you." The only sound was Tana's breathing.

"Let me out of here," said Sammie, her grip on Tana's neck tightening.

"Except," Dante continued, unnervingly calm, like a real-life hostage negotiator, "you threatened her, then you attacked her. You trashed her home. You frightened her children and injured her dog, Mr. Frisky, I believe?" He looked at Leeza.

"Inspector," she replied.

"Inspector Frisky. And you tried to kill your own father." The room halted with Dante's final words—four statues frozen in time: serious Rocky Horror Picture Show medusa transducer vibe.

Leeza remembered the gut-wrenching silence just before the artillery fire. It felt like only seconds passed between the start of the bombing and when the screaming bloody cots started to arrive.

When a young soldier hesitated, the platoon leader would yell: "*Deadline: two breaths!*" In that moment, she gave herself a deadline: two breaths. Breath number one, in through the nose, out through the mouth. She clenched her fist as tightly as humanly possible. Breath number two, in through the nose, out through the mouth. She trained her eyes on the side of Sammie's head, then thrust her body toward the bitch holding a switchblade to her best friend's throat. She swung her fist from behind in a direct line to Sammie's head, landing the punch above the right ear before any reaction. Sammie's head slammed sideways as the blade slid across Tana's throat, leaving a dripping red line in its path. Tana dropped to her knees, clutching her neck.

The switchblade hit the floor as Leeza landed on top of Sammie and got her in a chokehold. She forced her way behind her and lifted the dead weight of Sammie's body by her neck, standing her up and pinning an arm behind her back, lifting her heels off the floor. Sammie's face went red as the men watched. She gnarled her teeth like a terrified animal, kicking her legs as she clutched Leeza's forearm around her neck. The exchange of room air through her trachea stopped.

They waited. When Sammie's body gave up, Leeza dropped her, her head slammed against the wide-planked hardwood floor. The fat man in the Hawaiian shirt holstered the Glock.

A siren sped down the street outside. They took advantage of the break, listening until the cop car faded a few blocks away.

Dante dampened a towel and sat on the floor with Tana, propping her between his legs. The wound was superficial. He held light pressure as she calmed her breathing. He pulled back the makeshift dressing and kissed her head. "It's nothing," he told her.

Sammie coughed.

"Get up!" Leeza shouted.

Sammie glared at her, choking between breaths, still clutching her neck. She managed to get an elbow under her and prop herself up. "You sick bitch."

Sammie lunged at Leeza, swinging at her face with everything she had. Leeza ducked the incoming punch. They watched Sammie slam headfirst into the wall before falling back to the floor. As quickly as she was up, she was on her back. Her face went still; her eyes were vacant. Leeza stood over her. The only movement of Sammie's body was in her neck—the visible pulse of her carotid arteries.

The room took another pause. Dante tied the dressing onto Tana's neck with a handkerchief. He stood up and pulled her to her feet, wrapping his arms around her.

"That should do it," he said. "Tatiana. My beautiful girl."

"Gracias por nada (*Thanks for nothing*)," she said, holding the cloth to her neck.

"I wasn't worried."

"You're not normal," said Tana. Dante's Skeletor laugh filled the room.

"Te debo un favor (*I owe you one*)," said Tana.

"For this? It was nothing." He looked at Sammie. "Teníamos asuntos pendientes (*We had unfinished business*)."

Dante reached out to shake Leeza's hand. "Maybe we can do business someday." Tana held up her hand as if to say "*stop!*" and shook her head. "That would be a hell to the no."

He laughed as he pulled Leeza in for a hug. "See you two at the club."

"The club?" said Leeza, looking at Tana's neck. "You're not going anywhere until I take a look at that. I'll see *you* at the office."

Dante kissed Tana before turning to leave.

"Dante," said Tana. "Esa mierda del barco... (*That crap about the boat...*), really?"

"¿Qué? ¿No hay barco? (*What? There's no boat?*)," said Leeza.

"I'll tell you about it," Dante said to Tana with a wink.

The big man closed the door behind them.

Leeza knelt next to Sammie and softly pushed her hair back from her forehead. She looked into her half-open eyes while making a slow, circular motion around her throat. She could feel the air moving back and forth under her fingers. She slid her fingers laterally to the carotid artery and felt her pulse. As she reached into her pocket, Sammie's eyes opened. She grabbed Leeza's hand! *A bomb exploded just as the injured soldier suddenly grabbed Leeza's hand!*

Sammie landed a punch in Leeza's face, catching her nose and left eye. She writhed away from Leeza and swung around, a second punch locked and loaded.

Leeza thrust herself at Sammie and grabbed her throat with both hands, letting her body weight fall on top of her, the rage left in her soul fueling the chokehold. Sammie grabbed Leeza's forearms again, fighting to break free. She gasped for air, her face turning red.

"¡Basta! ¡No hagas que te mate! (*Stop it! Don't make me kill you!*)," cried Leeza. Their battle was fueled by years of pent-up rage from all the atrocities they had each suffered through. Leeza summoned strength in her arms that she had never felt before. She squeezed harder, shaking Sammie like a ragdoll. "¡No hagas que te mate! (*Don't make me kill you!*)." She knew only one of them would be left standing.

Leeza put her free hand on the soldier's neck and stared at his face, so young, with full cheeks that his mama used to pinch between her thumb and index fingers, followed by a kiss on the forehead. Her thumb encircled his Adam's apple. She could feel the air gurgling back and forth under her fingers as he fought for each breath. She leaned in, forcing her thumb into the soldier's neck with all her might, cutting off his airway. His grip tightened as his eye widened. Finally, the gurgling sound stopped, as did time. She hovered over him, staring—her mind was too exhausted to think. Then, very slowly, his hand released hers, and his body went limp as he let go of what was left of his fight for survival. Tears streamed down her face.

Leeza leaned into Sammie, her forehead pressing hard against her temple, pinning her to the floor. Their primal determination focused on one goal—the victor would reclaim a life free from the relentless fear of being hunted and, in turn, spare their families from unimaginable grief. Leeza's lips brushed Sammie's ear as she whispered a final chilling ultimatum: "Ya párale, o muere. (*Stop or die.*)"

A trickle of fluid dripped down from above. Tana stood over the entwined women and dripped the formula from the teacup into Sammie's mouth. Leeza's eyes, inches from Sammie's face, watched the amber paralytic glide past her tongue and into her throat. Leeza slowly eased her grip.

Sammie's grip relaxed as her body softened. Blood from Leeza's nose dripped onto Sammie's chin as she let Sammie slide back to the floor, paralyzed.

Leeza gave herself time to catch her breath, still staring. She rolled off and sat next to her.

"You and I are going to start seeing each other on a regular basis." She wiped her bloody nose on her sleeve, then reached into her pocket. She pulled out a small, empty insulin syringe with an attached needle. She pulled the plastic cover off with her teeth, pulled back the plunger, and drew up two cc's of air. She felt Sammie's carotid artery. As she moved her fingers away, the needle glided smoothly into Sammie's neck. A flash of blood spurted into the syringe. She injected the air into the artery, then withdrew the needle.

"It's what you've always wanted, right?" Leeza leaned down and kissed Sammie's forehead. She took Sammie's phone, dialed 911, then laid the phone on her chest. "Remind me to change my family's passcodes."

The exam room was eerily quiet in the after hours. The women didn't speak. Leeza lifted Tana's chin to examine the cut on her neck. She gently cleaned the skin of dried blood and applied a couple of Steri-Strips, just to keep the superficial wound from opening. Satisfied with her work, Leeza turned to the door but was stopped by a hand on her arm. Tana motioned for Leeza to sit on the exam table. She knew there was no escaping it: Tana had to see her leg.

As the pant leg slowly rose, revealing the blood-stained dressing, their eyes met. Tana bore the fresh mark of a razor blade on her neck; Leeza, the raw, ripped flesh from her brush with death by motorcycle.

35

I Am Not Crazy

Leeza stared at the return address of the oversized white envelope in her inbox:

National Institutes of Health
9000 Rockville Pike
Bethesda, MD 20892

Her hands trembled as she pulled out the letter, and for a fleeting moment, she was back in Beaufort, rifling through the mail for the envelope from Juilliard all those years ago. She held it in front of closed eyes and breathed in as deeply as she could, then held onto the breath as she held onto the memory. She opened her eyes and tried to focus. *She looked up at the blue sky, with its pillowy white clouds, and whispered...* "Thank you."

Two uniformed men stood outside the exam room. Leeza had seen them dozens of times. The embroidered patches on their shirts read: Medical Transport Charleston, SC. "Thanks, guys. Fifteen minutes, tops," she said, slipping into the room.

Inside the exam room, a patient reclined on the ambulance stretcher facing away from the door. Leeza stepped around to the side of the stretcher and stood next to her. Sammie's face was stonelike.

"Hi, I'm Leeza. You must be Rosario."

She scanned through Sammie's chart. "Embolic stroke following overdose. Hmmm... perplexing." She set the chart on Sammie's lap and checked her pupils with a penlight, their faces inches apart. There was a faint knock before Tana entered and stood next to Leeza. She took a long look at Sammie.

"We're going to keep a close eye on you, amiga," said Leeza, placing a stethoscope on her chest. "Strong heart."

"She always gonna be like that?" Tana asked.

Leeza draped the stethoscope over her shoulders. "MRI is underwhelming. All signs point to a full recovery." She exposed a small tube entering Sammie's belly. "She'll be walking around and eating solid food soon enough."

"Need anything?" Tana asked.

"We're good, thanks."

"Can't believe that skinny bitch got that shot in," Tana mumbled as she left.

Leeza leaned against the stretcher and put a thumb on each of Sammie's eyelids, raising them up to reveal her indifferent pupils. "Big news: the formula is over seventy percent effective. No more paralysis." She let the eyelids fall. "This—" Her voice caught, even though she promised herself she wouldn't get emotional. "This had nothing to do with the formula."

The yellow binder was under Sammie's chart. Leeza set it on the counter, then unfolded the NIH letter. "I just found out the National Institutes of Health approved my research grant—mine and three others. We're all researching the exact same thing." She read from the letter: "NIH RESEARCH PROJECT GRANT: Dopamine Receptor Manipulation and Paradigm Reprogramming for the Treatment of Non-organic Psychosocial Mental Disease. Basic Experimental Studies with Humans Required." She stared at the words and read them over again to herself.

Leeza washed her hands and turned her attention to the IV in Sammie's arm.

"Turns out there really is a correlation between dopamine receptor manipulation and paradigm reprogramming. Dopamine neurons of the ventral tegmental area harmonize cholinergic inputs to regulate functions of non-organic mental imbalance, such as..." she held up a finger for emphasis, "wait for it... motivation and goal-directed behaviors!" She shrugged and smiled. "Who knew? Studies have been done in mice—well, mice and me—but nobody knows that except us. I'm sure it'll come as no surprise that Sauvignon Blanc had nothing to do with it. And instead of classical music, the top five songs of the patient's choice from the year they turned eighteen. There will be a team of four of us; two MDs, a PhD, and, of course, a DNP. That's me. You see? I'm not the only one. Anyway, Phase III, Chica!"

She clamped the IV tubing and tossed the empty bag of lactated Ringer's with the antibiotic-piggybacked infusion in the trash.

"It's a breakthrough for me personally—fewer, less severe flashbacks. Less dependence on distilled spirits. Zero cravings after twenty-one days of abstinence." She leaned in, her mouth next to Sammie's ear, as if to tell a secret. But she didn't whisper; she declared, "I am not crazy." Sammie blinked. "Plus, I can't wait to rub it in Stephen's face." A deeper thought made Leeza pause. She reflected on her journey up to that moment. "This research will be a game changer for so many."

She pulled on a pair of gloves. "Have you heard that your dad is recovering in the hospital? If it makes you feel better, he did suffer. What he did to you wasn't your fault, Sammie. You are worthy of happiness in spite of your stolen childhood, and I suspect your trauma was egregious." Leeza caught herself. "That means horrible," she said as she slid the tiny catheter out of Sammie's arm. "If you can free yourself of that suffering and learn to live your best life, you will realize it's the greatest form of revenge. Do you remember when I told you that all your bad childhood memories are just cartoon characters that have no control over your grown-up life? Put that on a Post-it note, and someday you'll believe it." She held a small gauze on the insertion site, then wrapped it with an elastic bandage. "Pain is inevitable; suffering is optional."

Leeza saw the welling in Sammie's eyes. "Somebody's home." She lifted the hospital gown to reveal the dog bite. "I've never seen the Colonel bite anyone. Didn't know he had it in him. You didn't have to hit him that hard." She rubbed a finger over the oozing flesh and pushed down firmly on the wound. Sammie winced, letting out a faint cry. "They said all the Ativan in his system took the edge off the pain." Leeza chuckled and scoffed at the same time. "Poor little guy was dragging his ass for three days. You're going to need a different antibiotic."

Sammie's bottom lip curled into her mouth.

"All of this is a consequence of your own actions. You're too wrapped up in self-pity to see it. I borrowed that line from Artie's attorney, Victoria. Can you believe that bitch said that to me? Monster in a Chanel jacket. You can buy Tiffany and Dior, but you can't buy class."

Leeza gathered the gauze and elastic bandage. "In war, you never know which breath will be your last. You just know a bullet could come at any second, then agony, then nothing. Imagine existing like that." Leeza placed fresh gauze over the leg wound. "You know what's really messed up, Sammie? I was existing like that here at home. Because of you. Not anymore."

A single tear slid down Sammie's cheek, silent proof she was still there.

"I saved your ass. You would be on your way to prison." Leeza touched Sammie's forehead with the back of her fingers. "The stroke is transient... that means temporary. It was just a little air in the carotid. As expected, it settled centrally in the brain parenchyma, just a blip on MRI. Think of it as a gas bubble, like a burp, but in your brain. You're gonna be fine, guaranteed." She paused, leaning in. "And believe it or not, I've been saving the best news for last."

Leeza adjusted Sammie's pillow, then took both hands. "You were a partner in what is about to be one of the most significant breakthroughs in modern medicine. I couldn't have done it without you. I admit I was barking up the wrong tree for a minute, but we cracked the code. I even have a catchy title for the holistic psychotherapists: Surgical Orchestrators of Human Behavior—not surgical like an operation, it means... Never mind."

Sammie slowly raised a hand and touched Leeza's lips. Her fingers felt Leeza's next words: "I am indebted to you, and you will be taken care of." An immediate air of relief seemed to drift over Sammie as her hand fell back onto her chest.

"But you have to go home. You have to go to Hermosillo. You're not safe here. I'll get you out. You have my word. You can take care of your brother and sister and be near your real family." She kissed Sammie's motionless mouth. "We rise from the carnage," she whispered.

Leeza pulled a real estate flyer from the clipboard and held it up, showing Sammie the color photos of a house with a green yard and a porch swing. "I closed on the house." She pulled a small wooden box from her coat pocket and opened it, revealing the white powder, syringe, spoon, vial, and pills. "I was going to rent, but... anyway, great neighborhood. The biggest criterion was the porch swing." She dropped the syringe and needles into a bright red sharps container hanging on the wall. "The kids have their own rooms." She emptied the powder into the sink and ran the water, then straightened the spoon handle and dropped it into the sharps container, followed by the pills and vial. "They'll be with me most of the time. Artie doesn't know that yet; it's a long-range plan." She took a breath. "I keep telling myself he'll come around." She pulled off the gloves and dropped them in the trash. "Try to appreciate your life," she said, wiping Sammie's cheeks. "It can be wonderful."

She opened the door and gestured for the medical transport guys. Her fingertips slid down Sammie's forearm as they wheeled her out. *Rejoice in your salvation.*

"You did it, baby girl," her mama whispered as they rocked back and forth in each other's arms. "I got this for you," she said, holding

up a necklace. *"What is it, Mama?"* The rope chain held a silver grand piano engraved with 'Leeza'.

"The only one person in my whole damn life who ever told me I could be anything I wanted; that I was actually worth a damn thing."

36

Not Every Symphony Is Composed in C Major

An azure accent wall framed the cobalt-tiled fireplace in Leeza's restored nineteen-fifties craftsman. The Colonel stretched out under the dining room table, still wearing his soft e-collar—Leeza would be removing the stitches in a couple of days. She chopped garlic and onions as Tana paced anxiously over the newly refinished hardwood floors.

"The interview process for the new surgeon starts Monday," Leeza said. "I told Stephen you and I both will be joining the interview, AND the tour of Charleston, AND the dinner with the spouses."

Tana swooped into the kitchen and stopped at the counter where Leeza was working. "No way he agreed to that," she said.

"It wasn't a question."

Tana fist-bumped Leeza. "Bitchita!"

"I also told him the next partner needs to be a Neuro-Orthopedic Surgeon. It's all the rage."

"Okay, now you're just messin' with me."

"We're not waiting for him to hand us the keys, baby girl. Time for fresh blood in there. We'll be running the place long after Stephen's gone." Leeza tapped the chopping block. "Now chop these onions or sit your ass down."

Tana was gnawing on a thumbnail. "I don't know if I'm ready."

"Ready as you'll ever be. You're a different woman."

Once Tana got clean, Leeza became her tireless champion. She motivated her to go to nursing school, helped her study, and convinced her that she had what it took to succeed. But it wasn't until recently that Leeza finally convinced her that it was time to start working on a relationship with her kids, even if it was one at a time. Tana had resisted letting the kids know the truth—she'd screwed up so often, and she dreaded their questions about her past. Besides, Leeza and Artie had been perfect parents.

"Baby steps," said Leeza. "I got you."

"How much longer?"

Leeza looked at her watch. "Ten minutes."

"Dios mío (*My God*)." Tana sat at the kitchen table, blessed herself with the sign of the cross, and lowered her head. "En el nombre del Padre, del Hijo, y del Espíritu Santo (*In the name of the Father, the Son, and the Holy Spirit*)."

Leeza loved Tana with all her heart and was glad that her faith brought her peace, just as her own mama's faith had brought *her* peace. But she couldn't get past their go-to phrase for everything: the Lord works in mysterious ways. She wasn't wired that way; she needed proof, not faith. And yet, when Tana prayed over her in the office, she felt a peace that defied reason.

"Just so you know, you won't have to worry about Sammie anymore," said Tana.

"Is that so?"

"When Dante said he was gonna have her out on his boat... That's code for somethin' you don't wanna know."

"Sounds like some serious Dexter shit. Sammie must not have understood that when he said it."

"Trust me."

"Doesn't he know she's in rehab?"

"He knows exactly where she is every minute. Didn't you say the stroke is transient?"

Leeza knew she could get Sammie out of town before Dante could get to her. She controlled all of her appointments and knew where she would be before he could. He would think she ran away before being officially discharged, and Leeza would confirm it.

And it just dawned on her that she needed to be less concise with Tana.

"Do me a favor and don't tell me any details." She slid a chair back and motioned for Tana to sit. "I'm curious about something. Wasn't it his third strike when he went to Edgewood?"

"Dante has friends in high places," said Tana. "Put it this way—you're in the South—cops, preachers, politicians, and drug dealers, they are what we call first cousins around here."

"It ain't just the South, girlfriend."

Tana sucked her bottom lip, her foot tapping nervously as she stared out the front windows.

"Settle down, girl," Leeza told her. "It's gonna play out just fine."

Artie's SUV turned onto a street lined with classic Colonial, Craftsman, and Georgian-red brick homes, most with porch swings, all with landscaped lawns. Hedge maples and majestic oaks lined the streets, their limbs creating a canopy of shade as they conjoined above the cars and occasional pedestrians. A FOR SALE sign with a SOLD sticker was planted near the curb.

"There's something I've been wanting to tell you first," said Tana.

Artie pulled up to the curb, parking the SUV as the kids peered out the back window.

"It'll have to wait. It's showtime, Chica!"

Grant ran toward the house as Charlotte grabbed their backpacks and coats. Leeza stepped onto the porch; Grant barreled toward her. "Leesie!" He thrust a piece of paper at Leeza as Tana watched through the window. "I painted a picture, Leesie. It's for our new house!" Leeza held up the painting—a house with a mommy, two smiling kids, and a dog. "This is amazing, Dr. G. That looks just like the Colonel. I've got the perfect spot."

"It's Inspector Frisky!"

"Colonel," said Leeza.

"Inspector Frisky!"

"Colonel."

"Dork."

"Guilty."

"And I'm painting my room black. It's all the rage."

"You haven't even seen it yet." *And that's a hell to the no.*

"You'll have to trust me. Oh, and I'm shaving my head, so my chainmail armor hoodie fits better."

"Looking forward to those conversations—wait, did you say shaving your head for hoodie armor?" But he was already gone.

Artie leaned against the car, arms crossed, his gaze sweeping over the neighborhood.

Leeza joined him at the curb. "What do you think?"

He appeared lost in his own thoughts.

She hadn't been this close to him in months. The five o'clock shadow and the Pendleton Westerly sweater were a new look, and he rocked them both, of course. She didn't recognize the new cologne, a realization that hit her with a stab of jealousy—a vivid reminder of how much she'd lost.

"You've got a lot on your plate," she said, her voice softening slightly. "I want to give you time to process. I've filed a petition for custody with the court."

Artie was caught off guard. "Not likely. Do you actually think the court—"

"How's Marlie doing?"

He didn't miss a beat: "Sanctimonious isn't your color, all things considered."

Leeza chuckled. *He's not the pushover he used to be. That's hot.*

He was quiet again as he saw Charlotte heading toward them.

"Victoria is going to want to bring her A-game," said Leeza. "No mediators."

The air was refreshing and calm, and the neighborhood offered a quiet they didn't get in the city. Swaying tree limbs absorbed their words. In the city, private conversations bounced off buildings for everyone to hear.

"Do you want to see the kids' rooms?"

Artie gazed at Leeza's strange, perfect new home—the kids were acting as if they'd lived there forever. He caught a glimpse of a figure moving inside. *Tana.*

"I should probably go." As he turned toward the car, she saw his profile, and her heart fluttered. "The divorce isn't even final," he murmured, so softly he could have been talking to himself.

Charlotte grabbed Leeza's hand and pulled her toward the house. Leeza glanced over her shoulder at Artie as she was dragged away. "We'll talk."

"Can I ask about the spelling bee?" Leeza asked.

"Third runner-up."

"Stellar work! Next year you'll dominate!" Leeza shot her a sly grin, which was met with a famous eye roll.

"Ginnie Nguyen can spell words I've never even heard of."

Charlotte sat on the porch swing. Grant immediately sat beside her and was waving goodbye when the Colonel plopped down at their feet.

"Daddy made his girlfriend cry, and she hasn't been back," said Grant.

"That was a while ago," said Charlotte. "He says he's done."

"Whatever that means," Grant added.

Leeza looked in Artie's direction as the SUV pulled away from the curb.

"I think he's sad," said Grant. "He doesn't even brush his hair sometimes, which is totally weird."

"Gramma said she's gonna hook him up," said Charlotte.

"Whatever that means," Grant added. "Every time she brings it up, he gets mad. If I had a house like Gramma's, I'd be happy all the time. She said she can tell if we pee in the pool. Is that true?"

"I wouldn't test that if I were you." Leeza kept her eyes on the SUV until it disappeared into the canopy of trees.

Tana appeared in the doorway. The kids bolted up. "Tía! Tía!" cried Grant.

Charlotte hugged her as tightly as she could possibly squeeze. "Tía Tatiana!"

The scar on her neck was barely noticeable.

"¡Mis bebés! (my babies!)," cried Tana, her eyes welling up.

"Time to start working on dinner," said Leeza.

"Can we go out?!" asked a wide-eyed Grant.

"No. Tía Tatiana wants to teach you how to make arroz con pollo, so you've got a lot of work to do. But first, huddle up." Tana waited in the doorway as they assumed their positions in front of the coach.

"We're going to talk about the night when that lady broke into the house." Leeza watched their faces, giving them a moment to absorb the sudden shift. "I'm so sorry that happened to you."

"I thought she was your friend," said Grant. "We saw her at your apartment. Why did she break in our house? Why did she have a gun and hurt Inspector Frisky?"

"We had a misunderstanding," said Leeza. "She got upset. I made sure she got the help she needed, and I promise you it won't happen again."

"Inspector Frisky had to get stitches," said Grant.

"He's tougher than he looks. He's gonna be just fine. I hear he turned out to be a pretty good watchdog, huh?"

"Uhmmm, she was IN the house, soooo, no?" said Charlotte, avoiding Leeza's eyes. "And she had a gun."

"I know—"

"We didn't even hear her come in. How do you know somebody else won't do it? And Daddy didn't have a gun, and you weren't even there!" Her eyes were filling up. "I'm locking my door and I'm not turning off the lights!"

"Charlotte, listen. Have I ever lied to you about anything? Have I ever told you something would happen and then it didn't?"

"Uhhh, yes," Charlotte replied. "You said you were moving out for two or three months tops," her chin was trembling.

"I promise you it won't happen again." She lifted her chin until their eyes met. "It can't," she whispered. Leeza hugged both kids. "Grant, go help Tía Tatiana. We'll be there in a second."

Grant raced into the house as Leeza gestured for Charlotte to sit with her.

"I'm proud of you," Leeza said. "Your music, your grades, dealing with adults. It's been a tough time, and I'm sorry, I really am."

"It's all good. I keep picturing myself ten years down the road, living for myself."

Leeza took Charlotte's hands and spoke softly. "You're going to spend the night with Tía Tatiana, and when you get home, we'll talk."

Charlotte's mouth dropped open. "I knew it!" she exclaimed, her eyes filling all over again. A small "Okay," was all she could manage as her emotions took over. Leeza remembered the way Charlotte's eyes lingered on Tana during visits to the office, how she used to comment that their skin looked the same. But Tana was always too loud and too busy, and the two of them never found a quiet moment to talk. Charlotte admitted, however, that she looked forward to the visits anyway.

"Go wash up," said Leeza. "And don't tell your brother."

Charlotte and Tana passed in the doorway. Tana's eyes tracked Charlotte as she passed; Charlotte's glance was fleeting, nervous—she tried to smile as she ran inside.

Leeza wrapped her arms around Tana as they cried tears of relief. She looked over Tana's shoulder as they hugged, staring at the porch with the new paint and the beautiful swing, she could still see the broken one at the house in Beaufort. Tana pulled back and wiped her face. "I have something I've been meanin' to say."

"Hit me."

Tana took a while to gather her thoughts, stalling as if she were hiding a bombshell that would change the course of humanity. There were even a few false starts.

"Good Lord," Leeza said. "What have you got bottled up in there?"

"It was hard on me, finding out what you and Sammie were up to, and about the formula, the fight with Artie, and what she did to y'all." She wiped her cheeks again. "I could've lost you. And I can't lose you, whatever the reason." Tana broke down, having finally said it out loud. Leeza held her hands tight as she struggled to get the rest of the words out.

"Not too long ago, I started seein' a change in you, how you don't scare so easy," Tana continued. "There's a calmness that I hadn't seen in a long time. Confidence comin' back, little at a time. Somethin' happened. Feels like the Leeza I used to know." She let the tears fall as she squeezed Leeza's hands.

"I called Arthur," she said. A gust of wind lifted the canopy of ancient oaks and hedge maples, ruffling the branches and leaves like a flamenco dress. "And I told him what I know. He deserved that. You deserve that."

Leeza was emotionally spent. She heard the words, but there was no energy to react. Of course, she had told herself that she had a long-term plan, but she had finally faced the reality that her future without Artie had been determined; her marriage was history. The narrative that included Artie falling in love with her all over again had recused itself from the plot.

"The old things passed away; behold, new things have come," said Tana. She kissed Leeza on the forehead and went back to the house, leaving her best friend and savior with her own thoughts. Leeza wouldn't be standing there if not for Tana. And Tana wouldn't be there if not for Leeza. She walked across the lawn toward the curb. The red SUV was still sitting at the end of the street with the blinker on, but it wasn't moving.

She took out her phone and opened her photos. She swiped up the screen and watched as hundreds of photos sped by in a blur, like a slot machine teasing old ladies at a casino. As the photos slowed and finally stopped, she found herself staring at their wedding pictures. A lump hit her in the throat without warning. They looked so young. She lingered on Artie's face; he looked happy, and unaware of what she would end up doing to him and how the guilt would tear her apart. She looked down the street again at the SUV with its blinker, still contemplating the turn. *What is he doing?*

She sat on the curb and opened her contacts. Artie was always at the top. Her finger hovered over the phone when a sudden ringtone and vibration startled her, making her flinch, but she quickly recentered. It was Singh.

"Doc."

"Leeza, I got your email and thought I would reach out to see how you're doing."

"Just fine, thanks."

"You say you want to decrease the frequency of our visits."

"That is true."

"I would agree we've made significant progress, but there's still work yet to do, and we need to address the remaining challenges, particularly the last session. I want to explore the last regression. My suggestion would be—"

"You're driving down the street," Leeza interrupted, "and you notice a guy on the sidewalk next to a tent with a shivering puppy curled up at his feet. He's covered with tattoos, piercings, peculiar clothing choices. His face is dirty. You make eye contact. Then you notice your hand checking the lock on your door."

She looked down the street. Artie was still there. The blinker was still on. The bright white reverse lights hit her eyes and suddenly made her heartbeats slam against her sternum. The reverse lights were off again a second later. The SUV made the turn. Her face crumpled as he disappeared around the corner.

But you have the truth.

She forced herself to finish her thought with Dr. Singh, struggling with every word on its way out. "Why do we check the lock? Without even thinking? He's defenseless. We fabricate fear. And then we bathe in it." She hesitated before adding, "As for the last regression therapy session, the soldiers on the cots—I've been back since then—they wanted to thank me." There was a relieved sigh as she found the words, "Not every symphony is composed in C major." She touched the little red button and disconnected the call, then reopened her contacts.

She walked to the middle of the street and called Artie. The canopy of oaks and hedge maples rustled overhead in silent anticipation as his phone rang.

He picked up. *"Did you miss me?"*

She cupped a hand over her mouth, a sob catching in her throat as her eyes rimmed with tears. She stared at the thumbnail image, the one she took of him in Monaco with the tweed newsboy cap and racing gloves. She adored that picture.

"Always," was her answer, just like every time he asked that question.

Postlude

The Nomad

Josh worked the room at Friday night's open mic with a spot-on rendition of Jake Owen's "Down to the Honkytonk." A front-row table of Alpha Delta Pi wagered on whether he was a boxers or briefs kinda guy. Two placed their bets on "commando" based on the way his jeans wore him that night. The house was packed with students and tourists, and more than a few cougars on the prowl; the shots were flowing, and the feeling was fine. The final guitar chord lingered in the air until it was drowned out by enthusiastic applause and high-pitched whoops and hollers. The pitch of the hollers, Josh knew, was an accurate gauge of the room's blood alcohol level.

He flashed his boyish grin until the crowd settled just enough. "Thank you! Thank you!" He switched on the Clavinova digital piano and tapped a few keys for a sound check; the upper notes of the piano shot out from a dozen overhead speakers. The sound system could've handled concerts at the main stage of The Refinery Charleston, but at The Nomad, it was an immersive, mind-consuming experience when the show was good. And when Josh was onstage, the show was always good.

"Thank you. Thank you very much." He took the mic from the stand and cupped it in his hands at the front of the stage. "Love you, Josh!" A shrill voice screamed from somewhere in the room. "Back atcha," he blushed.

He cleared his throat and looked across the audience. "Several years ago, a very special person in my life was deployed to Afghanistan. I can't imagine what it was like over there, but I can tell you not a day went by that I didn't pray that God would bring her back home safe and sound." The room fell silent; there was only the clanking of glass from behind the bar. He stared at the back of the room. "We first met at a time when I was struggling—feelin' sorry for myself and questioning my purpose." The clanging of the barware seemed to soften. "I imagine we've all been there, but she sat with me, and she listened. And she encouraged me and tried to motivate me, right over there at the bar." A wave of laughter washed over the room. "Go figure," he chuckled.

Josh could barely make out Leeza's face at the back of the crowd, but when he squinted, he could tell she and Tana were holding hands.

"The first time we met, she gave me her number and told me to call day or night. It was the first time in a long time anybody made me feel worth a damn, and knowing her, I can only imagine how many other people she's touched in the same way."

He took a deep breath. "Tonight is a very special night for me. And believe me, this took some convincing, but it's gonna be a very special night for you too. Because that friend of mine is here tonight, and she's not only a war veteran, but she's also a musician." Applause and whistles flooded the room as the crowd looked around for the mystery woman that Josh was so worked up over.

"Leeza, would you join me, please?"

"Knock 'em dead, baby," said Tana, kissing Leeza's hand.

Leeza made her way through the applause to the stage and the waiting piano. The pendant necklace with the engraved silver piano was outside of her olive t-shirt, shimmering in the overhead recessed lighting in the shiny purple ceiling. She fell into Josh's outstretched arms, and the two of them hugged as the crowd cheered.

Leeza turned to the audience as Josh stepped down from the stage. She flashed a humble smile, then positioned the bench as if she, the piano, and the bench formed a dynamic trio, each with a crucial part to play. Deep breath; in through the nose, out through the mouth. Her hands rose ceremoniously above the keyboard. Seconds later, the agonizing radio silence was replaced by a mashup of pop songs and selections of Franz Liszt's *Transcendental Études*. The setlist included "Wrecking Ball" (*Mazeppa*), "Never Enough" (*Feux follets*), "Defying Gravity" (*Appassionata*), and finished with "Courage to Change" by Sia.

Soon her fingers were a blur, meticulously dancing over the keys with the quiet confidence of a child prodigy. Her body swayed and lunged in sync with the rhythm; her energy pushing the grand instrument to its limits.

The audience was mesmerized by the brilliantly intertwined classical and contemporary masterpieces—even the bartenders were frozen.

A sustained dramatic bass chord ended the fiery crescendo. She raised her hands triumphantly from the keyboard as the final notes dissolved across the cavernous hall.

There was a long silence as the piano's last vibrations seemed to hang in the very furthest corners of the room. The audience erupted into a standing ovation as Leeza opened her eyes. The rapturous applause, whistling, and bravos! washed over her. She squeezed the piano necklace tightly between her fingers.

Look, Mama.

Dante, Tana, and Artie were on their feet—cheering and clapping for their friend, bestie, and wife.

She was not alone.

About the author

Stacey began his medical career in the mid-80s, attending X-ray school in the U.S. Army. Following five years of military service, he spent the next three and a half decades in radiology, working in everything from X-ray to CAT scan and Ultrasound. He became a registered sonographer (RDMS, RVT) in 2003 and retired from the medical field in February 2024.

In 2019, Stacey finally began putting his story ideas on paper, and within a few years, he had several screenplays on the competition circuit. One of those screenplays, *Dissension*—inspired by actual events—won FIRST PLACE in a dozen contests around the world. Its success led to him being hired by an L.A. production company to write an original script for them (more to come).

Carnage in D Minor is a novel adaptation of *Dissension*, featuring a female protagonist. "This version tells the story of the character I always wanted to write: A strong Black woman, soldier, wife, mother, and successful healthcare provider. She epitomizes courage through adversity and perseverance through endless challenges. And she never loses the ability to see beauty amongst the carnage. I've known people like her, and their inspiration is what keeps me going."

Thank you for reading Carnage in D minor. I sincerely hope you enjoyed the ride.

Feel free to check out my YouTube channel: S. Alan Chronicles.
Say hello on Instagram - or by email - staceyalan38@gmail.com.
You can also stop by my website www.staceyalanspivey.com.
And don't forget to leave a review on www.amazon.com.

On borrowed lines...

Tana's affirmation for Leeza – *"I consider that the sufferings of this present time are not worthy to be compared with the glory that is to be revealed to me"* – Romans 8:18

Tana's affirmation for Leeza – *"He will cover you with his feathers. He will shelter you with his wings. His faithful promises are your armor and protection"* – Psalm 91:4

Miranda – *"But those who hope in the Lord will renew their strength. They will soar on wings like eagles; they will run and not grow weary; they will walk and not be faint"* – Isaiah 40:31

Dr. Randall to Leeza – *"Many are the plans in a person's heart, but it is the Lord's purpose that prevails"* – Proverbs 19:21

Tana – *"Blessed is the man who remains steadfast under trial, for when he has stood the test he will receive the crown of life, which God has promised to those who love him"* – James 1:12

Dante – *"...we must walk on in the days ahead with an audacious faith in the future."* - from Dr. Martin Luther King Jr.'s presidential address to the Southern Christian Leadership Conference (SCLC) on August 16, 1967, which was later published in his book "Where Do We Go From Here: Chaos or Community?" and the anthology "A Testament of Hope: The Essential Writings and Speeches of Martin Luther King, Jr."

Other works:

Dissension: A screenplay (spec script available in paperback)
A veteran Army nurse with PTSD becomes obsessed with finding a treatment to manage his condition. It's a race against the clock as he struggles with a failing marriage and an ex-lover-turned-drug dealer and stalker.

Carnage in D minor: A screenplay (spec script available in paperback)
Carnage in D Minor is a version of *Dissension* featuring a female protagonist. Though the protagonists grew up very differently, their lives are tragically similar following a deployment in a war zone.

The Last Lily of Savannah: A novel
Summer 2026
The story delves into a successful New York businesswoman's seemingly perfect life. But beneath the carefully cultivated facade, she is tortured by the fact that she was adopted, and that the truth surrounding her biological family's past has been hidden from her all her life. This story explores the primal need for adopted individuals to understand their origins. Unfortunately for our protagonist, sometimes it's best to let sleeping dogs lie.

Caduceus: A novel - Horror. Medical. Military. Stay tuned for details...

Coming to a theater near you...
Stacey has teamed up with a film production company to write a horror movie. As of this writing, the script is getting some final touches, and pre-production will begin in the near future. Updates will be shared on the author's website as they become available.

On another note,

The author lives in Vancouver, WA—just twenty minutes across the bridge from downtown Portland, OR. His screenplay *Dissension*, which is set in Portland, earned local acclaim as the Best Feature Script at the 2024 Portland Screenplay Awards. This follows a string of international wins, including Best Screenplay honors from the European Cinema Festival, Script Awards Los Angeles, and Bridge Fest, as well as top awards at the Bowery Film Festival and Austin Under the Stars.

Sidenote: The lowercase 'm' in the title *Carnage in D minor* is a stylistic choice, not a typo. (Just sayin')

www.ingramcontent.com/pod-product-compliance
Lightning Source LLC
Chambersburg PA
CBHW050026120726
47903CB00006B/1928